the
BOOKWORM
box

best laid plans

LK FARLOW

Best Laid Plans
Copyright © 2018 by LK Farlow.

www.authorlkfarlow.com

Cover design and formatting by Jersey Girl Design | Juliana Cabrera
Edited by Librum Artis Editorial Services | Gray Ink Editing

other titles by LK Farlow

The Southern Roots Series

Coming Up Roses
An Uphill Battle
Weather the Storm

Rebel Heart

To my Phoobs.
I'm so thankful life took my best laid plans and tore them apart.
After all, it led me to you.

best laid plans

prologue

Natalie

ALDEN WARNER. MY BROTHER'S BEST friend. The boy I've loved for as long as I can remember.

I've been watching him all night. Which is nothing new—my eyes are drawn to him anytime he's near.

From the very first time my brother invited him over after school, I was hooked. Even with our almost four year age gap, he didn't look at me the way Nate and all of his other friends did—with annoyance and frustration.

No, he always looked at me kindness and patience. Even when I was being annoying and clingy. Hell, even when I tattled on them, he never lost his cool with me.

But tonight, I'm not the only one looking. Nope. He's looking at me too, and good Lord, there's fire in his eyes.

At first when Mom said Nate would be chaperoning my party for me, I was upset. But then, Nate invited a few friends and seemingly forgot he was supposed to be in charge.

Currently, I'm in the middle of the living room dancing with my friend Alyssa. He's posted up against the wall in the corner of the room, his eyes freely roaming my body, transfixed as I roll my hips to beat of the music.

There's something in the air that feels charged. The kind of energy that says *anything could happen*. The song changes and I close my eyes, hoping like hell I'm not misreading him. Blinking them back open, I scan the room for my brother—he's nowhere in sight—good.

I set off toward Alden, hips still swaying, and he noticed. Oh, he notices. When I get close, he takes two steps bringing us toe-to-toe. "Small Fry," he murmurs, his voice a little slurred.

Feeling bold, I run the tip of my index finger down his chest. "Dance with me?"

He too scans the room before spinning me and pulling me into him. With my ass nestled against him...*oh, God...he's hard*. He grips my hips and we move together, every roll, every dip completely in sync.

I startle when his lips come down on my neck. "When did you get so fucking hot?"

My stomach—and things lower—clench. *This could be it! He's finally noticing you! The boy you've always loved is noticing you!* my brain shouts at me.

I grind back into him and turn my face up to his. "It's not my fault it took you so long to notice."

His lips descend on mine, capturing them in a kiss that turns my legs to jelly. I fall back into him, using the hard planes of his body as support. He nips at my lip before pulling back.

He smirks down at me, licking my kiss from his lips as he steps away. I instantly mourn the loss of his heat. But then, he takes my hand and sets off for the stairs. Before I know it, we're in the guest room he always stays in when he spends the night. He sits down on the edge of the bed and loops his index fingers in my belt loops, tugging me forward.

He flicks open the button to my jeans and I gasp, shocked and turned on by his boldness. A boy my age would never dare. When he begins pulling them down my legs, my breathing accelerates. Just as quickly, he strips me of my shirt, leaving me in nothing more than my matching bra and panty set—though, the bra doesn't last long.

I think I shock both of us when I say, "What about you?"

He drags his hands around to my ass, squeezing it, before trailing up over my sides and to my breast. "What about me, Small Fry?"

"Are you gonna take your clothes off too?"

He leans forward and takes one of my breasts into his mouth. I moan at the foreign sensation. I've heard Alyssa talk about how good it feels, but this...this is beyond anything I could have ever imagined. "Do you want me to?"

"Y-yes." I can hardly get the word out due to the sensations rioting through my body.

He quickly shucks off his clothes and strips me of my thong. He kisses my right hip and then lower before rolling us so that he is poised above me. I'm not sure which has me feeling more drunk—the two beers and shot I took earlier, or Alden's touch. "You sure, Small Fry?"

"More than ever," I murmur, meaning it with my entire being.

chapter one

Natalie

THE TO-DO LIST OF MY life definitely has "start a family" on it...somewhere way down near the bottom. You know, after things like college and getting married.

I absolutely imagined myself *out of freaking high school*, yet here I am, two towns over, buying a pregnancy test. And to top it off, my potential baby daddy—who also happens to be my older brother's best friend and what feels like a lifelong crush—has no clue we even hooked up.

Talk about mortifying.

I'm pretty sure I've been in love with Alden Warner since the very first day I met him. Thanks to his mossy green eyes and lopsided smile, I was absolutely enamored with that boy...still am, if I'm being honest. And I *finally* thought he noticed me. I finally thought he saw me as more than Nate's little pest of a sister. I was naive enough to think that growing boobs and losing my baby fat would make him suddenly realize he wanted me as much as I wanted him.

And I guess, in a way, he did see me. Only, he had his beer goggles on. We fell into bed together with him apparently unaware of my identity and me thinking he was nowhere near as intoxicated as he was.

What was meant to be the most magical night of my life—what I thought was the turning point in our relationship, so to speak—turned out to be nothing special at all. Sure, I lost my V-card to the boy of my dreams, but what's the point if he doesn't even remember it? He literally woke up the next morning with no recollection of the fireworks we created beneath the sheets.

The blank stare he gave me when he asked me why I was in the guest bedroom with him the next day will forever be etched into my mind as one of the top five most humiliating moments of my life.

It was around six-thirty in the morning when the need to pee forced me out of Alden's arms. I slipped on his shirt, along with my panties, before scurrying to the bathroom. I did my business and attempted to sneak back into bed with him. The thought of us waking up together after our night of bliss was something I was eagerly awaiting.

I could just see it so clearly in my mind: I would roll over to face him and he'd lazily blink his eyes open and run his knuckles over my cheekbone before drawing my lips up to his in a passionate kiss—morning breath be damned. Then, he'd declare his love for me, and we would make the long-distance thing, and the age-gap thing and the brother's best friend thing work. *Because, you know...love!*

Only that isn't how it went down. Nope. Not by a long shot. I snuck back into the room, and he lazily blinked himself awake and promptly asked, "What're you doing in here, Small Fry? Did Nate send you to wake me up? Lazy fucker couldn't even do it himself." She smiles a sleepy smile, his eyes roving over my body. "Hey, is that my shirt?"

In that moment, my heart shattered. He truly had no clue.

With my tears threatening to spill, I shook my head and dashed from the room, leaving him to his hungover ramblings.

I shake off the memory of that painful morning and snatch a two-pack box from the shelf and head to the front of the store. At the cash register, the clerk shoots me these knowing looks, and I want so badly to scream that these tests aren't for me, but that will only reassure her that they most certainly *are* mine.

As soon as she tells me the total, I slap down some cash, snatch my bag and dash out of the store—leaving my change and receipt behind.

All too soon, I'm home and pulling into my driveway. Luckily, I have the house to myself. My parents are at work, and Nate and Alden left the very same morning he unwittingly broke my heart to head back to college, to start his junior year.

I debate calling Alyssa, my bestie, and asking her to come over for moral support, but I don't. I think this is something I need to do on my own. After all, if I'm going to be a mother—a freaking teenaged mother—then I need to be strong and independent.

I rip open the box and remove the foil-wrapped stick, placing it on the countertop. After reading the pamphlet front and back, I take the test, cap it, and place it on the counter to wait.

With three minutes to kill, I set a timer and scroll

through social media. Bored with Facebook, I switch to Snapchat. The very first snap I see is from my brother. I open it and immediately regret it. On my screen is a short video loop of Alden and some random coed grinding on each other at a party.

My heart seizes painfully in my chest. And like a glutton for punishment, I switch back to Facebook and go to his profile. Right there, in bold, blue, soul-shattering letters, it says: *In a relationship with Mia Collins.* I stare at those six stupid words until my vision blurs with tears.

Finally, the sound of my alarm chiming breaks the spell. I close out of the app and steel my resolve. Whatever that test says, it's going to be okay.

Maybe.

I think.

I inhale a deep breath and release it, dropping my eyes to the pregnancy test on the counter.

Two pink lines.

Fuck.

chapter two

Natalie

IT'S BEEN A WEEK SINCE I found out I'm going to be a mother. Seven days since I became aware that I'm growing a life inside of me. One hundred and sixty-eight hours since I sat shell-shocked on the bathroom floor, clutching that stupid little stick to my chest, wondering *why me*. My salty tears were a confusing mix of emotions...

Sadness, for the loss of my youth.

Happiness, because I know that I'm going to be an amazing mom, because I learned from the best.

Fear, for all of the changes coming my way. *Will I be able to finish high school? Will my friends stand by me? Will my parents still love me?*

And anguish, because how in the hell am I supposed to explain this to Alden? *Hey, you don't remember this at all, but you took my virginity, and it was awesome, for me at least, and now we're gonna have a kid, so I hope your stupid girlfriend is down with being a stepmom!* Yeah...I think not.

The thought of telling him is daunting. So much so, it makes telling my parents seem like a cakewalk instead of the death march it should be. Or at least that's what I'm trying to convince myself as I walk down the stairs to face them.

They're in the kitchen when I find them. My mom is standing at the stove, minding her sauce pot. Dad is at the island chopping veggies with chef-like precision.

My dad notices me first. "Why the long face, Nat bug?"

I bite down on my bottom lip. "Uh. Well. I was hoping we could talk."

At my worried tone, my mom turns to face me, giving me her full attention; Dad looks my way but keeps chopping.

"What's wrong, Natalie?" Mom asks, motherly concern lacing her tone. *I wonder if I'll sound like her when I talk to my kid?*

"Maybe y'all should have a seat?" I scrunch up my nose. Why did I say that?

Mom walks over closer to me and wraps me in her arms. "Talk to us, sweet girl. You know we're here for you."

Deciding the Band-Aid approach is the best way to go, I blurt it out. "I'm pregnant!"

As soon as the words leave my mouth, my dad shouts, "Fuck! Goddamn it!" Apparently, my news caused him to miss the carrot and slice his thumb instead.

He should have sat down like I said.

"Oh, m-my God! Dad are you oh-okay?" I ask, my voice wobbly and tears streaming down my cheeks.

He grunts out some unintelligible reply and turns away from me.

Mom releases me from her embrace and passes him a dishtowel. He wraps it around his thumb, applying pressure. "Do you need stitches?" she asks.

Another grunt.

Taking my own earlier advice, I plop down onto a bar stool, tucking myself out of the way while Mom administers first aid to Dad. *Good thing she's a nurse, I guess.*

My eyes stay on my parents while my mom works, but I'm not paying attention to them—not really. My mind is racing a million miles a minute. I can't help but feel like I've let them down...like I'm a failure and a disappointment.

Before I know it, my silent tears have turned to gut-wrenching sobs. I know they say a parent's love is unconditional, but how could they possibly still love me?

How could anyone?

I'm so lost in my own mind I don't even notice that my parents have moved until I feel both of them wrapping me in their arms. Their comfort only makes me cry harder, because I know I don't deserve it.

chapter three

Natalie

"OH, HONEY," MOM WHISPERS BROKENLY into my hair, her voice clogged with emotion. "Let's go sit and talk."

I nod and they step back. In the family room, I claim the loveseat while my parents sit across from me on the couch. I can tell my dad is furious from the way his jaw is ticking and how he keeps clenching and unclenching his fists.

My dad is the first to speak. His tone is shockingly calm. "Nat bug, how did this happen?" I open my mouth to reply, but he cuts me off. The calm has worn off. "How the fuck did this happen? Your mother and I have provided for your every need, and this is how you thank us? By getting knocked up before you're even out of damn high school?" His face is an angry shade of red, and spittle flies from his lips as he yells at me.

Unable to take any more, I draw my knees to my chest and drop my head onto them, letting my hair fall forward like a curtain.

Taking note of me folding in on myself, Dad softens his tone...*a little*. "Are you sure you're even pregnant? Like one-hundred-percent positive? Who is the father? Why didn't you use protection? How could you be so..."

That cakewalk I mentioned early? Yeah, not so much. His rapid-fire questions make my chest feel tight, like an elephant is sitting on me, its weight slowly pressing the air from the lungs.

Luckily, Mom shuts him down...right before he could call me stupid. The word may have not left his mouth, but I know it's what he was going to say.

"Luke. Let's tackle this one issue at a time." She lays her hand on top of his, and he covers it with his other. Together, they're a united front, able to conquer any obstacle with grace—including their seventeen-year-old daughter being pregnant.

"Like your father was saying, you're certain your pregnant?" Her tone is soft, and it makes me feel so shitty, though I know that isn't her intention. I almost wish she would shout at me too. Her compassion is too much.

I give a small nod. "Yes, ma'am. I took two tests."

"They aren't always accurate!" Dad exclaims.

Mom gives him an indecipherable look. "That may be true, but that is typical with negative results. False positives are incredibly rare." His shoulders slump. "When did you take these tests?"

"A week ago."

"Well, you'll need to call the OB-GYN and make an appointment."

I want to argue and beg her to do it for me, but I don't, because if I'm going to be responsible for the life of another human, I sure as shit need to be responsible for my own.

"Yes, ma'am. I'll call first thing tomorrow."

She nods, pleased with my response. "Natalie, as much as I want to lecture you on poor decisions, waiting until marriage, and safe sex...it's obviously too late for that. So, instead we're going to talk about your options."

I blink at her. Surely she doesn't mean... "Options? Like abortion?"

"If that's what you want."

"I don't!" I rush out, my lower lip quivering. I'm all for a woman's right to choose, but it's not the right choice for me. Sure, I've only known I was expecting for seven days, but it only took minutes to know I loved this baby.

"There's also adoption. Have you spoken to the father?"

I shake my head. "N-not yet."

"So, you know who the father is?" Dad asks through clenched teeth.

I can't tell them that Alden is the father. Not only will my father murder him, it will destroy his friendship with Nate. Not to mention the havoc it would wreak on his new relationship with Mia...as jealous as I am over their relationship, I know he must really like her, because in all of the years I've known him, he's never publicly announced dating anyone.

So, instead, I hang my head and lie. "No, I don't." My voice cracks, right along with my heart.

Years from now, I'll regret this decision, but in this moment, it feels like the right choice. Alden has so much going for him, and I love him enough to not drag him down with me. No red-blooded, college junior wants to be a father.

Not to mention, if my parents wanted to, they could go after him for statutory, and that's not something I'm willing to risk. Alden Warner is a good man with a bright future, and I'm not going to jeopardize it over a night he doesn't even remember. Plus, this baby...our baby...will link me to him forever. Even if he is never aware, I'll always have a little piece of him to call mine.

"What do you mean you don't know?" Dad shouts even louder than before, causing me to cry harder. "How could you not know? You're better than this, Natalie. We raised you better than this!"

Mom tries to calm him down, but he's too far gone. As much as his words sting, I can't really blame him. If letting them think I'm a loose girl prone to bad choices protects Alden, then so be it.

Dad stands from the couch, refusing to even look my way. "Go to bed Natalie. We'll talk more tomorrow, but right now...I need some space." He stalks out of the room, not sparing even a single glance back my way.

Mom stands and walks over to me. "Give him time, sweetie. Give us both some time. I know this is hard, but we both love you very much."

I nod, too choked up to speak. She presses a comforting kiss to my forehead and follows after my dad.

chapter four

Natalie

Four Years Later

HOOPS OR STUDS? HOOPS OR *studs?* I repeat the question internally as I stand in front of my vanity holding one earring up to my ear before swapping it for the other. Good Lord, it's not like it matters. It's not like my earrings will make or break this date.

This date I'm already reluctant to go on. Because I already know exactly where it's going...

Nowhere.

I mean, Kevin's a catch—good-looking, employed, and gentlemanly to boot. But, they all seem that way at first. They all seem charming and attentive and interested until I drop the whole single-mom bomb on them.

Then they run weeping with their tails tucked. Typically, after some variation of: *You're a mom? But you're so young...but you're so hot*, and so on and so forth. Because apparently being old and dowdy is a prerequisite to childbirth.

For real, the fastest way to ruin a first date is to mention your kid. But, I still do, because I have nothing to hide. And anyone who tucks tail and runs at the mention of my girl isn't the man for me.

And before you think I'm some psycho out shopping for a father figure for my daughter, let me set the record straight.

While none of the men I've dated have *ever* met Tatum, much less seen her picture, I'm always upfront about her existence. Chemistry only goes so far, and at the end of the day, she comes first...even if that means the only action Mama gets is of the solo, battery-operated variety.

I finally settle on the hoops when I feel my rambunctious toddler rake her nails down my belly. "Rawr!" she yells as loud as she can. "Raaaawwwrrr!"

I pull my robe tighter and retie the knot, effectively blocking her access. "Whatcha doin' Tater Tot?"

"I's bein' the tiger that scratched you all up."

"The tiger? What tiger?"

"The one dat gave you all those marks on your tummy," she says, giving me a *duh* look that's far beyond her three years.

Ah. That tiger.

"Those are called stretch marks. When you were in my belly, my skin had to stretch to make room for you."

"See!" she squeals excitedly. "I the tiger!"

I run a hand through her messy curls—the exact same russet color as her father's. "You sure are." She follows me like a pint-sized shadow as I shuffle away from my vanity and into my closet. "Are you excited to hang out with Uncle Nate tonight?"

Like I flipped a switch, she begins jumping up and down, like a demented kangaroo. "Unc-ah Naaaaaate!"

"That's right, Tater Tot. He'll be here in about ten minutes. Why don't you go pick out a few toys to show him?"

With a yell worthy of a battle-cry, she darts out of my closet, presumably toward her bedroom. I soak in the peace and quiet for a beat—don't you judge me, I love the kid, with all of my damn heart, but she is loud—before flipping through the hangers in search of my favorite navy blue wrap dress. It's lowcut and clings in all the right places while still being modest—the perfect *I'm interested, but don't put out on the first date* dress.

Once it's on, I slide my feet into a pair of champagne espadrille wedges that make my calves look amazing while still being comfy. I assess myself in the mirror and smile—I'm no supermodel, but it'll do. I spritz myself with my perfume, slick a coat of shiny pink gloss across my lips and smile. *It'll definitely do.*

I can hear Tatum in the living room, and when I enter the room, it's all I can do to stifle a laugh. She has somehow managed to lug her tea set from her room, along with her Barbie castle, a plethora of stuffed animals, and four feather boas. "Wow, looks like you have big plans for Uncle Nate."

"Yes, Mama." She nods solemnly. "I does."

"You *do*," I correct her gently.

"Dat's what I said." She crosses her arms over her chest.

I squat down so that we're eye to eye. "You said *does* Tater Tot. When you refer to yourself, you say *do*. Does that make sense?"

She tilts her head to the right, thinking before replying—which is so like my girl. It's something else to watch her think through things. "I fink so."

I'm about to haul myself back to standing when there's a hard knock on the front door, followed by the sound of it opening. "Where's my girl?" my brother hollers as he steps into the room, and Tatum rushes to him, knocking me flat on my ass.

The *oomph* sound I make causes both of them to look my way. My brother tries to hide his smile, the faint laugh lines around his eyes give him away.

"Mama! Did I...*do*...that?" We both smile at her use of the word.

"It was an accident, baby girl. No worries," I say, soothing away any worries she may have had. Nate extends a hand down toward me and helps me up.

The second I'm steady on my feet, Tatum grabs the hem of my dress. "Mama! I gotsta potty!"

"Then go, Tater Tot! Call me if you need help." Like a flash, she takes off down the hall to the spare bathroom, leaving Nate and me alone.

He wastes no time grilling me. "So, who's the lucky loser tonight?"

"He's not a loser. His name's Kevin, and he's twenty-nine and works in accounting."

Nate scoffs. "Total loser. Bet he still lives at home too."

I roll my eyes. "He does not. His profile says he lives in the suburbs just outside of Bay Ridge."

"Suburbs totally equals his mom's basement."

"You dipshit, we live in South Alabama. We don't have

basements."

Nate holds up his index finger and tips it my way. "False. They aren't common here, but they exist."

"Whatever. Your argument's weak, and you know it."

"Your argument's weak," he whines, attempting to mimic me in that annoying way only a sibling can do.

"Mama! Mama! I did the poops!"

The toilet flushes as I walk down the hall toward the bathroom. "You did?" I ask enthusiastically, clapping my hands.

Honest to God, if someone would've told my seventeen-year-old self that I would be this excited over poop in a few years, I would have laughed in their face—and I mean laughed *hard*.

"I did! And I wiped my butt too!"

I widen my eyes and give a little gasp. "Well, aren't you just all grown? You know what this means right?" Tatum shakes her head. "It means...dance party!"

My little girl squeals and immediately we begin jumping around, waving our arms and stomping our feet. No doubt, we look nuts—but potty training this kid was tantamount to making water flow uphill. So, this is absolutely a dance-party-worthy feat.

At the sound of our commotion, Nate ventures back to the hallway, where we're shaking what our mama gave us. Ever the doting uncle, he doesn't come empty-handed. No, sir. He's armed with a glass of chocolate milk topped with whipped cream and a swirly straw.

Tatum looks up at him, all doe-eyed, batting her lashes. "Dat's for me?"

"Sure is. A little bird told me you're using the potty like an old pro!"

"It's true! I am!"

She reaches for the beverage, but I stop her. "Not so fast, Tater Tot. You gotta wash your hands first!"

Once she's as germ-free as a three-year-old can be, we retreat to the living room, where she instantly snuggles up to my brother on the couch. "We watch Poppy?" she asks, reaching for her chocolate milk.

"Poppy?" he asks. "Oh! You mean those things with the hair!"

"*Trolls,*" I inform him through a laugh.

"Yeah. That."

"It's on Netflix," I tell him, scooping up my purse from the table by the door. "Y'all have fun. I won't be late—call me if you need me." I walk over and press a kiss to Tatum's whipped-cream-sticky cheek.

Nate's voice stops me right as I'm about to step over the threshold. "Same goes for you. Call me if you need me."

chapter five

Natalie

KEVIN AND I MET THROUGH FindLoveOnline. Yeah sure... judge me, but how else am I supposed to meet men? At the grocery store? *Get real.* That shit only happens in books and sitcoms. Initially when we made plans for tonight, he offered to pick me up, but I declined and offered to meet him there, for two reasons.

One: the last time a date picked me up from my apartment, my overprotective brother—who's a cop, in case I forgot to mention—had his buddy run his tags and check him out. A gross misuse of power, if you ask me. Then again, homeboy ended up having a warrant out for his arrest. Turns out Paul liked to deal pot to high schoolers on his off days.

Which leads me to reason *numero dos*: Paul the pot dealer. He was a mega wake-up call for me. These dudes have no business knowing where I live, and I was incredibly naive to not suggest meeting them from the start—especially with Tatum.

I realize this makes it sound like I'm going out with random men nightly, so let me set the record straight—I go out once a month, if that! Between working at the café, my online classes, and my sweet Tater Tot...well, let's just say I'm busy as fuck. Truthfully, I wouldn't have it any other way. Even on the most stressful days—you know the kind...

You wake and you're out of coffee, your kid's favorite sippy cup is M.I.A., your car doesn't want to start, you manage to grab a coffee at the Circle K only to spill it on your shirt, aforementioned kid has the meltdown to end all meltdowns in the middle of the store, and by the time you finally make it home, the only thing that sounds good for dinner is half a bottle of wine, but you have to cook. Can't feed your toddler fermented grape juice for dinner—pretty sure that is heavily frowned up, not to mention illegal.

But even on the most hellacious of days, I wouldn't change a thing.

Well, maybe one thing...it'd be nice for Tatum's dad to know she exists, but that's a story for a different day. Thinking of Alden always makes me melancholy, and that's definitely not the right mindset for a first date.

Finding somewhere to park ends up taking longer than the drive over. After looping the block four times, I *finally* manage to snag a spot about half a block from South Bay Kitchen—the eatery we're meeting at. When Kevin suggested we eat here, I immediately said yes, as it's an absolute favorite of mine. Their chef uses only the best local ingredients and breathes new life into longstanding traditional Southern dishes.

The second I exit my car, the balmy late summer heat and humidity envelopes me, causing a fine sheen of sweat to dot my hairline. It's beyond gross...but that's the price you pay to live below the Mason Dixon line.

By the time I make it to the restaurant, I can feel little beads of sweat sliding down my spine. I pause outside of the entrance and fish my compact out of my purse. I use the powder puff to dab at my nose before swiping another coat of gloss over my lips.

I step into the dimly lit space; the aroma of freshly baked bread and sizzling herbs and spices fill my nostrils. On cue, my mouth waters. "Hello and welcome to South Bay Kitchen," the hostess greets me. "How many?"

Rising to my tippy toes, I glance over her shoulder into the dining area. "I'm actually meeting someone. We should have had reservations under the name Kevin."

She offers me a sympathetic smile before bending her head to scan her reservation book. "Yes, and it looks like he's already seated." She steps out from behind the podium. "If you'll follow me."

Zigzagging through the maze of tables, she leads me to a small two-top toward the back near the bar. "Here you go."

Kevin stands upon our arrival and...holy ba-jeezus, this man looks nothing like his picture online. I was expecting a good-looking man with tanned skin, blond hair, and startling blue eyes, who stands over six-foot-two.

What I'm met with is a balding man old enough to be my father with leathery skin. The only thing that matches is his eye color. Oh, my god—have I been catfished? Is that what is happening right now?

"Uh. Hello. I'm Natalie."

He flicks the tip of his tongue over his front teeth. "Phil." He shakes my hand and I cringe at the clamminess of his skin. "And, toots, the pleasure's all mine."

It's all I can do to suppress my gag. "You're not Kevin?"

He chortles. "Kevin couldn't make it tonight, so I came in his place. It's almost the same thing—the kid's a real chip off the old block."

I gasp and my stomach turns. "So...you're his...dad?"

"In the flesh." He grins, flashing me his dentures.

Oh, hell no. Thank God I never had time to sit. Without another word, I turn and walk right back out the way I came. What a sleaze. And who in God's name sends their dad as a stand-in on a first date?

Gross!

I drive around for a good half hour to pass the time. I know if I come this early, Nate will pester me with questions about Kevin-Phil. And, I'm in no mood to deal with that.

chapter six

Alden

GOALS. I'VE ALWAYS BEEN A fan of goals. Especially achieving them. Ever since I was a kid, there's always been something so fucking satisfying about crossing shit off my list.

In fifth grade, I wanted a dog. So, I put together a presentation on a tri-fold poster board and presented it to my parents after dinner one night. The left side highlighted all of the pros of pet ownership, while the right listed the cons. And if you think I held back or skimped on listing the downsides, *think again*. I wanted my parents to know I meant business.

The middle outlined all of the things I would be willing to do to achieve my goal of pet ownership—like getting up early to walk him, using my chore allowance for pet food instead of the arcade or dollar store, cleaning up after any accidents...shit like that.

Needless to say, I got the damn dog. Named him Oscar—God rest his little doggy soul.

That same tenacity and dedication followed me all throughout grade school and into high school. Don't misunderstand me, I still went out and partied with the best of them, and I definitely had my fair share of dates and hookups, but I also knew when to rein it in and dial it down.

Served me well, too. Got me into my dream school on a full ride, where I studied business. Extra perk, my childhood best friend, Nate, got in there, too, and he's every bit as driven as me. Since then we may have lost touch—thanks to him staying local and heading off to the police academy, where he learned to be a professional badass, and me shipping off to Europe to study under the bests in the culinary world—but that doesn't mean I don't have his back still, and Lord knows he has mine.

We pretty much lived at each other's houses in high school, and we roomed together in college. We may not talk every day like we did growing up, but we still text sporadically and comment on social media shit. And I know when we eventually hit the bar, we'll pick back up right where we left off, like we always do, distance and time be dammed.

My plan was always for me to end up back here in Bay Ridge, Alabama. Sounds insane, I'm sure. But like I said, *goals*. And I'm so damn close to achieving the grandest of them all that I can hardly stand it. Even though my parents have long since retired to Florida, all of my best childhood memories are here. Not to mention Nate and his family too—but I try not to think of his family too much. I love them, but thinking about them always leads me to think of his sister...his once annoying but blossomed overnight and now hot as fuck little sister. Thank God for social media for allowing me to creep.

Sure, there were some bumps and detours along the

way, but fate is smiling down on me, and I'm fucking here and ready to take back what should have never left my family in the first place—Bayside Café.

chapter seven

Natalie

IN THE WEEK FOLLOWING MY date with Kevin, every time my phone rang, I've In the week following my non-date with Kevin-Phil, I've decided to call it quits. I'm hanging up my dating hat—and by that, I mean deleting my online profile. I waffled on the decision, but a girl can only stand so many bad dates.

But you know what? I'm okay with that. Truly, I am. Any of the potential suitors I might have met on there would have been nothing more than a stand-in for the only man who's ever made my heart race.

For a while, I convinced myself that I didn't want passion and belly flutters—I fooled myself into believing lukewarm was the way to go...but I know that isn't true.

Deep down, if it isn't red hot and consuming, I'm not interested. Though, I'm pretty sure that kind of love only comes around once in a lifetime, and if that's the case, that's just fine too, because I'll always have my Tater Tot. Which is fine by me, because she's all the best parts of him anyway.

"Mama!" I hear, followed by the sound of Tatum's little feet stomping down the hall toward my room. "Mama!

Wake up! It's Us Day!" Tatum barrels into my room and up onto my bed where she burrows down under the covers next to me. "You up?"

"I'm up! Are you ready for our big day?" I ask, already knowing her answer.

On the third Saturday of every month, I'm off. Guaranteed, no matter what—and on that day, Tatum and I have a Us Day where we spend the entire day together, uninterrupted, doing whatever we damn well please.

"Wes have waffles?"

"We can absolutely have waffles. And maybe then we can go to the park."

Tatum nods her head furiously. "And to lunch and for ice cream and for shopping and for—"

I gently dig the tips of my fingers into her ribs, tickling her. "Slow your roll, Tater Tot. Let's tackle today one step at a time, okay?"

"Okay, Mama," she replies through peals of laughter.

Tatum begs and pleads to help with the batter, and as usual when letting a three-year-old work in the kitchen, more ends up on the counter and the floor than in the waffle maker. All the same, we end up with four perfect, fluffy waffles that we top with whipped cream, strawberries, and sweet, sticky syrup.

I send my little girl to wash her hands and brush her teeth while I quickly clean up the kitchen. Once I'm finished, I lay out her clothes before quickly working through my morning routine of washing my face, brushing my teeth and tossing my hair up into a messy-mom-bun—I call it a mom bun because it so *isn't* one of those cute buns you see girls on Instagram and Pinterest rocking—before throwing on a pair of drawstring linen shorts and a loose-fitting tank.

We exit our bedrooms simultaneously, only Tatum is not dressed in the outfit I laid out for her. Nope. Not by a long shot. My little girl is decked out in her frilliest dress-up dress, rain boots, and a tiara—with a smear of pink, glittery lipstick from cheek to cheek to finish her look.

"Don't I wook like a pwincess, Mama?"

"You absolutely do." I do my best to stifle my grin. I swear, this kid...she marches to the beat of her own bongo—because Lord knows, a drum would be too basic. "But do you really want to risk getting your royally beautiful outfit all dirty?"

Tatum taps her chin thoughtfully. "I guess not." Her little shoulders slump.

"I'll tell you what, you go change into the outfit I laid out for you. You can still wear your rain boots, and I'll do your hair up all pretty *with* your tiara. Bonus points if you wipe off the lipstick."

"But Mama! It's *sooooo* pretty!"

"You're right, it is very pretty. But I think I have a color that would match better, okay?" She nods and dashes back to her bedroom, and I do the same in hunt of my barely pink lip gloss.

We once again meet in the hall. "Dis better?" she asks, pouting slightly.

"Much better. C'mon and I'll braid your hair."

Tatum bounces on her toes. "Like Elsa?"

"Yup, just like Elsa."

Ten minutes later, Tatum is admiring her braid in the little entryway mirror. Finally, after checking it from every possible angle, she shoots me a thumbs-up and what I can only assume is a wink. It's all I can do to suppress a laugh, because the expression on her face makes her look like a hokey used-car salesman you'd see on a billboard somewhere.

We decide to take advantage of the good weather and walk to the park. Well, I walk. Tatum gallops, hops, and twirls her way down the sidewalk. Her enthusiasm garners us a few stares, coupled with friendly waves from others milling about outside. Being the little ham she is, Tatum eats up the attention.

At the park, Tatum goes straight for the big slide, climbing the rungs of the ladder fearlessly and then launching herself down the shoot. *My sweet, brave girl.* After about ten minutes she tires of the slide and sets off for the merry-go-round.

"Mama! Come spin me!"

Five spins later, she says she is too dizzy to keep going and we make our way to the swings. When she sees the tandem swing is open, she shouts with glee. "We swing togedder?"

"Sure thing, Tater Tot."

About an hour later, we have made our rounds through all of the playground equipment. "You ready for lunch?"

"Hmm." Tatum taps the little dimple in her chin. "I

stapose."

"You suppose? Well, what sounds yummy?"

"Ice cream," she deadpans.

"Try again kid."

"Fine. Grilled cheeses?"

"Now that sounds like a plan."

Thirty minutes later, we're both stuffed from our grilled cheeses. Tatum opted for the kid-friendly American cheese and white bread classic while I went with Gouda on sourdough accompanied by bacon, tomatoes, and garlic aioli.

"I eated it all." Tatum looks at me expectantly while patting her little belly.

"I see that," I say through a smile.

"So, do I gets ice cream?"

"That depends."

"On what, Mama? I'll do anyfing!"

"Anything? Oh, my..." I steeple my fingers under my chin, rubbing the tips against one another like a movie villain. Tatum looks at me with her beautiful green eyes. "How about you help me pick up your toys when we get home and no complaining at bath time?"

My girl nods her head furiously, almost to the point of looking like a bobblehead. "Yes! Yes! I can do that!"

I beam and hold my hand out to her, helping her down from her chair. "Then let's get to it, pretty girl."

We hop over to Scoops, which is conveniently located

right next door. After placing our orders, Tatum skips over to our usual table near the door while I linger at the counter, waiting for our order. I keep my eyes on her while listening out for our number to be called. By the time I have our sweet treats in hand, she's all but drooling.

Two bites in and my phone starts buzzing in my purse. I fish it out and check the screen, finding two new texts from Jenny, my work bestie. She and I started at Bayside around the same time, and being the new girls, we stuck together like glue. The fact that she's ballsy as all get-out, fun, and an all-around good person certainly doesn't hurt.

I press my right index finger to the sensor and unlock my phone before opening her message.

Jenny: Staff meeting Monday morning. 8 AM. Hiss, boo!

Ugh. Great.

Me: Thanks for letting me know. Any idea what's up?

Jenny: I've heard a few rumors about us getting new owners.

Ugh. Double great.

Bayside Café is a local institution and so much more than your average café. Or at least it was. The food used to be over-the-top small plates that were busting with flavors from all over the globe.

Growing up, it was owned by my longtime crush's—a.k.a. my brother's best friend—grandparents. From about age ten to fifteen, I imagined Alden and me getting married and running it together. From sixteen to seventeen, I became determined to make him *see* me. And he did. Through beer goggles. Our one and only hook-up ended with me knocked up and him with no memory of us even sleeping together, much less that he was my first...so no happy ending for us—obviously.

Even though there'll never be an Alden and me, my dreams of running Bayside persisted. Especially after his grandma passed away and his pops was moved to an assisted living community. The café was handed down to his uncle, who sold it—the rat bastard. Now, we serve deli sandwiches and soups of the day and fruit cups. And if we're getting sold again...well, there go my dreams of working my way up to running the place one day. Hell, I'll be lucky if the alleged new owner evens keeps the staff.

I tuck my phone back into my purse just as Tatum hops down from her chair. "All done! You ready?"

I scoop up the last bite of my mint chip and swallow it down. "Totally ready," I say with much more bravado than I'm feeling, and together we set off back toward the house.

chapter eight

Natalie

IT'S ONCE AGAIN ONE OF *those* days.

Even though I was in bed by eight, I overslept and had to rush through getting ready.

Tatum also wasn't feeling it this morning. She hated every outfit I picked out. She wanted her pink juice cup, but we couldn't find it. She wanted to bring her Troll doll to school, but it isn't show-and-tell day. It was one thing after another. All trivial things, mind you. But all together, they had my pulse racing.

By the time I got her dropped off at daycare, I was a hot, frazzled mess.

But, it's a Monday, so I'm cutting myself some slack. Plus, I still have fifteen minutes before the stupid staff meeting, and it's only a five-minute drive from Tatum's daycare.

So, yeah, totally winning.

I breeze through the employee entrance at seven fifty-five on the dot—thanks to hitting two red lights. Jenny immediately rushes over to me, practically bouncing on the toes of her black, restaurant standard, non-slip sneakers.

"Oh. My. Good. God. Girl!"

Grinning at her early morning enthusiasm, I arch a brow at her. "What's got you all excited?"

"Word in the kitchen is the sale is as good as done, *and* we get to meet the new owner today. I overheard Giselle saying she saw him and that he is fiiiiine." Mind you, her name is actually Jess Elle, but she says it isn't sophisticated enough and insists we all call her Giselle. *Whatevs.*

"Yeah, well..." I trail off. "I guess we'll see soon enough."

"Girl. You could at least pretend to be excited about some new eye candy."

I shrug my shoulders. As pathetic as it sounds, there's only one guy who has ever truly caught my eye, and last I heard he was in France and engaged to fucking Mia. Even now, after all these years, thoughts of her make me stabby.

At promptly eight o'clock, our daytime manager, Carlos, ushers us all into the dining room. Jenny and I snag a two-top near the back—that way we'll be able to whisper back and forth as this meeting drones on.

Before everyone even has a chance to sit down, Carlos starts. "Thanks for being here today guys."

"Like we had a choice," someone near the front mumbles.

Carlos pinches the bridge of his nose and continues. "As I was saying, I know it's early and a lot of y'all don't even work today, so I appreciate it. Before we get into the heavy stuff, I want to thank everyone who worked on-site at the Benson wedding shower last weekend. I know it was hot, but y'all killed it."

Don, our owner, who is every bit as lackluster as his

name, steps up behind Carlos. He taps his foot impatiently as Carlos continues. Finally, Don taps his shoulder. "All right guys—guess I'm going to turn it over to head honcho."

Don takes the mic and taps it three times, testing it as if Carlos wasn't just speaking into it. "I know there have been rumors about me wanting to sell this place. Well, they were true, and after noon today, I'll no longer be the owner of this dump."

His careless words spark a hot fury in my veins. This place wouldn't be a dump if it weren't for him and his apathetic, absent ownership. The only thing that jackass does is scrawl his name across our paychecks.

"Now then, let me introduce y'all to the new owner, Alden Warner."

At the sound of his name, I gasp, sucking air down the wrong pipe, causing me to choke so hard that I'm sure it looks like I'm sobbing. Hell, maybe I am. I'm certain my face is beet red, and I sound like a barking baby seal. My vision is blurred by my salty tears, but I can *feel* everyone looking at me. I cover my face with my hands in a paltry attempt to hide.

Right when I think my humiliation couldn't possibly get any worse, the universe decides to prove me wrong.

"Here, take a sip." Four words. That's it, and even though his voice is deeper—rougher—I'd know it anywhere. Alden Warner is right in front of me. Talking to me. Offering me a drink. Except I'm pretty sure he's the only thing that can quench my thirst. And the kicker—he probably doesn't even know who he's talking to. I'm just some nameless waitress he inherited when he bought the café.

Ignoring him, I continue choking and wheezing into my palms. There's no way in hell I can face him right now.

Undeterred, Alden pushes the cool glass against my knuckles. "Seriously, take a sip. Please."

There's something about the way he says 'please.' His voice dropped deeper and sounded so imploring, like his life depended on me drinking that water. Then again, he probably didn't want a waitress to die before the ink on the deed was even dry.

Slowly, I pull my hands from my face and take the glass from him. Bringing it to my lips, I take one small sip. And then another. Feeling brave, I sneak a peek up at him, but he's like the sun and looking at him dead-on hurts. So, I quickly revert back to staring at my lap. He probably doesn't even recognize me.

Except, judging by the, "No way," he murmurs, I know he did. He runs his index and middle finger down my jaw and under my chin, using them to tilt my face up toward him. "You work here?"

My words fail me, so I settle on a nod. A stiff, impersonal, awkward as hell nod.

"Holy shit, Small Fry! Get your ass up and give me a hug!"

I open my mouth to reply, but with catlike reflexes, Alden yanks me up from my chair and into his arms. Deciding to make the best of this unexpected but oh-so-welcome physical contact, I breathe him in. He stills smells the same—like spicy citrus and pure, unfiltered sex appeal. It's fucking deadly.

He holds me tight to his body—so close I can feel the lean muscles beneath his shirt. So close I might lose my mind and never let go if don't move away from him, pronto.

Finally, yet all too soon, Alden steps away from me taking his blessed body heat with him.

"Jesus, girl, it's been too long. How the hell are you?" he asks, sounding genuinely happy to see me.

However, instead of responding with a polite and rational reply like a normal fucking adult, my inner-teenager answers for me, sounding petulant and snotty. "Just dandy. How's Mia, your *fiancée*?" Even after all these years her name still tastes like poison

chapter nine

Alden

For a few seconds, the entire café is silent as if they're waiting with bated breath for my answer. I smirk at her, even though I know it's the wrong thing to do. I up the ante with a quirked brow, and I swear she's ready to spit fire.

"You think she'd appreciate you having me in your arms?"

"Honestly, I don't think she'd care one way or another." I let my words settle and then drop the hammer. "Seeing as we're not together any longer."

At that Natalie sputters, but she still hasn't pulled away. *Interesting.* "Wha...you're not? Since when? Nate didn't..."

"Nate didn't what? You been keepin' tabs on me, Small Fry?"

She rears back, trying to look angry. Hard thing for her to do, though, when we're so close she has to crane her neck to make eye contact. "Absolutely not. I...just..."

"It's all good, girl. I've kept tabs on you. Hear you got a little one?" The mention of her kid has her pushing away from me as if I'm fucking Michael Myers.

"Oh, uh...um...yup. N-Nate told you about her?"

It still blows my mind that she has a daughter. I'm not sure the world can handle two of her. She inhales sharply, and her cheeks redden. "What did he say? H-have you s-seen her?"

Weird questions, but okay. "Let's see, he says she is bossy and smart and cute as hell. Which, from the handful of pics he has sent over the years, I'd have to agree."

Sweat beads along her hairline. "Oh, okay. Good. Great." Her words are choppy, and she's acting a little psycho.

Natalie's reactions are so foreign, so fucking strange, that I feel like we should stick a pin in this topic and save it for when it's just the two of us. Sure as shit not on my first day as her boss, in front of all of her coworkers.

"Let's grab coffee one day this week and catch up." I know she's going to turn me down, so I pivot and saunter back to the front of the dining room in hopes of getting this meeting back on track. Though, judging from the whispers among the staff, I can see there's a fat fucking chance of that happening.

Nate and I have been trying like hell to get together, and tonight our schedules have finally aligned. We're hitting up Bennet's for a few drinks. It's pretty chill, seeing as it's a Monday night. Honestly though, after today's orientation meeting, a laid-back atmosphere works for me.

I stroll in at a quarter after seven and damn if this place doesn't look exactly the same as it did when we used to sneak our underage asses in here. I scan the space looking for Nate, and sure enough, he's seated at the bar sipping on his drink. He sees me and tips his chin in greeting. I cross the room and he stands, reaching out to shake my hand, but I pull his ass into a hug.

"It's been too long," I tell him as we break away.

"That it has. Catching up here and there wasn't working."

"I'm home and have no plans to leave."

"Look at us, living out our dreams."

I chuckle at his words, but damn if he isn't right. For as long as I can remember, Nate's wanted to be a cop. The desire to protect and serve flows through his veins the same way food flows through mine.

"How is it, being the local bacon?"

"Oink, oink, motherfucker. I'm living the dream."

"Glad to hear it. I will be, too, once I get Bayside up and running how it should be."

"Got big plans?" he asks, drumming his nails on the wooden bar top.

I flag down the bartender and order a Jack and Coke and pass him a ten-dollar bill. He returns with my drink and change, which I leave for him—if there's one thing the food industry has taught me, it's not to skimp on the gratuity.

"Hell yeah. You remember Carlos?" I ask, knowing it's a toss-up whether he will or not.

"I...I think so. He was a grade behind us, right? Always up at the café?"

"Yeah, that's right. His mom worked there, and he

went up there with her since she was a single mom. My grandparents kind of took him under their wing. Dude is as invested in Bayside as I am, and the minute he heard Don wanted to sell, he tracked me down on Facebook and that was it."

I sip at my drink. "I was already stateside, visiting my parents in Florida until I figured shit out, and this was just too good. The timing was perfect—I mean, shit, I came into the trust fund my grandparents left right as the café goes up for sale. Fucking kismet."

Nate signals for another round of drinks. "Please God, tell me you're fixing the menu."

"Hell yes. The minute I signed that paperwork I started crafting it. Gonna start implementing it as soon as I get my kitchen sorted."

"Glad to hear it. Natalie will be too."

"Speaking of, she's all grown up now, huh?"

Nate eyes me a little oddly. "Yeah, that's what happens. Time passes, we grow old, we die."

I bark out a laugh. "Jesus. Morbid much?"

He shrugs that classic Nate Reynolds shrug.

Our conversation turns from the here and now to reminiscing about the past, and I can't help but smile. Especially when Nate brings up one of my favorite memories of life here—even if it is for all the wrong reasons.

"You been to the river yet?"

"Nah, not yet. Man, we used to tear it up out there."

He lifts his drink to me, and we clink them together. "Hell yeah, we did."

"And Nat was always begging to tag along like the little pest she was."

"Nah, she wasn't that bad." Especially not when she was in her teeny little bikini, but I keep that thought to myself, seeing as she was fifteen, and I was headed to college.

"Bull. She's cool as shit now, but you've always had a soft spot for her, huh?"

If only he knew how he right he was. I've always been protective of my Small Fry, but as she grew and matured, so did my feelings, as wrong as they were. The heart—and body—want what they want, and from practically the day she grew tits, my body wanted hers. My mind joined the party a little later, but I never acted on it. I mean, hell, everyone knows your best friend's baby sister is no-fly zone...not to mention our age difference.

And good God if she isn't sexier now than she was then. Time has been good to the girl. And apparently so has childbirth. Her once-slim hips now have a delectable flare to them—the kind that's just right for gripping when I plow into her from be—

My inappropriate daydreams get cut short when Nate waves another Jack and Coke in front of me. "You all good, dude? You looked like you were somewhere else."

I choke back a laugh, because really, I was—but I'm definitely *not* telling him I was envisioning myself inside his sister. So, I lie. "Just thinking about work." An idea pops into my head. It's probably the alcohol, but fuck it, I'm gonna run with it. "Hey, speaking of work...you wanna let me get Nat's number?"

Once again, he cuts his eyes my way, really studying me. "For work, huh?"

I nod, not trusting my voice to sound convincing.

He hesitates, and I'm worried he's going to shoot me down. But then he slips out his phone and fiddles around on the screen. A few seconds later, my phone buzzes in my pocket. I check it, and sure enough, he sent over her contact card.

"Thanks, brother."

He's about to reply when a brunette with killer curves approaches us. "Hello there boys," she says, eyeing us both up and down like we're juicy, USDA Prime steaks.

Nate tips his chin to her, much the way he did to me. "Evenin'."

I lift my brows in a friendly gesture.

She twirls a lock of hair around her neon-pink-tipped finger. "My friend and I couldn't help but notice you boys were over here all alone."

"And did you ladies want to give us a bit of company?" Nate asks, his voice dropping an octave or so.

Brunette Barbie signals to her friend—who happens to look like an actual Barbie—to come over and join us. Objectively, they're both beautiful, but damn if my dick doesn't even take a lick of notice. Hell, after the shit Mia put me through, I can't say I'm surprised. Especially since she was so much like these two girls—sexy but calculating. Don't ask me how I know they are—I just know. Thanks to Mia, it's like a sixth sense now.

I stand from my stool and toss down a few more crisp bills. "Nate, I'll leave you to it; I've got an early morning."

He smirks, not minding one bit that I'm leaving him in the company of two beautiful women. "Talk soon."

By the time I Uber home, my buzz has mostly worn off. Not completely, but mostly. It's definitely still present enough that I'm fully blaming it for what I'm about to do...

Me: So, about that coffee?

She doesn't answer immediately, and I toss my phone down onto the ottoman, resting my head on the back of the chair. My eyes fall closed and almost instantaneously visions of Natalie filter through my head. And not just how fucking tempting she looked today in her black skinny jeans and black button-down. Hell, how tempting she's always been.

But shit like when she was eleven and broke her arm in a bike accident. Nate and I were riding down to the gully, and she was dead-set and determined to follow us. I remember suggesting to Nate that we should slow down and let her catch up, but like the know-it-all fourteen-year-old he was, he simply pedaled faster. So did Natalie. Her little chicken legs furiously pushed the pedals. She was so focused on catching up to us that she took the curve in the road too sharply. Down she went in a sickening crunch of aluminum and skin scraping across asphalt. In that moment, I felt fear like never before.

Fear that she was seriously hurt.

Fear that her mom and dad were going to kill us.

I remember pulling my handle brake so hard that I skidded to a stop. I threw my bike down and hauled ass to her—thank you, JV track—where I gave her a quick once-over before dropping down beside her and scooping her into my arms while Nate raced back home to his parents.

Her arm was bent at an unnatural angle, and I know she must have been in so much pain—hell, it hurt me to even look at it. But even still, she buried her face in my chest and cried quietly until her parents arrived.

I guess you could say I've always been protective of Natalie. Even when I was with Mia, I found myself checking up on her through social media. She never posted too much, but each and every picture she did post was like a man being stranded in the desert and finding an oasis. And seeing her today and knowing she's a single mother to what I'm sure is a sweet little girl has me feeling some kind of way.

The sound of my phone pinging draws me out of my thoughts, and I rush to grab it, hoping like hell it's her.

Natalie: Uh...who is this?

Me: It's cute that you're acting like you don't know.

Like I said, we're blaming the alcohol. I try and convince myself of that as I wait for her reply. When it doesn't come as quickly as her first, I wonder if I pushed her too far. But then...the typing bubbles appear.

Then they vanish.

Appear.

Vanish.

Too impatient to wait for her reply, I fire off another text.

Me: How about tomorrow? Around ten.

Natalie: I have to work. Sorry.

Me: Nat, come on. I'm your boss. I know the schedule. You gotta do better. Let's meet at the little shop near the café.

Natalie: Make it eleven and you'll have yourself a deal.

I pump my fist in victory, considering this round won. With our plans in place, I weave my way through my unpacked moving boxes toward my bedroom, more than ready for bed.

chapter ten

Natalie

The thought of meeting Alden for coffee has termites swarming in my stomach. Or at least that is how it feels. My insides are a jumbly mess, and it feels like my nerves are eating away at me from the inside out.

Now that he's back, I have to tell him. However, the million dollar question remains...*how?*

Oh, and when?

I'm torn between ripping off the Band-Aid and easing into it; I also know the longer I wait, the angrier he'll be. And seeing as I've already kept him in the dark for four years...let's just say I'm not expecting him to be super understanding.

My only true hope is for me to be able to persuade him to see things from my point of view—to get him to see that I was a teenaged girl with a serious case of hero worship, who was terrified and embarrassed.

Over the years, I thought about reaching out. Especially after Tatum was born looking just like her daddy. I was tempted again around her first birthday; I even wrote him a letter, but when I asked Nate if he knew his address, he looked at me funny before informing me Alden has just moved to Europe and he didn't know his mailing address.

Shortly after that news of his engagement broke, I made the decision—as stupid and shortsighted as it may have been, especially now—to say nothing. What man wants to celebrate his upcoming nuptials with the love of his life by getting a card in the mail saying: *Congrats, and, oh, you're a dad!*

No man, that's who.

Now, though, I wish I would have tried harder. Partly because I'm terrified to tell him now, but mostly because he truly had the right to know. For so long, I thought I was protecting him, but really, I was only protecting my heart.

Gotta love hindsight.

I stroll into the coffee shop at ten till, thinking that if I get there first I'll have some sort of advantage. Only, Alden's already seated in a cozy wingback chair tucked away into the corner. He locks eyes with me and pats the seat cushion of the identical chair next to him.

With a shaking hand, I gesture to him that I'm going to order first. Lord knows I'm going to need some caffeine to get through this. I wonder if they serve Irish coffee?

At the counter, I order my usual hazelnut iced latte with a pump of vanilla before moving down toward the pick-up area to wait. The entire time I keep sneaking surreptitious glances at Alden. Age has certainly done him well. His once-lanky frame is now sculpted with lean muscle. His boyish and shaggy hair is now cropped close on the back and sides with just enough up top for me to run my fingers through. His jaw is cut from granite and covered in stubble so sexy it causes my thighs to involuntarily clench.

In fact, I'm so caught up in cataloging all of his yummy physical changes that I completely miss my name being called for my order. Naturally, Alden *doesn't* miss it, nor does he miss the way I'm gobbling him up with my eyes.

Sometime between imagining his scruff leaving my skin pink and my name being called out, he must've walked over to me. His oh-so-yummy and familiar scent invades my senses, and I jump when I feel his hand land on the small of my back. I break out into full-body shivers when he leans down and whispers in my ear. "You wanna stare at me, I'm not gonna stop you. But the ice in your latte is melting."

A rock to crawl under would be really nice right about now.

I open my mouth to reply, and close it—twice. I'm positive I look like the damn goldfish Nate won for Tatum at the county fair last year. Alden slides his hand from my lower back and slips his thumb through my belt loop, snagging my sweating latte with his other hand before tugging and guiding me to the little alcove he's claimed as ours. The action catches me off guard, as it's hands-down the most intimate we've been since *that* night

Whereas I'm an awkward, fumbling mess, Alden's the picture of cool, calm, and collected, slouched back in his chair with his beverage balanced on his knee. The silence stretches out between us, his eyes fixed on me, burning me from the inside out. I'm embarrassed he caught me staring, but more so by my apparent loss of motor skills *after* he caught me. I mean, *come on!* I've practically known Alden my entire life, so there's no reason for me to be acting so nuts—you know, other than the massive secret threatening to spew from my lips at any moment.

Alden lifts his cup to his lips—his luscious, kissable looking lips—and takes a few sips, his eyes never leaving me, even over the rim of his mug. Finally, he speaks, but I really wish he wouldn't have. "This weirdness between us isn't gonna work for me, Small Fry."

Deny, deny, deny! my mind demands. "Weirdness? Pssh. What weirdness?" I wave my left hand in the air as if I'm shooing away a fly.

He smirks. "*That* weirdness." He leans toward me, placing his coffee on the table, and grabs my hand, effectively halting my fidgeting. "Seriously, who are you, and where's my Natalie? You're acting like you've been body snatched. What gives?"

My brain trips over the *my Natalie,* and I know my cheeks have to be crimson. Sure, his voice sounds sincere, but the gleam in his eye shows me he's enjoying himself, even if it is a little at my expense. "I-I guess it's just nerves." I release a long exhale.

"Why? What's there to be nervous about?"

Well, mostly because you're the father of my child, and the secrets and lies are slowly driving me insane. Speaking of insane, I pull my hand back from him, because *why are we still holding hands anyway?* "I don't handle change all that well. And even though Don's an asshole, he's always been good about working around my schedule." I nibble on my lower lip, drawing his eyes. They dilate; I pretend not to notice.

"Natalie, if you're worried about—"

I cut him off, not wanting to elaborate any more on Tatum—I'm already near my breaking point and hearing him speak her name will surely rupture the dam. "I don't expect special treatment. I want you to treat me like any other employee. So, if my schedule has to change or you have to let me go, I get it. It'll epically suck, but I get it. Business is business, and your friendship with Nate shouldn't change anything." My words come out so fast and jumbled that by the end of my tirade I'm breathing heavily. I probably sounded like a freaking auctioneer.

I'm not sure what type of reaction I'm expecting from Alden, but it certainly isn't laughter. All the same, his low, husky laugh meets my ears, sending tingles down my spine, all the way to my toes.

"For real, girl?" He crosses his right leg over his left, propping his ankle on his knee. "First off, my relationship with your entire family, not just Nate, has no effect on your continued employment—your job performance, on the other hand, does. You do your job and do it well, and you'll stay on the staff. It's that simple." He leans forward, assessing me. "As for your schedule, I don't see any reason for it to change. So, we good?"

A small smile graces my lips. "Yeah, Alden, we're good."

He eyes me, then his gaze flits to the window. He almost seems nervous, but I can't fathom what he has to be nervous about. It's not like he has some fifty-ton secret crushing *his* chest. "Wonderful," he murmurs, his voice dropping deliciously low. "So, since we're good, you'll let me take you to dinner one night so we can catch up some more?"

"Dinner? Let's just catch up now." *Seriously, who goes to dinner?*

Alden makes a big show of checking his watch. "Well, I'd totally be down for that if I didn't have to be at the café at noon." *Holy shit! Noon? That means we've been here for almost half an hour!* "So, like I was saying, dinner..."

"I'll probably be busy," I say, deflecting.

He shoots me a sly grin and places his hand on my knee. The contact heats me straight through. I want to wiggle and shrug his touch away, but at the same time, it is the sweetest kind of torture. "I haven't even said when, Natalie."

"Oh, right." I look down to my lap, far too embarrassed to meet his eyes "When?"

"How about next weekend? That should be plenty of time to request off and secure a babysitter, right?" The corners of his mouth tip up. He knows he has me. I'm but a fish on a line, and he is reeling me in.

Dammit! He's thought of everything; I don't really have a way to say no! "Yeah...sounds great."

He stands and extends a hand down to help me up. "Great. It's a date."

I yank my hand back from him so hard that I slam back down into my chair. Alden quirks a brow at me. *Gah, somehow this only serves to make him look hotter.* "Nope! Not a date!"

Yet again, my outburst has Alden in stitches. "Easy there, tiger. It's not a date."

"Promise?"

He shakes his head back and forth. "You're bad for my ego, Nat, because gotta say, I've never had a girl beg me not to take her out on a date."

Ugh. The thought of all of the girls between Mia and now makes my stomach churn. Not with jealousy, but with...well...*something*. "Well, there's a first time for everything. And I'm betting your ego can handle it."

chapter eleven

Alden

WHILE I WISH I COULD say taking over Bayside has been a breeze...I'd be lying. Truthfully, it's been more of a hail storm—as soon as I think I'm in the clear, another chunk of ice pelts me. With the way good old Don was running things, it's honestly a miracle they're still open.

As if serving bland, basic recipes made with second-rate produce wasn't bad enough, the dumbass didn't enforce any type of written disciplinary policy, and he allowed the staff to set their own schedules. Luckily, I'm well on my way to fixing the first issue with a total menu overhaul.

Which leads to an entirely different issue. Yesterday I promised Natalie her schedule would stay the same. If I make everyone else change theirs and keep her as is, will it look like favoritism? But, if I change hers, I run the risk of severely pissing her off, maybe even losing her as an employee, and undoubtedly losing my date with her next weekend.

How much of a shit does it make me that the date is what I'm most worried about? Even if it is only as friends. Everyone's gotta start somewhere, and I have no qualms about working my way up from the bottom.

I've been holed up in my office all day sorting through the mountain of unorganized paperwork. Applications are mixed in with invoices, the schedules are handwritten and barely legible. This is a veritable shitshow. Of epic proportions.

Three hours later, I have ninety percent of the papers sorted—wouldn't have taken quite so long if my staff would stop interrupting me for shit they should be able to handle on their own. Speaking of my staff, I don't have applications or tax information on file for half of them. I'm talking no contact information, no emergency contact, no W2—nothing. *Seriously, how the fuck did Don keep the doors to this place open?*

Fed up and in need of a break, I slip my phone from my pocket and dial Nate. He answers on the third ring. "'Sup? How's the café?"

"A headache. It's a headache."

He chuckles. "C'mon, it can't be that bad."

"You're right. It's worse. At this point, banging my head into the wall sounds more appealing than dealing with all of this."

"Gonna be worth it, though."

"If I can get everything straightened out." I fill him in on all of the bullshit, hoping he'll have some advice for me. Luckily, he does.

"All right, listen. You already know you're going to have to thin the staff. Have everyone fill out an application—that way you have their contact information and whatnot. Once you figure out who you're keeping on, take care of tax forms. It's that easy."

"Easy for you," I grumble.

"Hey, this is your dream—man up and put the work in."

I scrub a hand over my face. "You're right. I just..." I trail off, debating whether or not to mention the debacle with his sister. "Here's the thing: I promised Natalie her shifts could stay the same. But..."

Nate lets out a slow exhale. "You know I can't really be objective here, right?"

"Yeah, I know. I'll figure it out. Drinks again soon?"

"Actually, I was thinking...why don't you come out to the house this weekend? We can invite a few people over, celebrate your ass coming back home."

I turn his idea over in my head for all of two seconds before agreeing. "Yeah. That sounds great."

It's finally Friday, and I've spent the past two days re-interviewing my staff. At this point, I'm legitimately wondering how some of these people were hired. I'm ninety-nine percent positive two of them showed up high. And I don't mean like a few tokes high, I mean a few blunts and a couple of bong hits high. The smell was so strong, they may as well have lit up in my office. And FYI, Axe Body Spray doesn't mask the scent—it intensifies it.

Don't get me wrong—I don't give a shit what my employees do in their own time, as long as it doesn't adversely affect business. They wanna party...go for it. They wanna dance with Mary Jane...not my business. Real talk: every restaurateur has had an employee or two like these guys.

It is, however, my business when they show up so high that instead of answering my questions, they cackle like fucking hyenas. How in the hell can they provide exceptional service when they can't even remember their own fucking names? And don't even get me started on their droopy-ass, bloodshot eyes.

Now, I'm down to the final three interviews—Carlos, who is more of a formality than anything else, that dude's not going anywhere; some dude named Steve, who I don't think I've even met; and Natalie, who I saved for last.

Not that his position was ever in question, but Carlos will definitely be staying on here at Bayside, only he's been promoted from the daytime manager to the general manager. The well-being and success of Bayside runs through his veins just as it does mine.

Turns out Steve is a standup guy. He is an older gentleman who busses tables because, as he so eloquently put it, *retirement is a fucking snore*. I told him bussing was better suited for teens and asked him how he felt about a promotion. Steve is now our expeditor—which really couldn't be a better position for him, seeing as how he used to write for a foodie magazine back in the day. So, dude knows quality food when he sees it.

For some unexplainable reason, waiting for Natalie to step into my office has me feeling anxious. Even though I'll be able to keep her schedule *mostly* the same—thanks to some insider info from my best friend—my posture is rigid, and my jaw is tense. Not because I think things won't go well, but because...hell, I don't even know why.

Maybe it's the fact that the sound of her voice lights me up from the inside. Or maybe it's the way the sound of her laughter erases all of my worries. More than anything, though, it's probably the fact that I want her in ways that would have her brother kicking my ass—especially if he ever realized that she was still in high school when she caught my eye.

But hell, I pretended for years that she was more like a sister to me than anything else...so why am I struggling now? *Because she's a grown-ass woman now,* my mind counters, fucking with me.

I'm about to tell my mind to eff right off when there's a knock at the door. "Alden?" Natalie's honeyed voice sounds from the other side of the door.

"Come in," I call out, my voice deeper than usual.

She steps through the door, smiling bright, and it's like a shot to my gut. *She's so damn beautiful.* "Having a good day?"

I nod. "How about you?"

"Yeah, um, yes." I smile at her rambling. I can't put my finger on it, but I like the way I make her nervous.

"I'm not gonna beat around the bush here, Nat. Your schedule is going to have to change—but only a little and only temporarily."

"Change how?" she asks, sounding mildly irritated.

"I'm going to need you to close at least one night a week."

She blinks at me. "That's it?"

"That's it. I was thinking Wednesdays?"

"That's actually perfect. I have online classes on Tuesday and Thursday nights—well, I mean, those are the days I set aside for it—but Nate is off early on Wednesdays, so he should be able to get Tatum."

I nod, like this is all news to me, when really, I chatted with Nate a few times to make sure everything would work. *But what she doesn't know won't hurt her, right?*

"Oh! Wait," she murmurs. "I guess I should actually ask Nate first. Is that...is that okay?"

"Of course, Natalie. Why don't you go ahead and give him a call?"

"My phone's in my purse in my locker, since I'm on the clock. May I?" She glances down at the office phone sitting in the cradle; I lift it and slide it her way, flipping open my laptop to give her a little privacy to call her brother. Thankfully he answers, and like I knew he would, he tells her he is absolutely fine with picking up Tatum on Wednesdays. She breaks out into a brilliant smile and thanks him. She's in the process of saying goodbye when her brow quirks.

"Uh, well. Um." Her words stop, and she listens for another beat. "That's j-just really short notice, Nate. I'm not sure I'll be able to get a sitter."

A quick glance her way shows me she's nervously wringing her fingers in her lap. Obviously, I can't hear his side of things, but she follows up whatever he says with, "Oh, are you sure? I...I guess that'll work. I'll see you then."

She ends their call and places the phone on my desk. "We're good to go, and apparently Tatum and I will s-see you at Nate's this weekend!"

"Glad to hear it," I tell her, leaving her to assume I'm referring to Wednesdays when really, it's the thought of seeing her two weekends in a row out of work that's got me feeling some kind of way.

chapter twelve

Natalie

WHEN NATE ASKED—NO, DEMANDED—THAT I come out to his place tonight for Alden's welcome home party, my insides basically melted like an ice cream cone—a freaking emotional ice cream cone—on a hot, summer day. And now, that sticky, feely-feels mess has me cycling through a riotous mass of emotions. At the forefront of them all is apprehension.

Coupled with a whole lot of reluctance.

Followed by a healthy dose of hesitation.

Pretty much, I'm nervous as fuck and have transformed into even more of a hot mess than usual. Which is saying a lot, because most days I feel lucky to leave the house in one piece. I was such a wreck heading into work this morning that even my mom picked up on it when I dropped Tatum off with her. I could tell from the major side-eye that she wanted to ask what had me wound so tight, but mercifully, she didn't.

I managed to calm down a little when I realized Alden wasn't there, but still, every worst-case scenario raced through my mind all day, leading me to make simple mistakes and mess up some orders. Finally, after the lunch rush, Carlos cut me early, and I rushed to pick up my little girl, seeking the comfort only her sweet toddler scent and cuddles can give me.

After eating a snack, we watched *Trolls*—again—before taking a nap together in my bed. Well, Tatum took a nap. I laid there and worried.

I mean, what if Tatum doesn't like him? Hell, what if he doesn't like her, because, *holy shit, I don't even know if he likes kids, much less wants one!*

That would certainly make telling him the truth a whole lot harder. It wouldn't stop me—made that mistake already—but *gah*, it would suck. At this point, my biggest concern is panicking and spilling the truth at his feet in front of everyone in some horrible nerve-induced word vomit.

I'm in the kitchen starting an early dinner—because Nate's food is rarely edible—when Tatum yells out for me from somewhere in the apartment.

That's her new thing. Hollering loudly enough for me to hear her instead of stopping what she's doing and coming to speak to me. I've told her countless times that's not how we talk to people. So, instead of replying, I go on about my business as if I hadn't heard her at all. *Mean, maybe. But...*

Not even two minutes later, the sound of tiny feet padding across the carpet meets my ears. And then, a tug on my shirt tail. "Mama! Did you heard me?"

I pivot to face her, and when she extends her arms up toward me, I reach down and pick up her, depositing her into the countertop. "I did hear you, Tater Tot."

She pouts. "Then why you not answer?"

"Why do you think?" I ask, with a smile in my voice. I don't want her to think I'm scolding her when I'm only teaching.

"A'cause I didn't come to you?"

"Bingo." I boop her on the nose, and she giggles. "What'd you need?"

"I not remember," she mutters, displeased to no end.

"It'll come to you. Why don't you go play while I cook?"

"I help?"

"Absolutely." I set her back down onto the floor before pulling her step stool out of the laundry room. "Wanna help me mix?"

"Yes! I'm a good mixer! Da best!"

She stands patiently in front of her stool as she waits for further instruction. "You are. Let me get you something to stir with." I grab her pink and red whisk that came in a Mommy-and-Me set I saw at Target. She also has her pint-sized apron and oven mitts. Yeah, I might've gone a little overboard the second she showed an interest in cooking—so much like her daddy.

I add our ingredients to the bowl: one cup of shredded, skinless rotisserie chicken, one cup of mixed garden veggies, and three-quarters of a cup of cream of chicken.

"All right, get to mixing!"

She hops up onto her stool, and I stand behind her, bracing her while also supervising her mixing. Once she has everything *mostly* folded together, I sprinkle it all with poultry seasoning and pepper and instruct her to give it one last stir.

Then I sprinkle a little flour onto the countertop, which Tatum thinks is hilarious. Through stitches of laughter, she informs me I've made a big mess, but I only smile. Once she gets her wits about her, she helps me roll out the store-bought crescent dough. I grab a glass down from the cabinet and use it to cut out six perfect circles of dough. I lay each one in its own spot in the muffin tin.

"Hey, can you do Mama another favor?"

She nods.

"In the drawer right next to the fridge, there's an ice cream scooper. Can you grab it for me?"

Another nod.

With the scooper in hand, I guide her through adding the creamy chicken goodness on top of each circle of dough. "What's we do with those?" Tatum asks, gesturing to the little leftover strips of crescent dough.

"Ah!" I exclaim. "Those are the most important part." We place two strips on top of each scoop of chicken and then step back to admire our handiwork. "Well, Tater Tot, nothin' left to do but to bake it now."

With the fun part over, Tatum retreats to her room, and I slide the pot pie muffins into the oven, setting the timer.

I decide to make the best of wait time and paint my toenails. Anything to keep me busy—to keep my mind occupied. And when I'm done, I paint my daughter's too.

The timer goes off right as I finish polishing Tatum's little piggies. "Stay here," I tell her, knowing she'd be sad if she smeared her polish. I walk to the kitchen mostly on my heels, with my toes spread apart—I'm sure I look nutso, but hey, I don't want my pretty pink polish to get messed up either.

After dishing up one muffin for Tatum and two for myself, I cut up an apple and grab us each a piece of cheese. *Dinner of champions, y'all.* I carry our plates to the table and then make the short trek back to the living room to grab my girl.

Once we've both joined the clean plate club, as my mother would call it, I tell Tatum it's time to get dressed to go to Uncle Nate's. She pumps both of her little fists over her head and squeals, her excitement palpable. If only I were confident in tonight going off without a hitch. If only I had her childlike naivete. *If only, if only, if only...*

We go through the same song and dance of getting dressed like we always do...I lay out an outfit for Tatum, and she dresses herself anyway. Then, we compromise. Tonight, that leaves her wearing a rainbow tulle skirt and a neon pink graphic tee proclaiming *a little kindness can change the world*—and Lord knows that's true. Her hair is styled into pigtails, with the right one sitting a smidge higher, with mismatched bows. Which is all too fitting when you take in her mismatched Converse as well.

Compared to her, in my white skinny jeans, casual gray knotted-front top and nude flats, I'm plain Jane and boring. In an effort to spice things up, I tease the crown of my hair and gather it into a messy, high ponytail. I coat my lashes in mascara, swipe some berry-colored gloss over my lips, and grab my olive-green slouchy cardigan because Nate keeps his house roughly the temperature of a walk-in fridge.

I throw an extra pair of panties and a pull-up into my bag for Tatum, along with her juice cup and a baggie of cinnamon Goldfish crackers. I start to holler for Tatum, but quickly clamp my lips shut, knowing it will undo my teaching her *not* to yell through the house. Instead, I set off in search of her, finding her in her bedroom packing her own bag. And—spoiler alert—it's full of toys.

She turns her big doe eyes my way and sticks out her lower lip. "It won't zip, Mama!"

"That's because it's too full. How about we pick three?"

"Four?" she hedges.

"Sure, four. But hurry, or we're going to be late."

Then again, maybe I should ask her to take her time. Hell, maybe I should call and say she's sick. I'm sick. We need to be quarantined.

Sigh, I wish.

The drive to Nate's house flies by, and before I know it, I'm pulling directly behind my parents' car in front of his little blue Craftsman-style bungalow. By the looks of it, we're one of the first to arrive or this little get-together is more intimate than I was led to believe.

I'm a bundle of nerves as Tatum and I walk up the little sidewalk leading to the porch. The door swings open before I even get a chance to knock, revealing Nate standing there with open arms, waiting for a hug from his niece.

He wastes no time scooping her up and twirling her

in a big circle, the sound of her laughter beckoning to my parents, wherever they are inside. As soon as Nate sets her down, Nana and Popsie are there waiting to dote on her. It's honestly like some sort of toddler receiving line, and at the end of it is Alden.

chapter thirteen

Alden

FOR SOME UNEXPLAINABLE REASON, THE thought of meeting Nat's daughter has me tied in knots. Or maybe it's merely the idea of seeing Natalie as a mom with my own two eyes—*fuck, does that make her a MILF? Because I'd definitely like to...*

A flash of headlights through the front window derails that train of thought...thank God. The last thing I need is to pop a boner in front of the entire Reynolds clan when I'm about to meet the youngest member of their family.

Nate makes his way to the door, opening it before they even have a chance to knock. Instantaneously the sound of sweet, high-pitched laughter floats through the house. Luke and Melanie are quick to head for the door, ready to smother their granddaughter with hugs and kisses.

Once she's had enough, the little girl draws back but stops when she sees me. Her mossy green eyes study me. She starts at my scuffed-up boots and slowly works her way up, taking me in. When her eyes land on mine, something tight pinches in my heart. I don't know this kid from Adam, but damn, I can just tell she's something special.

She tilts her head to the side, further assessing me.

"Who's you?" she asks with all the honesty of a toddler.

I crouch down in front of her so that we're eye level. "I'm Alden, and you are?"

"Tatum. I's Tatum."

I shoot a quick glance to Natalie, who has her left palm pressed firmly to her chest, before extending my hand toward Tatum. She looks at me funny before placing her tiny, slightly sticky hand into mine. I shake it. "Nice to meet you, Tatum."

She blushes and pulls her hand back from mine. I rise to standing, my eyes landing once again on Natalie. Despite looking stunning in her tight white jeans, she looks a little green around the gills, like she's two seconds from either puking or passing out.

I walk over to greet her. "You all good, Small Fry? You look—" I don't get to finish my sentence because suddenly Tatum is running circles around my feet.

"Small fwy? For reals? My mama calls me Tater Tot! Which do you like better?" she asks, moving at what seems like a speed her short legs shouldn't be capable of. "Fwys or tots? I like dem both with ketchup. I looove ketchup. Do you?"

I want to answer her, but I'm too hung up on Natalie calling her Tater Tot. I guess she didn't hate that silly nickname as much as she led me to believe when we were growing up. *How interesting.*

Finally, Natalie finds her voice. "Take a breath, child." Tatum stops her circles and does exactly as her mother says, inhaling deeply through her nose and exhaling through her mouth. "Good girl. Now, let's all go sit down, and maybe then you can ask Mr. Alden a few questions."

Mr. Alden...I ruminate, turning that over a few times in my head as I trail behind everyone toward the family room. Somehow, it just doesn't feel right.

Nate and his parents settle onto the couch while Natalie snags the recliner, pulling her little girl onto her lap, leaving me to occupy the loveseat. Mrs. Reynolds is asking me about how I'm liking being home when Tatum shocks the shit out of all of us, by scooting off of her mother's lap, grabbing her backpack, and climbing up next to me.

Natalie is quick to protest, but her voice comes out more wobbly than firm. "T-Tatum, Mr. Alden—"

"It's fine," I rush out, cutting her off. "It's totally fine, and you can just call me Alden."

I feel like my words shock her as much as they do me. Hell, they probably shock everyone. It's like not like I'm particularly familiar with children, but she's a tiny charmer, and something tells me she'll soon have me wrapped around her little finger, like everyone else in this room.

Nat looks like she's on the verge of tears, which is fucking odd, but Tatum simply nods happily. "Okay, Alden. Wanna see my Poppy Troll?"

I have not a single clue what that means, but all the same, I find myself saying, "I thought you'd never ask!"

Conversation continues around us as she excitedly unzips her bag, but swear to God, if quizzed, I couldn't tell you a word anyone else has said. This sweet little girl has me completely under her spell. I *ooh* and *ahh* appropriately when she pulls out a pink doll in a blue dress with a fluff of hair resembling cotton candy. "Dis is Poppy. She's a pwincess."

"Like you?" I ask, serious as can be.

Tatum breaks out into musical laughter. "I not a pwincess. I'm a Tatum."

"That's the silliest thing I've ever heard. You can be a Tatum *and* a princess. In fact, I'm pretty sure *all* Tatums are princesses. Didn't you know?"

Her eyes are as wide as saucers. "I do have sparkly dresses and a tiara and pretty lipsticks." Her pitch rises with every word. "I *am* a pwincess!"

I tap my pointer finger to the tip of her nose. "Hell yeah, you are, and don't ever let anyone tell you different."

She sucks in a sharp breath. "You said a no-no word." It takes everything I have not to laugh at how absolutely scandalized she sounds.

"I guess I did. I'm sorry."

"It's okay, Alden. Mama says we all make mistakes sometimes. She says it's part of being hooman."

I grin. "It sounds like your mama is raising you right."

Natalie

Watching Alden with my—*our*—girl has me feeling like Humpty Dumpty after he had his great fall. I feel emotionally fragile, like at any second I could shatter into pieces.

As she blabbers on about nothing and everything,

he never once looks bored or put out. No. It's quite the opposite. He looks enthralled—like every word from her mouth is the single most important thing he'll ever hear. And while I should be over the moon that they've already managed to bond, I'm gutted.

Absolutely gutted. Because now a whole new bout of issues is plaguing my mind. *What if when he finds out, he decides he wants nothing to with her? What if he tries to take her from me?* The what-ifs are as endless as the ocean, and the more I think about them, the more it feels like I'm drowning.

Right when I think I can't possibly take it any longer, my mom extends me a life raft in the form of a question. "Natalie, I know you asked if we could keep Tatum next Saturday for a few hours, but I was thinking maybe she could sleep over?"

"Sure. She'd love that."

Mom claps her hands together in delight before scooting to the end of the couch so that we're closer together. "Aren't Tatum and Alden precious together? He'll make a fine father one day." She gives me a little wink.

I choke on air at her words, because *Jesus, that hit too close to home*. All of this regret is like an anvil around my ankle, dragging me to the bottom of the river. That feeling of suffocating is back, and I'm so beyond desperate for someone to talk to, but there's no one here except us.

"Nate!" I call out my brother's name in a tone that's just too loud for the small space. All talk ceases, and everyone turns to look at me. *Kill me now.*

He whips around to face me with mirth dancing in his eyes. "Yes, Natalie?"

"I-I thought you said this was a get-together. Where's everyone else?"

Nate scoffs, pretending to be offended. "What, the company of your family isn't enough?"

I clench my jaw, speaking through gritted teeth. "Not what I said."

"But it's what you meant," he goads. *What is it about big brothers getting so much pleasure out of antagonizing their little sisters?*

"Not what I meant, either. I was just expecting more people."

"I invited a few other people, but they all had some reason or another they couldn't make it." Nate shrugs. "Which is fine by me—more food for us!" His words are in perfect harmony with the oven timer in the kitchen.

"Food?" I ask. "Tatum and I ate before coming over."

Giving me the stink-eye, my brother grumbles, "Why? My food not good enough?"

I can't help but to laugh. "Nate. You can burn water."

"Yeah, well, we can't all be fancy-schmancy cooks like you and Alden Gordon Ramsay over there."

At the sound of his name, Alden breaks away from his conversation with Tatum and turns to look at us. "Huh? What's going on?"

"Natalie was complaining about my kitchen skills."

Alden barks out a low, sexy laugh. "What kitchen skills?"

"See!" I exclaim, air fiving Alden.

He returns the gesture with a wink, causing my heart to drop to my stomach.

"I'm so hungry I don't care if it's a soggy grilled cheese—let's eat!" my dad says as he stands and leads the way into the kitchen.

We all follow suit. Nate opens the oven door with a flourish and pulls out two frozen pizzas that are slightly charred around the edges—case in point. Wanting to be a gracious-ish house guest, I keep my smartass comments to myself. Alden and my mother, however, do not.

"Nathanial Reynolds! You do not invite guests into your home and serve them store-brand freezer fare!"

"Right? Up high, Mrs. Melanie." Alden and mom slap their hands together. "Dude, you have to know I would've cooked."

"It didn't feel right asking you to cook for your own party. That's like wrapping your own Christmas gifts."

Tatum puts a stop to everyone's bickering. "Peoples! Who cares? It's pizza!"

"That's my girl," my dad bellows as he scoops her up and pretends to fly her to the eat-in table. "Quit your bit—whining and eat!"

After the pizza is long gone, it's past Tatum's bedtime, and her temperament shows it. Gone is my sweet, smiling girl, and in her place is a grump monster of epic proportions.

She's currently snuggled up in my dad's lap with him soothing her little tantrums as they come. Every couple of minutes her eyelids droop closed before she bolts upright, a new bout of tears welling in her desperation to fend off sleep.

Quietly, I excuse myself from the table to gather her

toys. Once I'm positive I have everything, I make my way to the front door. Only a deep, masculine voice stops me in my tracks.

"Going somewhere?"

Looking back over my shoulder, I see Alden looking like a freaking Adonis, propped up against the little half wall-bookshelf-mah-jig between the entryway and the formal dining room that never gets used. Well, at least not for eating—Nate has a freaking pool table in it.

My eyes eat him greedily, loving the way his dark wash denim hugs his powerful thighs. *Gah.* He's seriously too sexy for his own good.

"Just taking everything out to the car so I'll be able to carry Tatum."

"Look at you, girl." He pushes off of the wall and steps toward me, grinning. "Beauty and brains."

His playful words make my heart stutter in my chest. *Did he just call me beautiful? Holy shit...*

Apparently, my face gives away every thought racing through my brain, because Alden laughs as he slips Tatum's bag from the crook of my elbow. "You really are beautiful, you know that, right?"

I can feel my cheeks turn rosy and warm with equal parts embarrassment and delight. Because let's be real—there's something so validating about your lifelong crush finding you attractive. Even if nothing will ever come of it, because you're a lying liar who lies—even if your intentions were misguided but pure.

"C'mon, Small Fry. I'll help you get everything loaded up."

I want to argue with him, to send him away and do it myself—I mean, there are only two bags—but I don't. Because my time with him is precious.

We walk side by side to my car, his arm occasionally brushing against mine. I feel like a teenager on a first date, which is ridiculous. Alden pulls open the passenger door, and we toss the bags into the car. I start back the way we came, but he stops me with a hand to the wrist, gently tugging me back to him.

I spin to face him, and he drags his eyes over me like he's committing every detail to memory. His tongue darts out, running across his full, kissable lower lip, and I swear on all that's holy, my thighs clench together. *That's how you know it's been a while...when a guy licking his lips gives you a lady boner.*

"I gotta tell you, Nat, Tatum is something else. She's so smart and articulate for a...what, three-year-old? And she's so damn funny. Almost everything she said had me in stitches. I can tell a lot of that is how you have raised her; you're an amazing mother."

I'm gonna puke. Exorcism style. I try to open my mouth to reply, but a small sob gets stuck in my throat. Alden, misreading my reaction, wraps me in his strong arms. "Shh. You're good girl; you're good."

But he's wrong. So wrong. I'm far from good, and when he discovers all of my truths, he'll see.

"Th-thanks." I pull out of his embrace, even though it feels more comforting than hot cocoa on a rainy winter day. "I-I better get Tatum...it's p-past her bedtime."

He can tell something's off with me—hell, I'm acting

like I'm fresh out of the loony bin—but he nods all the same as he presses a hand to the small of my back and guides me to the house.

Back inside, I quicken my pace, causing his hand to fall away. Being this close to him is not good for my sanity. Working with him his bad enough, but physical contact... yeah, it's too much.

We find everyone exactly where we left them, gathered around the kitchen table. My brother catches my attention, his eyes narrowed at the two of us like he just caught us toilet papering his house. I hope he's not putting together any of my puzzle pieces—I'd like to keep them scattered for now, thank you very much. I shrug, and he arches a brow, silently saying *we'll talk later*—though to which one of us, I'm unsure.

Tatum is seemingly out cold. Now, I just have to hope she doesn't wake up when I move her. I attempt to gently lift her from my dad's chest, but she instantly wakes, letting out an ear-piercing shriek.

I gently pat her lower back and rock her a little in my arms while whispering soothing words into her ears, but my girl is having none of it. She rubs at her eyes with her tiny fists before pointing toward Alden, muttering something under her breath between bouts of angry-tired-toddler sobs, but I can't quite make out what she's saying.

"Say that again, Tater Tot. Mama can't hear you."

This time she speaks clearly. "I. Wants. Alden." With her arms stretched wide, she flings herself in his general direction, her momentum causing me to topple. Luckily, Alden is close enough to stop me from tumbling to the floor.

He smoothly takes her into his arms, and she contentedly snuggles into his chest, her eyes already slipping shut.

I shoot him an apologetic look, but he only smiles. And I mean he really smiles, beaming from ear-to-ear. After making the rounds of telling my parents and brother goodbye, Alden yet again walks out to my car with me. I watch on in awe as he effortlessly deposits her into her car seat. He makes an attempt to buckle her in, but laughs and steps aside. "I think this part is best left to the pros."

Once she's safe and secure, I back away, and Alden softly shuts her door. "Thank you for—"

"Don't worry about it. Like I said earlier, that girl is something special. I'm shocked she doesn't have your dad and Nate more wrapped around her little finger than she does."

At that, I laugh. "Don't let her fool you. You just distracted her tonight."

His upper lips curls in a half smile. "Not gonna complain. She was the best part of my entire week."

I smile and wonder if he'll feel the same once he knows she is his. Because ready or not, it's time for Alden to know the truth.

chapter fourteen

Alden

AFTER THIS PAST WEEKEND, THOUGHTS of Natalie and Tatum have taken up residence in my brain, and like squatters, they refuse to leave. Saturday night after everyone left, Nate cornered me and asked me what was up with his sister and me.

Wanting to keep my balls, I lied. Told him I didn't know what he was talking about. Told him she was an employee and a friend and nothing more. Utter bullshit, because I can totally see Natalie becoming my *everything*.

And her little girl? Damn, I may have only just met Tatum, but I already feel fiercely protective of her. Maybe it's because she doesn't really have a father figure, or maybe it's because she's Natalie's kid. Hell if I know. We just *got* each other. It's like her brain and mine connected on a whole other level.

One thing's for sure, I'm honored to know her, and that's not something I *ever* thought I'd be saying about anyone's kid other than my own.

Still, I can't stop wondering about Tatum's father—no, not father, sperm donor. How *any* man could leave those two is beyond me. Nat is sexy, smart, selfless, funny, driven...

the whole fucking package. And Tatum, my God, I've only met the kid once and can already tell she's amazing. She possesses all of her mother's best features and for some reason, we just *got* each other. It's like her brain and mine connected on a whole other level.

I asked Nate about the father when he broke the news all those years ago that Natalie was going to have a baby before she even finished high school. He said she didn't know for sure who her baby daddy was...or she wasn't telling.

Hell, I even shot her a message asking about it all, and while it was read, it went unanswered.

But what reason would she have to keep it under lock and key? I know for damn sure if I knocked someone up, I'd want to know. I'd want to be present and to help...to know my child. I swallow down the bitter memories that threaten to invade. It's fucking crazy how Mia has managed to poison so much of my life with her lies.

For real, though, that shit pretty much blew my mind. My Small Fry has always been a good girl, and the thought of her letting some dude between her legs when she probably should've been studying lowkey pissed me off. Which is kind of absurd. What right did I have to be upset over her doing the same things I was doing at that age? I told myself I was merely feeling overprotective of her—like a brother. Except, the uninvited thoughts I had of her from time to time were far from brotherly.

Natalie

It feels like my entire body is being poked by a million pins and needles anytime I'm in Alden's vicinity at work. If he gets too close, my skin feels too tight, my gut like lead, and my brain turns to mush.

I'm ninety-nine percent sure it's my guilt slowly eating its way through my internal organs, working to consume my soul. Which is why I'm coming clean Saturday night at dinner.

I know it's going to be painful and awkward, but hopefully in public, the inevitable fallout won't be too catastrophic—though, I definitely deserve his anger. And I'm prepared for it. Obviously, I'm not expecting him to throw his arms around me and thank me for taking on the hard parts alone. I'm not stupid, and he's not a martyr.

Nope. Just a girl prone to making monumentally poor decisions.

Unfortunately, I came to this decision over coffee on Sunday morning while standing in Tatum's doorway watching her sleep. So far, she's never asked about her father, or where he is, or why she doesn't have one. But, one day, she will. And I'm doing them both a major disservice by holding onto the truth.

So, Saturday night it is.

Downside, it's only freaking Wednesday, which means I get to help Alden close tonight. Like I said...pins and needles. And because of that, I can't seem to get my shit together enough to put up a front of being cool, calm, and collected.

It's like that one time in high school when I drank for the first time. All of my friends were having a good time, but I was jumpy and paranoid that we were going to get caught and grounded for all of eternity.

So far, thanks to Jenny running interference, it's been easy to avoid being completely alone with him. When I asked for a helping hand, she looked at me a little funny but agreed anyway. *Thank you, girl code.* But the fact that he just told her to go home early tells me he's onto my avoidance tactics and that some one-on-one time is inevitable tonight.

I mean, she was in the middle of her freaking side work, for Pete's sake, but Alden didn't even blink about cutting her. Told me to take over and her to see Carlos for tips and to vamoose.

The sounds of the kitchen crew breaking down for the night filter out into the dining room, letting me know that soon they too will be gone.

All I have left to do is clean my section and stack my chairs, and then I'm home free. Only thing stopping me from doing so is the fact that I have to go to the supply closet right next to Alden's office. The very same office where I know for a fact he's holed up doing end of day paperwork and God knows what else.

But, it's the only way I'm getting out of here, so I need to put on big girl panties—so to speak—and deal with it. Plus, maybe with a little luck, I can creep by really quietly, and he won't hear me.

I tiptoe through the dining room, probably looking like a cartoon villain, checking over my shoulder every few steps as if he's going to pop up out of nowhere. I've almost made it when he steps out of his office, causing me to shriek. "Jesus, Alden! You scared me!"

He blinks innocently at me, but the spark of delight in his eyes isn't very convincing. "Did I?"

"Ugh, yes! I about jumped out of my skin." Luckily the startle has overridden some of my nerves. I better hurry before the effect wears off.

"Sorry 'bout that, Small Fry. You about done for the night?"

I give him a tight smile and nod. "Yep. Just gotta clean my section."

He moves past me, grabs the cleaning caddy, and passes it to me. "I'll help. Two sets of hands are better than one, right?" It's on the tip of my tongue to tell him no, but... *technically* if he helps, I'll finish faster. And plus, we won't be able to talk over the vacuum.

"S-sure. Sounds good." I turn on my heel and head back to start wiping down my tables and chairs. Alden follows, vacuum in tow. I wait to hear the whir of the vacuum, desperate for some sort of noise to drown out his presence. But it never comes.

Determined to ignore the tension blanketing the room, I move to the next table, scrubbing away at a wine stain. "Natalie," Alden speaks my name, and even though it hits me like a dart, I ignore him.

"Nat, please look at me?" he asks, his voice softer than before.

I'm well on my way to my third table when I feel Alden standing behind me. He's so close that my body is absorbing the heat from his. If I were to move back even an inch, we would touch. Intent on continuing to ignore him, I vigorously scour the already-clean table.

Displeased with being ignored, he clears his throat. I spin to face him, and he steps into me. I try to move back, but the table digs into my ass, stopping me. "Wh-what do you want?" I whisper, terrified by his nearness and turned on all the same.

"This."

He cups the back of my neck, pulling my face to his. The next thing I know, his lips are descending onto mine, claiming them in a hungry kiss. He nips at my lower lip, tugging. I open my mouth, intent on stopping him, but he takes it as an invitation and deepens our kiss. His tongue moves against mine in the most sensuous dance, robbing me of my words. He shifts his hand from my nape, trailing his fingers down my spine, settling his hand on my waist, pulling me into him. I gasp as his much-larger-than-I-remember erection brushes against my belly.

That's all the encouragement he needs. Using his free hand, he threads his fingers through the end of my ponytail and fists my long locks, guiding me to the position he wants me in.

I'm all but ready to rub up on him like a cat against a tree when he pulls away. "What was—" I start to ask, but he shushes me with one last chaste kiss, followed by parting words that cause my heart to drop.

"Head home, I've got this." I start to walk away, and he reaches out and snags hold of my wrist. His touch is like fire and ice all at once. "Oh, and Nat—plan on us picking up where this left off on Saturday."

chapter fifteen

Natalie

IF I THOUGHT GETTING READY for my date with Kevin was hard, it's got nothing on this. I mean, what do you wear to tell the man of your dreams he's unknowingly the father of your toddler? Somehow, I don't think there's an outfit in existence that says *I'm sorry for not telling you, please don't hate me.*

I settle on dark indigo wash skinnies with a chambray boyfriend-fit button-down. A statement necklace and pointy-toe nude heels complete the look. It's casual and comfortable and maybe it screams *I'm not a total monster...*or at least I hope it does.

I'm ready with twenty minutes to spare, which is no good since Tatum is already at my parents' house. I'm anxious and restless, like a caged lion. I've been pacing the short hallway for at least five minutes when I decide a glass of wine to take the edge off is exactly what I need.

Moving to the kitchen, I grab the bottle of Riesling from the fridge and a stemless glass from the cabinet, pop the stopper, and pour. I take a sip, relishing the burst of crisp fruit across my tongue.

Yes. This is just what I needed.

The temptation to pour a second glass is strong, but I recork the bottle and rinse my glass in the sink. I want to dull my nerves, not get white-girl wasted.

I resume my pacing until a knock at my door lets me know it's showtime. Hindsight, I should have insisted on driving myself instead of letting Alden pick me up. But he used his charm like a weapon and wore me down, plus I've known him forever. But, it's still a bit weird. I'm pretty sure the last guy to pick me up for a date was pot dealing Paul.

I debate simply not answering the door, but knowing Alden, he'd find a way in. I crack my back, neck, and knuckles, and head to the door.

On the other side stands Alden, dressed in a pair of Nantucket red chinos and a navy and white buffalo check button-down. Sounds like it wouldn't work, but my God, it looks like it was made for him and him alone. He honestly looks so damn fine that my words seem to dry up and desert me.

Alden, on the other hand, not so much. "Damn girl. You look so good." He leans in for a kiss, but I sidestep him. He chuffs out a laugh. "Okay then, Nat. We'll play it like that." Ever the gentleman, he opens my car door for me and helps me into my seat. His hand on the small of my back sends sparks racing through my bloodstream and to my heart.

Alden tries to start up a conversation on the drive, but I stick to one or two word answers. I can tell he's confused by my erratic behavior, but my God, this feels more like being led to stand before a firing squad than a dinner between old friends, much less a date.

I think he's pretty much resigned to our night being a flop by the time he parks. He's taken me to R Bistro—a personal favorite of mine, due largely in part to their steaks being so tender you can cut them with a spoon. Not that we'll be here long enough to order. I try to offer him a grateful smile, but it's most likely more of a grimace.

Even with me acting like I have split personality, Alden opens my door and helps me out. *Gah!* He even takes my hand in his, and like the selfish bitch I am, instead of pulling away, I savor it, knowing it will probably be the last time.

Inside, Alden informs the hostess he called ahead for a table, and she takes us right back. We're in a little alcove; it's private and romantic and all wrong for what's about to go down.

"What are you in the mood—"

Our server arrives, cutting him off. "Welcome to R Bistro. My name is Jamal, and I'll be taking care of you this evening. Tonight, our specials are a blackened red snapper served atop a bed of wilted greens and whipped purple cauliflower puree or a pan-seared filet of beef with sweet potato mash and broccolini. But for now, may I take your drink orders?"

Alden orders a pale ale while I opt for a glass of water. My beverage choice earns me a brow quirk, but I can't stomach the thought of anything else at the moment.

Our server heads off to retrieve our drinks, and I decide it's now or never. "I...I have something to tell you."

Alden nods, encouraging me to continue.

"Y-you're not gonna like it." I lick my lips nervously. "In fact, you probably won't like me."

"You're freaking me out, Small Fry."

I pinch the bridge of my nose to keep from crying at the use of his nickname for me. *Might as well add it to the list of shit that ends tonight...*

"It's about Tatum."

Alden immediately looks alert. "What? What's wrong? Is she okay?"

This. This right here is what dying must feel like. "Oh, no. She's...she's fine. It's just that..." I let my words fall off, wondering how in the hell to say this.

Impatient, Alden prompts, "It's just what, Natalie? You're building this up to something momentous and freaking me the fuck out."

I cringe. *Ugh*, I'm messing this all up. "It's about her dad..." I lock eyes with him. "You're her dad."

Whatever reaction I was expecting, Alden's laughter was *not* it. Only it's not humorous laughter, it's dry and decidedly dark. "Not funny, Natalie. Get real." He runs his fingers through his hair, tugging hard on the ends. "Jesus. I thought you really had something to tell me."

I swallow over the lump in my throat. "I'm being real. You're her father."

He looks almost sick to his stomach as he eyes me skeptically. "You do realize *sex* is required to procreate, right?"

I nod, my eyes welling with tears. "You—" My voice breaks. "You remember that night the summer before my senior year when you woke up, and I was in the guest room with you?"

His stare is blank, almost as if he's somewhere else.

"Yeah, Nat, I do."

"Wh-what else do you remember from that night?"

Alden

My jaw ticks. What the fuck kind of game is Natalie playing right now? Whatever it is, I'm not interested. After everything Mia put me through, I vowed no more bullshit, and this conversation reeks of it.

"Honestly, not a whole lot. It was a long time ago, and I had been drinking."

Natalie sucks in a deep breath, her eyes wet with unshed tears. "We slept together that night. I came onto you, and you seemed into it. Into me. I-I didn't realize just how m-much you'd had to drink. It was my first time and yeah..."

Her first time? What the...is that why she had on my shirt and was in the guest room with me? No. No way. Thinking back, I realize the timing is spot on, but still...this can't be real, can it? Hell, I was so drunk that night, I couldn't tell my ass from my face. Could I really be Nat's baby daddy? And if what she's saying is true, what gave her the right to deny me a spot in my daughter's life?

My heart stops. Time stops. The fucking world stops.

"Holy shit. You...you're serious, aren't you?" My gut and her eyes say she's telling the truth—that we did sleep together. But that sure as shit doesn't make me her baby daddy. Hell, for all I know she sees me as an easy target. Lord knows Mia did.

She nods, her tears finally falling, running down her cheeks and dripping from her chin.

I drop my head into my hands, massaging my temples... how is this even real? "I...I have a daughter," I murmur to myself, testing out how it feels. My initial instinct is to call her on a bullshit and leave, but something keeps me from doing so.

"I have a daughter." My shock quickly gives way to anger. "How could you not fucking tell me? What right do you have to keep something like this from me?" Jesus, do I know how to pick 'em or what? My ex was the single most conniving woman on this earth, and Natalie, well, I'm not sure yet, but she could be a close fucking second. Because even if this shit is true, she kept it from me for four fucking years.

"It's n-not l-like that," Natalie hiccups out. "I-I never—"

I scoff, hardly able to even look at her, sitting there sniffling like she's the wronged party...like she's some delicate little flower that got trampled on. When in reality, she's nothing more than a liar and a thief of my time. "You never what? Thought this day would come? You never thought you'd have to come clean?"

"No!" she shakes her head rapidly. "No, that's not it, I swear."

I cross my arms over my chest and sit back farther into my seat to create more distance—emotionally and physically—between us. "You might want to explain what it *is* like, really fucking fast, Natalie."

She blinks through her tears and glances around the alcove like the answers she's looking for will magically appear. *Too bad, sweetheart, ain't gonna happen.*

"I...I was so young and sc-scared, and I know I made the wrong choice. I know I should have t-told you."

I pound my fist onto the table, causing our glasses and such to rattle. "You're damn right you should have!"

My hard, angry tone makes her jump back in her chair. I'd feel bad if I wasn't so damn furious. And hurt. This sense of betrayal and loss is so potent it's almost choking me.

"I'm sorry. So sorry."

"Save your apologies, Natalie. They don't mean shit to me. There's nothing you can say that will fix this. You robbed me of three years of *my* daughter's life. All those firsts you got to cherish? I. Missed." I grit my teeth together. She continues to cry and apologize, but I ignore her. My head is spinning, but I know if I don't get the fuck away from her, this is going to get ugly. Sliding my phone from my pocket, I tap the Uber app on my home screen and order her a car.

With that done, I push back from the table and grab my wallet, throwing down a twenty-dollar bill.

"Wh-where are you g-going?" she asks through her sobs.

"Away from here...from you. I can't stand the sight of you right now."

"Wha—"

I speak over her, not interested in anything else she

has to say. "I ordered you a car. Don't come into work on Monday." I push past her and stalk out the bistro, ignoring the curious stares from other patrons. To say this is not how I saw the night going might just be the understatement of the year. I feel blindsided and deceived and so fucking angry.

Who does shit like this?

Natalie fucking Reynolds—that's who.

Once in the privacy of my car, I break.

Shock like I've only ever felt once before flows through my veins, igniting and bubbling to the surface. I slam my fist into my steering wheel, desperate to dull the emotional ache. When that doesn't work, I do it again and again until my knuckles are red and raw.

How could she do this? How could she be so deceitful? And why? Why keep my daughter from me? I mean, Jesus, the only people she's hurting are Tatum and me. Surely, she isn't that selfish...then again, it seems like she is. It's Mia 2.0, and I truly don't know what I've done to deserve this shit.

The real kicker is this: the one person I want to talk to about this is her fucking brother. I can only imagine that conversation will go over about as well as a bowling ball to the head.

All of my feelings still bubbling just below the surface, I know I need to find a way to cull them. I need to numb them. To silence them. Luckily, I know just the place.

Destination in mind, I crank the ignition and head toward Bennet's, where I know my old friend Jack Daniels will be waiting.

chapter sixteen

Natalie

WELL, THAT WENT POORLY, IS all I can think as I wait on the sidewalk for my Uber. Then again, what did I really think was going to happen? If anything, it could have gone worse. He could have flipped the table. He could have thrown his drink in my face. He could have left me stranded to find my own way home.

In all of the years I've known Alden, I've never seen him that upset. I know I'm devastated over what just happened, but it's nothing compared to how he must be feeling.

Finally, a black coupe with the company logo on the door pulls to the curb. I waste no time getting in, and the driver wastes no time pulling back into traffic. I'm guessing he can tell from my puffy, raccoon eyes that I'm in no mood to talk.

When he idles the car in front of my building, I move to get out, but he stops me. "Hey, no one hurt you, right?"

I offer him a sad smile. "No, this is of my own doing."

He nods, and I close the door, hastily retreating to the safety of my apartment. It's just like Alden to be mad at me and to still be concerned for my safety. What other guy would make sure a girl got home okay after dropping the kind of bomb I did? I certainly can't think of a single one.

Then again, I guess that kind of stuff is the reason I've always crushed on him. He's been the ideal I've measured every other relationship against, and every single man has fallen short. *Jesus, if I weren't all out of tears, I'd cry at how pathetic I sound.*

I march straight back to my bathroom, where I strip out of my clothes and start the shower. I may not be able to wash off the sins of my past, but I can at least take care of my ruined makeup.

I stand under the spray of the scalding water until it runs icy and cold—much like Alden's feelings toward me. The crushed look on his face plays on a loop behind my closed eyelids. I can't recall a time that I've ever seen him so upset. Not even with his grandparents passed away. And knowing I'm the cause kills me.

Dried off and dressed for bed, I grab my phone, hoping and begging for a missed call or a text from him. But there's nothing.

No shit there's nothing, my brain shouts at me.

But my heart's not having that, so without thinking too much about him, I dial his number. The line rings and rings until voicemail picks up. "Al-Alden...it's me, Nat. Call me?"

Foolishly, I sit and wait, hoping he'll call. I try and distract myself with some Netflix. When that doesn't work, I pick up my Kindle and dive into my latest read—*Breakaway* by Heather M. Orgeron—but even still, my heart hurts. I toss my reader into my bedside drawer and decide to check out social media. But when I open Facebook, the first post I see is a check-in from Alden at Bennet's Bar. *Well, shit.*

Now I'm even more worried. Logically, I get that he's mad at me, and hell, maybe I'm even a little mad at him. I mean, it's not like he really gave me the chance to explain much of anything...*or did I just not try hard enough?* Either way, the thought of something bad happening to him has me nauseated.

I do the only thing I can think of—call my big brother.

"Sup, Nat?"

"I...I need a no-questions-asked favor."

"Whoa. Why—okay, what's up?"

"I need you to go to Bennet's and check on Alden."

Nate's heavy breath comes through the speaker. "I know you said no questions, but Nat, what—"

"Please? Please just do this for me? I'll owe you! Anything you want!"

He leaves me hanging, but only for a minute. "Fine. But when it's time for me to cash in, remember this shit."

"I will," I whisper into the phone before ending the call.

chapter seventeen

Alden

I'M SIX SHOTS DEEP, AND I'm fucking sure lucky number seven will be the one to make me forget...to make this shit go away. I raise my hand to signal the bartender—*since when are there two of him?* I blink twice and rub at my eyes to clear my vision. *False alarm, still only the one guy.*

He takes his time working his way down to my end of the bar, where I've been guzzling whiskey like my life depended on it. Which, I guess, in a way it does. Lord knows it's the only thing keeping me from losing my shit right now.

Once he ambles down to me, I push my empty shot glass toward him across the sticky, wooden bar top and slur, "Anudder! And keeps them coming!"

He grabs the bottle from the shelf and pours two more shots. "No more after this."

I slam them back to back, relishing the burn, loving the way it chases away the ache in my heart over Natalie and Tatum. *My Tatum.* Before he has a chance to walk away, I ask him, "You gots any...any kids?" He meets my eyes before looking over my shoulder. As he fixes a glass of water, I continue babbling drunkenly, desperate to get some of this crushing weight off of my chest. "I do. A daught-daughter. She's three and d-doesn't even know I'm her d-dad. How f-f-fucked up is that?"

Instead of acknowledging what I've just said, he keeps his gaze over my shoulder and asks, "You know him?" A pause. "Good. You got him?" Another pause and then he just walks away. I turn to the patron next to me—a grizzled old man that probably eats nails for breakfast. "Guess he doesn't like kids?" I slur. He grunts in reply.

I go to sip the water he left behind when a voice low and lethal whispers in my ear, "You wanna explain the shit I just heard come out your mouth?"

I attempt to spin to face the voice, but I tilt sideways off of the stool. Two strong hands grip the front of my shirt and haul me upright. The room spins, and my stomach churns. I pinch my eyes shut and let the sensation pass. When I open them, my best friend is right in front of me, all up in my space and glaring daggers.

"Gonna say it one more time; wanna explain that shit I just heard you say?"

Unsure of how he knew I was here, much less what to say, I simply blink up at my best friend, swaying slightly. He tightens his hold on me with one hand and uses the other to retrieve his wallet. He throws a few twenties onto the bar and hauls me up to standing.

Wordlessly, Nate manhandles me out of the bar and into his truck. I got a bad feeling about this...

Nate

ALDEN AND I HAVE BEEN friends for a long fucking time; in that span of time, we've had our fair share of disagreements, but never once have I wanted to deck him like I do now.

The shit I heard him saying just doesn't make sense. There's no way he's Tatum's dad. Like, my brain is screaming *does not compute,* because in order for that to be true, that means he fucked my sister. My still-in-high-school-at-the-time little sister.

Speaking of, how in the hell did she know he was here? How did she know he needed checking on? How did...*oh shit.*

No questions asked, she said. Guess I know why now. But here's the thing, I've got a lot of fucking questions.

Such as, if Alden's drunk ass is Tatum's father, why the hell hasn't he been pulling his weight and helping out? I glance over to where's he slumped over in my passenger seat, sleeping like he doesn't have a care in the world— which is utter shit, seeing as he's most likely the deadbeat mystery father of my niece.

I decide to bring him back to my place instead of taking him home. My face is gonna be the first thing his ass sees when he wakes up, and he's going to answer *all* of my questions, hangover be damned.

Hell, at this point, he deserves worse than nausea and a headache. My sister has spent the last four years damn near breaking her back to provide Tatum with a good life while this dickhole's been gallivanting through Europe with his cunty, psycho ex.

By the time I pull into my driveway, Alden's starting to wake up. "Huh?" he slurs. "Wh-where am I?"

I ignore him and exit the truck, coming around to his side. I fling the door open and find him fumbling with the buckle. *Jesus. How much did he drink?* I reach around him and hit the button to release it. He tumbles out, barely landing on his feet. "C'mon asshole. You're crashing here tonight. And in the morning, we're gonna have words."

With a reluctant arm around his waist, I help him into the house. Inside, I shove him—maybe a little harder than necessary—down onto the couch. I grab a blanket from the hall closet and throw it at him before locking up and heading to my room.

I grab my phone from my pocket and dial Natalie—*no questions asked, my ass.* She's got some explaining to do.

chapter eighteen

Alden

I WAKE GROGGY AND DISORIENTED, and I'm pretty damn sure an entire group of death metal bands has taken up residence inside my head. Hell, maybe my stomach, too, judging by the way it roils when I move.

Slowly I open my eyes, only to immediately close them—*so bright!* I'm in rough shape, but the question is...*oh shit*. The events of last night come rushing back.

Dinner with Nat.

Learning that I'm a dad...*Tatum's* dad.

Shots. Lots of shots.

Nate dragging me out of the bar.

No, no, no. This is not good. Especially if I am where I think I am. I force my eyes open, and sure enough, I'm on my most likely former best friend's couch. I'm half tempted to sneak out, but I'm not that chicken shit.

I move to sit up, and the room spins a bit. Coffee. I need coffee. Dragging ass, I stumble into the kitchen, where I start a pot. Hopefully after a cup or two, I'll feel slightly more human. While it brews, I help myself to the guest bathroom, splashing water on my face and gargling some mouthwash. It's not perfect, but it'll do.

Back in the hall, I hear Nate moving around in the kitchen. Looks like it is time to face the music.

"Morning," I greet, testing the waters.

Instead of replying, he grabs an insulated tumbler down from one of the upper cabinets and proceeds to pour damn near the entire pot of coffee into it. Guess that answers how this is going to go.

"Take a seat," he says, using what I like to call his bad cop voice.

My fight or flight is whispering *don't do it*, but like I said, I'm no chicken shit. So, I sling back a chair and sit. Nate, however, remains standing. No doubt to intimidate me.

Not gonna lie, it's working. Dude could probably kill me and get away with it; his police buddies would definitely help him dispose of my body.

"Talk," he clips out, sticking with one-word commands.

"Any chance I can get some coffee first?" I ask, halfway serious, halfway stalling. Nate narrows his eyes in reply. "Yeah, okay, fine. Honestly, I don't know where to start and probably have as many questions as you do."

"The fuck's that supposed to mean?"

I prop my elbows on the table and hold my head in my hands. "It means...I only learned of my apparent dad status last night. Hell. I didn't even know we—" I let my words fall off, not quite wanting to discuss *that* part of things with Nate.

"Yeah," he says, sounding as uncomfortable as I feel. "That's what Nat said too, but I figured she was lying to save you from me kicking your ass."

"Nope. Not lying."

"This is some fucked-up shit," Nate mutters, pacing the length of the kitchen. I nod my agreement, watching him wear a path in the tile. "So, what are you gonna do? Swear to God, you better do right by them. You wanna be mad at Nat, go for it, but you will *not* take your feelings out on Tatum."

"Jesus, Nate. Of course not." I let out a humorless laugh. "And to answer your question, I guess I'm going to do my best to get to know my...daughter. Shit, that feels weird to say."

A few silent minutes tick by—Nate sipping his coffee, and me wishing I had some—before I speak again. "I just wish I knew *why* she did this? Why she kept this from me? I don't get it."

Nate shakes his head at me. "I tried talking to her last night after I dropped your drunk ass onto the couch. She was crying something fierce and kept telling me she had good intentions, but wouldn't say much else. No matter how much I begged her to explain it, she wouldn't."

I mull over his words as he starts another pot of coffee. Looks like we're good after all. Two minutes later, the weird gurgling sound that signifies the end of brewing fills the kitchen, and Nate pours me a mug.

The first sip scalds my tongue, but I don't care. I take two more and then ask, "How did you know where to find me, anyway?"

Nate darts his eyes to the ceiling. "Natalie saw your Facebook post and begged me to check on you."

The idea that even after what went down she sent her brother to check on me has my heart swooping low in my gut. But I shut it down, because either way, she's still a goddamn liar.

chapter nineteen

Natalie

LIKE AN IDIOT, I CALLED Alden twice more after asking Nate to check on him. I even fell asleep with my phone clutched to my chest. When it rang in the middle of the night, hope soared in my heart thinking it was Alden. No such luck though—it was only Nate.

Which is an entirely different can of worms. It seems Alden has loose lips when intoxicated and some the things he said led Nate to bombard me with questions. Lots and lots of questions that I was in no way—even still—prepared to answer.

After a lot of deflecting and begging for a reprieve, Nate ended the call, leaving me to steep in my regret as I cried myself to sleep.

Dreams of Alden plagued me all night. Dreams of us as a family together. Nightmares of him taking Tatum from me. It made for a restless night, and it's hitting me like a ton of bricks this morning. I fell asleep with my hair in a wet bun, and now it's a rat's nest on my head. My eyes are puffy and the tip of my nose is red from crying so much.

Hindsight really is a bitch. At the time, at seventeen, I adamantly believed I was doing the right thing—that I was protecting Alden. Down to my very marrow, I believed it. But, with time comes wisdom, and my God, it's true that ignorance is bliss.

In the moment, Alden's words stung last night. But in the harsh light of day, they ring true. I *did* rob him of time with his daughter. And more importantly, I kept Tatum from knowing the love of the amazing man that—albeit, unknowingly—helped create her.

It's a bitter pill to swallow, but I am determined to make it right. Obviously, I can't give him back the time he's lost, *or can I?*

With that thought in mind, I fly out of my bed and into Tatum's room. I drag the rocking chair over to her closet and climb onto it. Balancing precariously, I brace myself with one hand and feel around the high shelf until my fingertips brush against the thing I'm looking for. I shift my weight forward, causing the chair to recline, hoping it will give me that slight extra boost I need.

No luck.

Carefully I bring my other hand up, praying like hell for the chair not to move. With a surer grip, I slide the heavy book toward me. Victory is in my grasp when the edge of it meets the lip of the shelf. I slide it toward my chest and slowly lower myself down to my knees.

Over the years, I have obsessively chronicled every single one of Tatum's firsts. From her first poop blow-out, to her first tooth, to her first epic meltdown. I know it's not the same as being present, but maybe it will help all the same.

I dash back to my room and dial Alden. Straight to

voicemail. I do as the robotic feminine voice instructs and leave a message after the beep. "H-hey Alden, it's me. N-Natalie. Um. Please call me when you get a chance. Please?"

I hang up and toss my phone down onto my fluffy white duvet. God, could I have sounded any more idiotic? *Yes,* my brain answers. *Yes, you could have.*

Which I prove to myself a mere two hours later when I fire off two text messages to him—both of which go unanswered.

It's around five o'clock when Mom drops Tatum off. Like usual after time with Nana and Popsie, my Tater Tot is on a serious sugar high. You'd think my mom, being a nurse, would keep her from consuming so many sweets, but she's a total pushover for this little girl.

"Mama! Mama! Mama!" Tatum chants my name, bouncing like she's on a pogo stick.

I gently place my hands on her tiny shoulders to stop her jumping. "Yes, baby?"

"Did Nana tell you about da muffings?"

"You mean muff*ins*?" I ask. Tatum nods furiously. "Nope, will you tell me?"

"We's made dem! But instead of booberries we used chocolate chips! And when Nana wasn't looking, I sneaked in some chocolate syrup! They were so yummy!"

"Whoa! That's a lot of chocolate, Tater Tot. Guess we better make a healthy dinner."

"I help?"

"Yeah, baby. Mama would like that very much. Go wash your hands and we'll get started."

Tatum tears off down the hall while I set about gathering ingredients. By the time she enters the kitchen, I have the chicken defrosting and I'm chopping up some broccoli.

"What we making?" she asks.

"Chicken and broccoli alfredo."

"Yum! I love dat!"

I move around her and get a pot of water going on the stove.

"Oh! I forgot to grab the butter. Will you get it, baby?"

She dashes over to the fridge and grabs a stick of butter—mind you, it's one I intentionally moved to where she could reach it while she was washing her hands. She brings it to me with a wide grin on her face.

"Thanks!" I move her stool over so that it is in front of the stove. In one pot we have our noodles boiling and in another our butter melting. When the microwave dings, I grab the chicken and add it to the pan of sizzling olive oil. I don't let Tatum up onto her stool to help until the chicken is finished—I would hate for the oil to pop her.

After I transfer the chicken to a plate, Tatum climbs up onto her stool. I slide the broccoli off of the cutting board and into the pan the chicken was in. Then I let her help me add a little chicken broth to it before covering it with a lid.

I also let her help me stir in the heavy cream for our sauce, as well as the parmesan cheese.

I once again have Tatum hop down from her stool so that I can safely drain the pasta. When I finish that, I turn off the burners and together we pour the noodles into the sauce and add the chicken and broccoli. "It smells good,

Mama!"

"It does," I agree, an idea sparking in my mind. "Hang on, okay? Don't move!" I grab my phone up from the counter. "Okay, baby, give everything a good stir for Mama!" I snap a few shots of Tatum at the stove stirring our dinner and attach them to a text to Alden that reads *She may not know you as her father, but she is so much like you. Can we please talk soon?*

chapter twenty

Alden

NATE DROPPED ME OFF AT my car after our chat. Things may be okay between us, but I can tell he's not totally okay with all of this. Hell, I'm not even sure *I'm* okay with it.

I mean, it's a lot to digest. Not only did I sleep with my best friend's little sister, but...*oh shit*. She said it was her first time. *I was her first*. Knowing that is kind of a mind fuck. On one hand, that caveman that lives inside every red-blooded, breathing male wants to stomp and shout in victory of claiming unconquered land.

But the sane, rational part of me also knows that has to be a shitty thing for her—for me not to even remember it, and then get knocked up on her first go. Knocked up with my kid. That she kept from me. At that, I tell the sane, rational part of me to fuck right off. She didn't have to be a single mom. All she had to do was fucking sit down and talk to me—I would have been there for her, come hell or high water.

In an attempt to clear my mind, I kill a few hours driving aimlessly. My plan backfires spectacularly, though, when I cruise past a playground and instantly picture myself pushing a chubby, red-cheeked baby in a swing. It gets worse when I pass the ice cream shop my grandparents always took me to growing up. I can't help but wonder if Tatum likes ice cream, and if so, what's her favorite flavor? Is she all about the classics or is she more adventurous in her flavor choices? Toppings or no?

My low fuel alert dings, breaking me from my thoughts. But, hell, even the gas station has me feeling nostalgic. As soon as we were allowed to ride our bikes out of the neighborhood, Nate and I would pedal down here to get glass bottle Cokes and peanuts. Nate got his roasted and put them in his Coke; I got mine boiled. Meanwhile, I have a daughter and don't even know if she has a peanut allergy—or any allergies, for that matter.

It's late in the afternoon by the time I make it back to the house. The silence inside mocks me. It tempts me to delve into my psyche—into the issues that I love to bury and pretend as if they don't exist. Issues named Mia.

But, after last night, I'm in no frame of mind to defuse that particular bomb, so I do what I do best, and mentally stick her back in her box, sliding it back up onto the shelf. She's an entirely different issue for an entirely different day.

I wash my hands over my face and take a deep breath, noticing for the first time that I smell like a distillery mixed with stale cigarette smoke—gross. I toss my keys onto my dresser and plug my phone into the charger before shucking off my clothes and hitting the shower.

The hot water soothes my body but does nothing for my mind. I waffle back and forth between shock, anger, and denial.

Shock that I have a daughter.

Anger that I'm just now finding out about her.

And denial...well, this one's a bit trickier. Because as much as I want to deny she's mine, I can feel it in my soul. Not to mention, her features favor mine more than Natalie's. Even still, maybe I should ask for a DNA test to be sure...even though I'm pretty damn positive of what it's going to say. After last time, I'd be a fool not to cover all of my bases.

When the water runs cold, I step out, towel off, throw on a pair of sweats, and face plant onto my bed. The urge to sleep is strong, but I roll over and snatch up my phone and power it on.

As my home screen loads, notifications ping. A total of five missed calls—all from Natalie—along with a slew of texts, though shockingly only half are from her. The rest are from Carlos.

I open his thread, not ready to deal with Nat's bullshit.

Carlos: Tara no called, no showed her shift tonight.

Carlos: Called her. She sounded drunk. This is her 2nd time pulling this shit.

Carlos: Also, you texted me some crazy shit asking me to find someone to cover Natalie's shift last night...wanted to let you know Jenny agreed to.

Jesus. I quickly scroll up, making sure I didn't make a total ass of myself, and for the most part, I'm okay. You know, aside from texting my GM at ten o'clock at night asking him to alter the schedule. I text him back a thumbs up emoji and toss my phone back down, still not ready to deal with Natalie, or anything really.

I know we need to sit down and talk, calmly and rationally, but I'm finding it really fucking hard to be either of those things at the moment. Instead of reading her texts, I pad out to the kitchen and whip myself up some dinner. I keep it simple, making quick work of a bowl of creamy avocado pasta, because as much as I love being in the kitchen, cooking for one isn't all that satisfying.

I take my dinner out onto the patio and eat it to the sounds of my quiet, sleepy street. It's peaceful, but would certainly be better enjoyed with company. Involuntarily my mind drifts to Natalie. I picture her and Tatum out here with me; the sounds of their laughter warming my belly far more than the meal.

Suddenly my appetite is ruined. I head back inside and toss my bowl into the sink—I'll wash it tomorrow. Back in my room, I finally decide to man up and read her texts.

Natalie: I'm so sorry. Please know that.

Natalie: Alden, I'm worried. Are you okay?

Natalie: What a stupid question, of course you're not. Please give me a chance to explain. Please?

The last message contains a picture of Tatum smiling and stirring a pot of what appears to be alfredo. The text attached fucking guts me.

Natalie: She may not know you as her father, but she is so much like you. Can we please talk soon?

I might come to regret this, but I pick up my phone and dial Natalie. The quicker I sort shit with her, the quicker I get to know my little girl. I've already missed out on enough. I'm not going to miss any more.

With every ring, my heart feels like it's going to crack my ribs and beat right out of my chest. Finally, on the fourth ring, she answers.

"H-hello? Alden?"

"Yeah." My voice comes out gruff. "We need to talk, Nat."

I hear her exhale softly. "Yeah, we do."

"Come by the café tomorrow for lunch—eleven-thirty. We'll talk then."

"Sure. S-sounds good. I really am sor—" I hang up before she can apologize...again.

chapter twenty-one

Natalie

I HARDLY SLEPT AFTER MY very brief but nerve-wracking phone call with Alden last night. Instead of getting much-needed sleep, I laid in bed and picked apart every last little detail of our conversation.

He didn't sound as mad as he had the night before. Not happy, by any means, but less like he wanted to snap my neck. So, that's a plus, I suppose. And he actually wants to talk. That has to be a good sign, right? Either way, that's what I'm telling myself, because the alternative is downright unbearable.

It's been less than an hour since I dropped Tatum off, and I'm already on my fourth cup of coffee. Usually I would be getting ready to head into work, but since, Alden *gave me the day off*, I have a bit of free time.

Mind you, every bit of that said free time will be spent obsessing over our lunch meeting. It really could go either way, but I am determined to think positive. I mean, it's not like I expect all to be forgiven and forgotten in two seconds flat, and I certainly don't expect him to ever want to pursue something romantically with me, but...I do expect him to want to get to know Tatum, and to do that, we at least have to be civil. Baby steps and whatnot.

I decide to make the best of my free time and do a little laundry—Lord knows it is easier to do while Tatum isn't here. She likes to help fold, only we have *very* different definitions of the word.

With two loads down and one in the dryer, I hop in the shower. I take my time, washing and scrubbing and shaving. I'm hoping the whole look good, feel good can somehow extend to my meeting with Alden. If I look good and feel good, maybe things will go...good.

After drying off, I wrap my hair in my towel and slather on some lotion. I start on my makeup immediately after, opting for subtle and soft. I decide to toss my still-damp hair into a braid so it can air dry into waves. A few squirts of my sea salt spray and I'm good to go.

I check the time when I step back out into my bedroom. It's only half past ten; that gives me plenty of time. I dress in a pair of black skinnies that are slightly distressed in the knee, pairing them with a simple slub knit gray top and gold sandals.

I still have about fifteen minutes to kill after getting dressed, but I'm too antsy to wait around. I grab my purse and head out to my car. The drive seems shorter than usual, but I'm not sure if its nerves or an actual lack of traffic—either way, I find myself rolling into the Bayside employee lot at 11:15 a.m. I guess in some circles, fifteen minutes early is considered on time.

So, with that in mind, I take down my braid, finger comb my hair, and head on in.

Giselle is at the hostess stand, and she greets me with

a plastic smile. I used to think it was fake, but eventually learned it's just her smile. "Hey Natalie, I thought you were off today? Lord knows Carlos called us all looking for someone to cover you. Is everything okay? Is Tatum okay?"

"Oh, yeah. Um..." *Jesus, this is awkward.* "Yeah, Nat's fine. Um..."

Jenny walks up and saves me from answering. "Girlfriend. We need to talk."

"We do?"

She nods and pulls me away. "Yes ma'am. I texted you this weekend and you never replied."

I give her a sheepish look. "Did you? I'm sorry, J. This weekend was...a mess."

"Yeah, yeah. We'll talk tonight."

"Sounds good." I start to talk away, toward Alden's office, but Jenny speaks up, stopping me.

I slow my pace as I approach the office, taking a deep breath before approaching. The door is partially open, but I knock anyway.

"Come in," Alden's deep, masculine voice calls from inside.

I take a timid step into the room, taking great care to leave the door exactly as it was. "Hey," I say lamely.

"Take a seat, Nat." His voice is borderline emotionless, and that worries me.

"S-sure." I lower down into one of the chairs on the opposite side of his desk, looking everywhere but at him.

For several tense moments, we sit in silence until finally Alden stands. "Let me grab our food and then we can talk."

He stalks out of the room, and I use the time he is gone to give myself a little pep talk. "You've got this, Nat. Just tell him your side of things. It's okay."

Alden steps back into the room, and I zip my lips. Unlike me, he doesn't leave the door cracked. He shuts it completely, and I gulp.

"Hope you're in the mood for a grilled shrimp Caesar." He casually drops the plate in front of me along with a roll of silverware.

"Sounds great, thank you."

I dig into my food, mostly to have something to do. I expect him to do the same, but instead, he slides open a desk drawer and pulls a bubble mailer from within it and sets it on the desk between us.

"You say she's mine, and I believe you—mostly. But I'd be a fool not to get proof. I don't want to drag this shit before a judge, so here." He gestures toward the package. "I've already swabbed myself. All you need to do is swab her and mail it."

Slowly, I pull it toward me and peek inside. A paternity test. My heart sinks a little, but deep down, I know he's right to ask for this. Especially with him not remembering even sleeping with me. Still, it hurts, just a little.

"Sure."

"If she's mine, you're not going to keep her from me, Nat." His tone is hard and cold and so unlike the boy I fell in love with.

"That was...no. Never." I stumble over my words and he scoffs.

"Never? That's fucking rich."

My eyes fill with tears, and I tilt my head back, desperate not to let them fall.

"Jesus Christ. Do you ever get tired of playing the victim?"

My sadness and hurt morph to anger. "Do you ever get tired of making assumptions and not letting people speak?"

"There's not a damn thing you could say to justify keeping my daughter a secret from me for four goddamn years!" He yells the words, slamming his palms down onto his desk.

I shove my chair back and stand, getting in his face. Fuck being nice and understanding. "Did you ever, even once, stop to think I was seventeen and alone and scared? Did it ever fucking occur to you that I was trying to protect you?" I'm so mad that I'm crying. I fucking hate angry crying.

"Protecting me? Get fucking serious! The only person you were looking out for was you!"

"Right. You called it. I was looking out for me by going it alone. I was looking out for me by not getting any parenting support, much less fucking child support. You're absolutely right. It was so easy and breezy for me."

"Always the martyr, huh, Natalie?" He pitches his voice to mimic me, "Oh, poor me. I'm a single mom and my life is so hard."

"Fuck. You." I spit the words in his face like they're venom. "I was terrified and so infatuated with you that I suffered the humiliation of letting my parents think I was a whore just to save you!" He starts to rebut, but I yell over him. "I was seventeen, Alden. You were twenty! I was scared you'd be charged with statutory rape and that your entire future would be destroyed. So, yes, you asshole. I. Was. Protecting. You!"

By the time I'm finished, we're both breathing heavy. I'm still crying, and he looks utterly broken and on the verge of totally losing his shit. He parts his lips to speak, but the door flies open, silencing him.

We both turn and watch in horror as my father bursts in, looking ready to kill. My mom lingers outside the office with wide, worried eyes, while my brother is right behind Dad, grabbing him by the collar of shirt just as he rears back to punch Alden.

This day just went from awful to *fucking awful* in about two seconds flat.

chapter twenty-two

Alden

I LISTEN MUTELY AS MR. Reynold's hurls insults my way left and right. "You sorry, sad sack of shit! You take advantage of my goddamn daughter after we practically raised you as one our own?"

Nate keeps him physically restrained, but barely.

This, right here, is my worst nightmare come to life. I'm honestly closer to the Reynolds family than I am my own. The love and kindness they showed me growing up was no different than the love they gave their children— unconditional. But here and now, I can see that there absolutely are conditions. And sleeping with their little girl, fathering her child, and—as it seems to them—skirting my responsibilities, breaks those conditions.

"Dad, please," Natalie sobs, but it's no use. Mr. Reynolds is past the point of no return.

"It makes me sick to think of all the time we allowed you into our home. All the times you spent the night."

I don't bother trying to defend myself. He's not going to listen to a word I say. Thankfully, Nate speaks up. "That's. Enough." His voice is deep and commanding, and his father instantly stops.

Natalie is quietly crying, her mother now consoling her while the three men in the room engage in a testosterone stare down, none of us willing to be the first to speak.

Carlos steps into the room, cutting the tension—slightly. With eyes straight on me, he says, "I'm gonna go suggest y'all either take this elsewhere or take the volume down. Customers and staff alike can hear every word. And while we want to be talked about in town, let's reserve it for our food, not our gossip." Just as quickly as he entered, he leaves, shutting the door behind him.

I collapse back into my chair. "Fuck," I groan out, elongating the word.

"If I let you go, will you stay put?" Nate asks his father.

Mr. Reynolds grunts and nods.

Nate releases him and he lunges, popping me in the jaw. "Goddamn it, Dad!" Nate yells, yanking him away from me. Mrs. Reynolds begins to weep as well. I rub a hand over my aching jaw, and Natalie moves closer to me, placing her hand over mine.

"I'm s-s-sorry. This is all my f-fault." Her words are barely understandable, and her touch feels like fire and ice. I want to haul her in closer and shove her away all at once. One thing's for sure, though—this is her fault.

Yet, somehow, I find myself sympathizing for her, which pisses me off. I turn my head from her, causing her hand to fall away. She gets my message loud and clear and steps back. Nate guides her down into a chair, repeating the motions with his mother.

Together, we sit in my office, me on one side, the Reynolds clan on the other. This feels like the meeting from hell, with sides clearly drawn—it's me against them.

The patriarch of their family goes to speak again, but his wife quiets him. "Luke, I think it's safe to say there's a lot more going on here than we know."

Mr. Reynolds disagrees. "I know all I need to know."

"You really don't, Dad. You know what you overheard, which isn't much."

Her dad pins her with a glare so icy it could sink the Titanic. "Then start talking, little girl."

Natalie

Oh. Jesus. I've never in my life regretted keeping this secret more than I do in this moment. Talk about a colossal fuck-up on my part. "If you're going to be mad at anyone, be mad at me."

My dad glares. "Oh, I am." My mom lays her hand on his, and he simmers down.

"When Alden and I...when we..." I struggle to find the right words, finally settling on, "That night, I came onto Alden. I'd had the biggest crush on him for as long as I could remember, and I finally decided to act on it—that it was now or never.

"He...he seemed into me, and one thing led to another." A quick look around the room tells me this is as awkward for everyone else as it is for me. "I didn't realize how much Alden had drunk that night, and the next morning, he didn't even remember anything happened between us.

"It stung, but I figured no harm, no foul. And then..."

"And then you found out you were pregnant," Mom supplies.

I nod, feeling microscopically small.

"I really thought I was doing the right thing. I see now that I was wrong and incredibly misguided. I was scared Alden would get in trouble, among other things."

Alden speaks up. "What other things?" I shake my head, not wanting to answer. "No, c'mon, Natalie. Cards on the table: what other things?"

"Things like Mia," I whisper.

At her name, Alden's gaze turns hard and dark. "Mia. Got it."

He seems angry about this, which baffles me. "You guys had started dating and I didn't want to come between y'all."

He lets out a low, humorless laugh. "Thanks, Nat. So much. Really appreciate it."

I'm not sure where this particular brand of hostility is coming from, and I don't appreciate it. "How many times do I have to say sorry? I know I was wrong, and I have apologized countless times—and yes, I know *sorry* doesn't make it all better! But, I refuse to be your emotional punching bag. You may not remember that night, but you *were* a willing participant like it or not. Not to mention, the age I am now, is basically how old you were then! I messed up. I'm owning it and trying like hell to make it right. Either accept my apology or don't, the choice is yours. But this shit? It's not going to happen."

My words shut him up. They shut everyone up.

Mom is the first to break the silence. "Obviously y'all have a lot to talk about. Nat, why don't you walk your father and I out?"

"Yeah, sure."

The three of us stand and exit the office. I can feel the eyes of seemingly everyone on me, and it makes me squirm. I'm a fairly private person, and now every employee on shift and patron knows my business. *How mortifying.*

I walk my parents all the way to their vehicle. The air around us is thick and tense.

My mom steps to me and wraps me in her arms, pressing a kiss to my temple. "It will be okay. Everyone makes mistakes, kiddo, but I have to say, you may have taken the cake." *Leave it to mom to attempt to joke at a time like this.*

She squeezes me one last time and gets into the car. Leaving just me and my dad. My very angry, surly dad. "I'm disappointed in you, Nat Bug. Real disappointed." He turns and gets into the driver's seat, not even looking at me, much less giving me a hug.

Guilt and sorrow churn in my gut as I head back into the café. I was prepared for today to be hard, but my family's presence only served to further complicate our already difficult situation.

As I approach the office, still-raised voices greet my ears.

Great.

I linger, not wanting to interrupt. I'm in the process of turning to walk away when my brother's voice stops me in my tracks. "Here's the thing, Alden. Even if you were hammered, you wouldn't have made a play for my sister unless you were already thinking of her like that when you were sober. I know you, brother, and that's just who you are."

It wasn't my intention to eavesdrop, yet here I am, waiting. In all honesty, I feel like a dog with a treat on her nose, waiting to be told to *"Get it!"* Only, Alden's reply is my *it* and I'm downright salivating for it.

"You really are like a brother to me, so I'm gonna shoot straight here and not give you any bullshit. Yes, your sister caught my eye on more than one occasion. I can't pinpoint the exact moment my feelings for her changed—I just know that one day she went from honorary sister to something more. I swear though, I never *knowingly* acted on it. Age difference aside, I'd never betray you like that."

I suck in a sharp breath at Alden's confession. *He had feelings for me?*

chapter twenty-three

Alden

I FEEL IT'S ON ME to be honest with Nate about being into his sister back then. But vague is the way to go. He doesn't need to know the extent of my— mostly former— infatuation.

He doesn't need to know that when she turned sixteen and sprouted breasts that I could hardly tear my eyes away, as sick as that is. And he absolutely doesn't need to know that every time I...took matters into my own hands...it was her fantasized about.

Nope. No way in fucking well. I'm keeping that shit under lock and key. Hell, maybe in a fireproof safe.

"I know you wouldn't," Nate says, lifting a boulder off of my shoulders. Legit, I feel a hundred pounds lighter.

A knock sounds from the other side of my office door. Nate quickly stands. Awkwardly, I extend my hand toward him. But instead of a handshake, he pulls me in for a bro-hug. "I'm gonna get out of here and let you and Nat talk."

"Sounds good." He walks over to the door, but I stop him before he can pull it open and leave. "Hey, Nate, thanks."

He opens the door and leaves, and his sister enters the

room, taking the seat he just vacated. "That was...a lot," she murmurs, breaking the ice.

I stare at her, seated across from me, looking frazzled and puffy-eyed, but still so fucking beautiful. The fury I want so desperately to cling to begins to slip away. I'm not sure that I'm actually ready to let it go, but I can see the pain and regret so clearly in her glassy eyes.

"One way of putting it." I drop back down into my chair. "I want to get to know Tatum."

"Yes! Yes, of course. I really, truly would never stand in the way of that." She pauses, wiping her palms across her shapely, denim-clad thighs. "And I want you to know, I don't expect anything from you. Between us or monetarily. The only thing Tatum needs from you is your time—time I have already unfairly taken from y'all."

The remorse in her voice is so strong that I physically feel it, and it makes me ache. "I'm gonna be real with you, Nat. I'm not as mad as I was. But, I can't say I'm ready to forgive and forget. It's going to take time, but I will never let the shit between us bleed over into my relationship with Tatum."

She gives me a sad smile. "That's all I can ask for."

"Let's hammer out a schedule then."

Natalie digs her phone out of her purse, and I run my index finger over the touchpad on my laptop, waking it from its sleep. I key in my password and open my calendar.

"W-would it be okay for the first visit or to two for me to tag along?"

My first instinct is to tell her to fuck off, but I refrain. I imagine this has to be hard for her—even if it is of her own doing. "Sure."

"Really?" She sighs, and I watch her posture visibly loosen. "Thank you so much. Maybe we...we could make you dinner?"

I don't particularly want to go to her house, but I agree to because I know it is where Tatum will be the most comfortable. I offer the same one-word answer as before, but she smiles like I just told her she's won the lottery.

"Thank-you-thank-you-thank-you!" She leaps from her chair and moves around the desk, wrapping me in a hug. Her nearness feels better than I'll ever admit out loud; it feels like carbonation bubbles bursting against my tongue after that first sip of Coke.

I gently move her back from me. I can't think for shit when she's that close. It's like my body and my brain go to war, and her little body and her warm skin on mine feel so good that my brain waves the white flag of defeat within seconds.

Fuck that noise.

She looks a little hurt at the distance I've forced, but she'll get over it. "How about dinner tomorrow?"

She returns to her seat and nibbles her lip. "I have one of my classes."

"That's not a problem for me. I'll keep an eye on Tatum while you do your class. Maybe Tatum and I can cook for you." As soon as the idea forms in my mind, I like it. "Really, it's the most favorable option, Natalie. I get time with her, but we're under the same roof. It's a win-win."

"Yeah. You're right. But listen, we need to handle telling her *who* you really are delicately."

I fight the urge to roll my eyes. I may be new to the whole parenting thing, but I'm not an idiot. "I agree. I'll spend time with her first and let her get to me, and when it feels right, we will tell her together."

"Yeah, okay." She stands, grabbing her bag. "I'll see you tomorrow. My class starts at six, so maybe a little before?"

"I'll be there."

"Oh, and Alden." I glance up to find her fishing something out of her bag. It looks like a...scrapbook? "I-I brought this for you. It's a book of all of Tatum's firsts. I know it's not the same as *being* there, but hopefully it'll help a little." She places it on the edge of my desk and walks away, closing the door behind her.

I pull the memory book toward me, with great caution, like it's a coiled snake, ready to strike and inject me with deadly venom at any time. Flipping it open, I'm immediately met with a picture of Tatum as a newborn laying on Nat's chest. I'm awestruck by how similar we looked as babies; if anything, it reaffirms what I already know in my heart to be true—she is mine.

I flip through the pages, one by one, soaking up every entry. I have to give Natalie credit, she truly kept up with every single first. Even a few I could have went without— first diaper blow-out? *No thanks.*

chapter twenty-four

Natalie

I'VE SPENT THE ENTIRE DAY cleaning like a maniac. The carpet is the cleanest it's ever been, the countertops are spotless and the tile is sparkling, yet I keep scrubbing. I'm on my hands and knees in the kitchen making sure the oven is in tiptop shape in case they bake anything when Tatum walks in and says my name. I turn to look at her banging the top of my head on the stove.

"Ouch! Shit!"

"Dat's a no-no word, Mama." She shakes her head back and forth at me as if I've severely let her down with my foul mouth. "Nana says its un...unbetumming."

I stifle a laugh—she's so precious it hurts. "Unbecoming? That's an awfully big word, Tater Tot."

She beams. "I smart."

"Very much so."

"What's you doing?" she asks, scrunching up her nose.

"Cleaning."

"Why?"

"Alden is coming over." Before I can get another word out of my mouth, my girl is full-on happy dancing. I'm talking head-bobbing, booty-shaking, foot-stomping, hand-clapping dancing.

"You excited?"

"Yes!" she squeals, throwing her tiny arms around me, knocking me onto my ass and my head into the stove for a second time. "I'm so 'cited! I gotta get dressed, Mama! Like a pwincess!"

She takes off toward her room, and I push myself back up onto my knees. I give the oven one last appraisal—it looks almost new, despite its years of use. Gripping the lip of the counter, I pull myself to standing and check the time. "Oh my God! It's already five!"

I haul ass down the hall, pausing outside of Tatum's door. "Mama's getting in the shower. I'll leave the door open!"

I turn the knob, shuck off my clothes, and hop in before the water even has a chance to get warm. "Cold, cold!" I squeak, but I power through. By the time the water runs warm, I'm finishing up and hopping out.

I forego a towel entirely, drip-drying as I make a mad dash to my closet. I toss on my undergarments, shimmy into a pair of leggings, and pull a tank over my head. I toss my wet hair up into a bun and rush back to check on Tatum.

Unlike me, she is a picture of pure perfection, decked out in a lemon-colored flippy tulle skirt, a pastel pink cap sleeve top with a silver glitter heart on the front, and a pair of purple high-top Converse.

"Fix my hair, Mama?"

I check the time on my phone. Five-forty. "Sure baby." I follow her into her room and take a seat on her bed, where she already has her brush and hair elastics waiting. She stands between my knees as I brush her hair, smoothing it away from her face. I do a pretty waterfall braid and then secure the ends into a side pony.

"You done?"

"I am. Go look."

She rushes over to the mirror and squeals at her reflection. "Thanks, Mama! It's perfect!"

I put her brush and extra elastics in her top drawer and drop a kiss to her forehead. "Glad you like it, baby."

We both freeze when the sound of the doorbell echoes through the apartment. Tatum recovers before I do, making a break for the door. I trail after, more apprehensive than excited. But, I know this is the first step in mending all that I broke.

I gently scoot my girl out of the way and open the door. The sight of Alden damn near takes my breath away. He's dressed in a pair of navy cargo shorts and a weathered gray graphic tee that reads, *You are what you eat.* Nothing special, but my God, it's mouthwatering all the same.

"Hey," he says casually.

"Hi."

"Alden!"

"Hey there, Princess. I've got something for you. If your mama ever asks me in I'll give it to you."

If the floor could swallow me up right about now, that'd be great. I open the door wider and gesture for him to enter. Tatum wastes no time leaping into his arms, knocking the reusable shopping bag he's holding from his grip. "Alden! I missed you!"

I see some unidentifiable emotion pass over his face, but it's gone in the blink of an eye. I pick up the bag as he hugs her closer and twirls her around. "I missed you too, pretty girl! You ready to see what I brought you?"

He sets her down and she's almost vibrating from excitement. It kills me to know that this could have been the norm for her. "Yessssss!"

He kneels down and reached into his pocket, retrieving a small organza drawstring bag. He tugs it open and spills the contents into his palm and presents it to Tatum.

Tears threaten when I see what he's presenting her. In the center of his hand sits a rose gold charm bracelet with one single, solitary charm attached. Upon closer inspection, I notice it is a princess crown. *Jesus, this man.*

Tatum looks from the bracelet to him with awe in her eyes. "Dat's for me?"

"It is," he tells her, smiling at her reaction.

Just like earlier in the kitchen with me, she launches herself at him. Unlike me, he keeps his footing and hugs her close. After a small eternity, she pulls away and holds out her wrist like the little diva she is. Alden fastens the bracelet, his sturdy fingers fumbling a little with the lobster clasp. Once it is secured, she turns her wrist this way and that, admiring her new pretty.

"What do we say, Tater Tot?"

"Thank you! I loves it so much!" She hugs her wrist to her chest and bats her long lashes up at him. And just like that, I know he, too, is under her spell.

I check the time again and realize if I don't get moving, I'm going to be late for my class. "Well, uh. I would offer you a tour but, I gotta log on..."

Alden shoos me away. "You're fine. Go. Tatum and I have things on lock, don't we?"

"On. Wock. Mama!"

"Okay. I'll be in my room if you need me."

"I won't. I haves Alden!" My heart rattles and I nod, turning to head down the hall.

chapter twenty-five

Alden

Tatum's words echo through my mind, rocking my world on its axis. *I won't. I haves Alden.* Already she trusts me to have her best interests at heart. *Damn.* I could tell from the guilt-stricken look Natalie desperately tried to hide, Tatum's words affected her too.

Tatum, though? Not so much. That kid is business as usual. "Wanna see my room?"

"Sure, I'd love to." She wraps her small hand around my pointer finger and pulls me behind her down the hall. Her door is the first on the right. She pushes it open, and the first thing I notice is that it looks like a rainbow exploded inside her room. Her walls and carpet are the only neutrals in the entire space. Her curtains are purple and blue, her rug is a rainbow shag, her bedding is pink and orange polka dots, and she has throw pillows in every color in the Crayola box. It's a lot to take in, but it screams *Tatum*.

"Whoa, Tater Tot. This room's amazing!"

She darts past me and climbs up onto her bed where she starts bouncing. "You likes it?"

I scoff. "Like? No. I love it!" I let her bounce a few more seconds before swooping her off of her mattress and into my arms. I set her down and take a seat on her bed, and she shows me her most favorite toys. After a few minutes, I ask, "You wanna help me make dinner?"

She looks up at me like I'm some kind of hero. "You likes to cook?"

"I do. I like it so much I went to school for it."

"I go to school! But we just pway!"

"Oh yeah? Nothing wrong with that. What did you do at school today?"

She pauses, thinking over my question. "Today I got marrieds Clark, he's my number two hubband."

I practically choke on air. "Married, huh? Does your mom know?"

Tatum smiles a smile so saccharine my teeth hurt. "Nope. It's our secwet, Alden."

I lift my brows in surprise. "Got it." I pinch my fingers together and hover them over my mouth and mime locking a key. "My lips are sealed. Now, let's go cook!" I grab my bag from the floor by the door and meet Tatum in the kitchen. I'm immediately impressed by the way she knows where everything is—from pots and pans to utensils to spices. This kid is familiar with her kitchen.

I start arranging the items from my bag when Tatum tugs on the hem of my shirt. "Tie my apwon?" I look down, and clutched in her grasp is a miniature apron covered in flowers and polka dots.

"Of course."

It's then I notice she's already wearing the apron she wants tied. Which must mean... "Here. Dis one for you." Dutifully, I put on the child's size smock with a smile.

"Dat's perfect! What's we making?"

"I was thinking we could make breakfast. How does that sound?"

"Like yum!"

"Have you ever had eggs benedict?" She shrugs her little shoulders. "Well, you're in for a treat." *I hope...do kids like hollandaise sauce?*

Tatum stands on her stool at the counter, and I show her how to separate egg yolks from whites. "Dis feels yucky," she squeals, and I agree.

Once our yolks are safely in the blender, we add two teaspoons of water using her special rainbow set of measuring spoons, along with salt, pepper, and a pinch of cayenne. Switching gears, Tatum drags her stool over to the stove and we set to work on step two of our sauce, melting the butter until it's nice and foamy.

When it's just right, I help her slowly pour the butter into the blender as well before securing the lid. I show her which button to press, and she squeals when the loud mechanical whir fills the room. She then helps me transfer the sauce to a small bowl, and I cover it with plastic wrap.

"What next?" she asks, her voice bubbling over with excitement.

"Now we poach our eggs." The hot water makes me nervous, so I only let her watch with this part, but I still explain every step. "You don't ever want the water to be boiling, just a few bubbles. You got that?"

She nods like a scientist checking an experiment. "Bubbles, not boils."

We set our eggs onto a paper-towel-covered plate

and start on toasting our English muffins. While they get golden and crispy, we fry up some Canadian bacon.

"We done?" she asks, looking at the plates of food on the counter.

"Not quite. Now we have to assemble them."

"Ah-swimble?"

"Assemble. Or...build them. Kind of like blocks."

I show her the order to stack them with the first one and help with her the second, but the third...the third I let her try solo.

The tip of her tongue pokes out in concentration as she sets an English muffin onto the plate in front of her. She moves the Canadian bacon with surgeon-like precision. It's the egg that trips her up. She sets it down a little too roughly, and the yolk bursts.

Suddenly, my worst fear is coming true. Her big green eyes are full of tears. "I broke'd it," she wails, absolutely distraught.

Without even thinking about it, I wrap her in my arms and hug her tight. "It's okay," I soothe, "I promise. It's okay."

"But now da yolk ran away," she sniffles.

"It did. But it didn't get far." I show her how the yolk is pooling around the bread. "It will still taste just the same. In fact, I think I want to eat this one. Can I?"

Her tears wane, and she looks at me with pure joy. "Really?"

"Really-really. Now, let's finish up. Your mom should be ready to join us soon."

We crank out the remaining Benedicts, and I carry

them to the table just as Natalie enters the room. "Mmm, something smells good!"

Tatum rushes over to her and drags her to the table. "We made eggs...uh, eggs..."

"Benedict," I fill in. "And Tatum helped every step of the way."

Natalie shoots me a knowing look. One that says, *that's because she takes after you.* My throat clogs with emotion, but I swallow it down. "Let's eat!"

chapter twenty-six

Natalie

I TYPICALLY FINISH ASSIGNMENTS LONG before the allotted time runs out, but tonight I am down to the wire. Every little sound Alden and Tatum make distracts me. *What are they doing? Are they having fun? Are things going smoothly?* I try my damndest to focus, but *gah! The distraction is real!*

At the last minute possible, I click submit and push back from my small, cramped desk. Standing, I reach my arms over my head and arch my back in a stretch worthy of a cat resting in the sun. I give myself a mental pep talk, pumping myself up for whatever they've been up to and head out toward them.

All the pep-talks in the world couldn't have prepared me for the sight that greets me, though. I linger at the end of the hall and watch them for a few. I watch how he takes his time and talks to her like she's an adult, not in that patronizing tone some adults use with kids. I watch as he comforts Tatum and wipes away her tears after she drops... what looks like an egg? And that apron hanging from his neck...I can hardly handle that fucking apron.

He's patient and calm and him stepping into this dad role so flawlessly is some kind of sexy. If I wasn't one-hundred-percent positive he wanted jack shit to do with me, I'd climb him like a tree.

As Alden brings the plates to the table, I step out of the shadows, not wanting to be caught. "Mmm, something smells good!"

Tatum runs to me and drags me to the table. "We made eggs...uh, eggs..."

"Benedict," Alden provides. "And Tatum helped every step of the way."

My insides turn to mush. My girl is so much like her father it is insane—and such a blessing.

Alden looks as though he's about to say something, but seems to rethink it and instead says, "Let's eat!"

Tatum and I claim our usual seats, with me at the head of the table and her to my left. Alden opts to sit to my right. The three of us seated together like this—like a family—causes a flutter in my belly. Which is absurd. The man can barely tolerate my presence after the shit I pulled.

But when he pulls her plate toward him and starts cutting her food without anyone asking, I'm helpless to resist. The flutters turn into a full-blown flap as the butterflies riot in a mass swoon.

Desperate to mask the emotions simmering within me, I dig into my food with gusto. The flavors burst on my tongue, simple yet homey and delicious. "Oh," I moan around my fork. "This is delicious."

My girl smiles widely. "Alden showed me how to make dis. We poached da eggs, Mama!"

"You did, and they are delicious."

"Thanks!"

The food is so good that even Tatum's chatter falls away as we devour it. That is, until she asks, "You wants to stay and watch a movie?"

Alden's fork audibly scrapes against his plate, and I swear he swallows so loudly the upstairs neighbors can hear it. I can tell from his rigid posture he's not totally down with spending more time with us—though it's probably spending time with *me* that's the issue.

Not wanting him to be the bad guy, I speak up. "Oh, Tater Tot, it's pretty late already. You still need a bath and everything."

She narrows her eyes at me and pouts. "But Mama! I don't want him to go!"

She's gearing up for a meltdown, and as stupid as it is, I'm worried it will send Alden running for the hills. What if he's the kind of dad who's only in it for the good and easy? *No!* my brain shouts. *You know better than that, stupid girl!* But still, the worry lingers.

"I actually have to get up pretty early tomorrow too, pretty girl. But, what if I stay for a little longer?"

"You puts me to bed?" she asks, using her sad eyes like a weapon.

Alden rubs at his throat. "Uh, sure. If it's okay with your mom."

Tatum speaks for me. "It is!" Alden swings his gaze to me, and I give him a subtle nod letting him know that I'm good with it.

I push back from the table and stand. "Okay, now that that's settled, you need to get your behind into the tub!" Alden stands, too, and begins gathering up the dishes. I drop my hand on his, stopping him, and he stiffens at the contact. "I'll get these later. You cooked."

"I've got it. You take care of her." His robotic tone causes my shoulders to sag.

Luckily, Tatum lightens the mood. "You swears you won't go nowhere while I gets clean?"

"Yeah, pretty girl. I swear."

Pleased with his response, Tatum skips off down the hall and I follow after. We fly through her bedtime routine, at her insistence. Once she's dressed in her jammies and her hair is combed, she takes off in search of Alden.

We find him in the kitchen loading the last of the dinner dishes. *That man.* He turns at the sound of us entering. "You squeaky clean?" he asks.

"Uh. I just clean, not squeaky!"

"Good enough for me." He walks over to her, and she reaches her arms up for him to hold her. He scoops her up. "Now, about that bedtime book..."

He sets off down the hall toward her bedroom, where he deposits her onto her bed. She scrambles underneath the covers, pulling them up to her chin.

I hand him the book she's favored lately, and he lowers himself down onto the edge of her bed, opens the book, and begins reading. Reluctantly, I step out of the room, giving them their privacy.

And by privacy, I mean I hover just outside the door, listening as he reads to her, taking the time to do different voices for all of the characters. Her eyes are drooping when he turns the last page, but she sleepily demands an encore.

She loses the battle to sleep less than two minutes in,

and my heart feels like it weighs a million pounds in my chest as I watch him lean down and press his lips to her forehead. He pulls back and stares at her a few moments before setting her book on the nightstand. I haul ass and hurl myself onto the couch, not wanting him to know what a creeper I am.

Though judging from the look on his face, he's fully aware—then again, my labored breathing is probably a dead giveaway that I haven't been sitting here calmly waiting.

"So." He tucks his thumbs into his front pockets and rocks back on his feels.

I stand. "So."

Lord, this is painfully awkward. "Any chance I could use your restroom before I head out?"

"Oh, yeah. Okay. Sure. It's the door across from Tatum's."

Alden

Turning on my heel, I walk to the hall bath. I turn on the faucet and splash my face with some cold water. Tonight has been a lot to take in. But, Tatum is...she's magical. And something in my gut is saying she's mine.

I'm about to head back out when something in the trashcan catches my eye.

"What the..." I crouch down to get a closer look. Sure as shit, it's the paternity test I gave her. A wrath like I've never known lights my insides in a blazing inferno.

I storm out of the bathroom and stalk toward Natalie, a.k.a. Mia 2.0—it's fitting, seeing that she's a lying, conniving bitch. "You really thought you could fucking fool me?" I'm up in her face, begging for a fight.

"Wh-what are you talking about?" she asks, sounding genuinely confused. But, I know all too well how deceitful women like her can be. To think she almost had me fooled... What's that fucking saying? *Fool me once, shame on you. Fool me twice...* Well, thank God I discovered the truth before twice could fully hit.

"That's cute, Nat." I laugh a hollow laugh. "Keep up the innocent, woe is me act. But I gotta be real, it's not very becoming on you."

She looks up at me with wide tear-filled eyes, but I can't seem to find it within me to care. "Al-Alden, I r-really don't know what you m-mean."

I scoff, disgusted with her antics. "I saw the paternity test in the garbage. There's only one reason you'd toss it. You figured you had me snowed and didn't need proof anymore."

I'm expecting her to beg for forgiveness and understanding. I'm expecting her to plead her case in a mess of snot and tears. But she does neither of those things. Nope. She shoves past me and marches down the hall toward the bathroom.

She returns, box in hand. "This, Alden? You mean this?"

She thrusts the box into my hands, her face red and tears running down her cheeks. It's then I notice it's...empty.

"I sent the samples in this morning! I'm not trying to hide anything from you. I made that mistake once already and look how well that turned out."

Her words, so full of conviction, take the wind out of my sails. "What?" I ask, my brain not quite comprehending what she's saying.

"I have nothing to hide, Alden." Her words are a quiet whisper.

Deflated, I drop down onto the couch and hang my head in my hands. "How did everything get so messed up?" I mutter the words more to myself than aloud, but she still hears me.

"This is my fault. All of it. I should have been honest from the start. I know I've said it a million times, but I really am sorry."

I scrub a hand over the stubble on my jaw. "No. Well, yes, but it's more than that. The way things ended with Mia really fucked me up."

Natalie cautiously claims the seat next to me. "What's Mia have to do with us?"

A long, weary sigh escapes my lips. "Nothing. Everything. Fuck."

"Talk to me, Alden. Please."

"She...she was pregnant." Natalie gasps, her lips forming a perfect "O." She lifts her right hand to her heart, looking stricken. "Only it wasn't mine. She cheated on me. Said I wasn't attentive enough but figured I was a more... suitable...father figure than the actual father. She lied so convincingly and I followed her blindly.

"We weren't really in the right place to start a family, but

Natalie, I was ready and willing to step up and do whatever it took. All she ever did was take and take and take, but like an idiot, I always gave willingly. She needed money to see the doctor, I handed it over, no questions asked—not even when she came home with a new designer bag or shoes. It never once crossed my mind that insurance would have covered most of her appointments. I just wanted her to be happy

"I was so fucking blinded back then. It took me catching her with him to figure it out, and I swore then and there that I would never be so stupid again. And now—"

Natalie sniffles next to me. "And now, here I am crying *baby daddy* like the boy who cried wolf. But Alden, from the bottom of my heart, I'm not lying to you." She stares down at her lap, looking so, so sad. "The...the results will be here in about five days. You'll see."

A mix of emotions are clouding my mind, so much so that I'm not sure I know up from down. "I'm gonna head out." I stand and head to the kitchen to grab my bag. "I'm sorry for jumping to conclusions tonight."

"I deserve it, so..."

I sigh. Again. For what feels like the billionth time tonight. "Natalie, I'm sorr—"

"Please don't apologize. Knowing about you and Mia really helps me to see why you feel the way you do. And I don't blame you for being suspicious. But, she is yours Alden, through and through."

Deep down, I know Tatum's mine. Which is why I ask, "When can I see her again?"

Natalie sucks in a shuddering breath. "Maybe we can

all go to the park Sunday?" Hope tinges her tone—most likely hope that I'll agree to another group activity.

I glance up at the popcorn ceiling, then back at her. "Sure, Nat. See you around."

chapter twenty-seven

Alden

SPENDING TIME WITH TATUM LAST night was all that I imagined it to be and more. The amount of stress and anxiety I felt leading up to it is almost laughable now. That kid is every single good thing in this life all rolled into one. She is so honest and pure—it gets me feeling fuzzy to know she's mine.

Even after everything with Natalie—and telling her about Mia—I'm still on cloud nine.

What brings me down a little is the thought of calling my parents and breaking the news. But, I know I have to.

The phone rings twice and my mom picks up. "Alden, sweetie. How are you? Is everything okay?"

I guess her Spidey senses must be tingling.

"Good. Uh. Mostly. Is Dad around?"

I hear shuffling and then, "Yes, dear. We have you on speaker."

"Son. What's going on?"

"I...I have." My words break off. Damn, this is harder than I thought. "I have a daughter."

I met with nothing but dead silence, and then the sound of my mother wailing—if they are tears of sorrow or joy is yet to be determined. "My baby has a baby. Oh, Lord. Oh, Lord, I knew this day would come." My mom continues on with her emotional rambling.

"Her name's Tatum. She's three. And she's...absolutely amazing."

My dad steps in as the voice of reason. "Gonna need more information here, son. Such as, *how* do you have a toddler and with who? Are you sure she's yours?"

This conversation is going about as well as I thought it would. "Mom, Dad. Listen. N-Natalie Reynolds is her mother and—" I pause. I may not be scientifically sure, but my heart is absolutely certain. "Yes, I'm sure."

At that, my mom truly goes off the deep end, but I can't really say I blame her. "Natalie? Little Natalie? Nate's sister?"

"Yes. That Natalie."

I hear my dad mumbling, and I know what's coming next. "You said the girl's three. That puts you at what, twenty, when she was...conceived? Son, correct me if I'm wrong, but that's statutory."

Yep. Called it. I go on to explain the ins and outs of mine and Nat's incredibly delicate situation. Our conversation is long and, rightfully so, my parents have a lot of questions. I answer them all to the best of my ability, and when we end the call, it's with the promise of a video chat date soon so that they can meet their granddaughter.

I tried my best not to paint Natalie in a bad light to my parents, but I'm still holding a slight grudge toward her, and I'm sure it shows. I'm trying not to, but *fuck*, easier said than done.

To make things even more confusing, a few times during dinner tonight, I caught her giving me these looks—on the scale of one to ten with one being *awe, that's sweet* and ten being *holy shit take me now,* she was a solid eight. Which took my brain nowhere good. I guess I get it though. Though things are tense between us, my body still reacts to hers—much to my mind's dismay. I can't help it; she's just so effortlessly sexy. She always has been. Natalie's the kind of girl that you fantasize about and take home to meet mother—basically, she's the whole package—you know, aside from being a liar.

But is she really a liar? I mean, on the one hand, fuck yes, she lied to me and everyone about who Tatum's father was. However, the more I think about it—the more I try and put myself in her shoes—the more I *get* where she was coming from. And really, it was more of an omission of the truth than an outright lie. Doesn't stop me from being salty about it, though.

It's been eight days since I went over to Natalie's house. To say that things have been tense between us ever since would be an understatement. Hell, I'm pretty sure the tension swirling around us is so thick that everyone in the same vicinity as us can feel it.

The fact that the paternity test results should arrive any day now also has me feeling like I could crawl out of my skin. Which explains why I'm holed up in my office, anxiously waiting for her to arrive for her closing shift.

Will she have the results, or won't she? What's even more strange is that I think I'm more nervous about seeing her than I am about the test—probably because deep down, I already know the answer.

To make matters worse, my mind keeps reliving our last closing shift together. If I think hard enough, the memory of how her body felt pressed against me and the sear of her lips on mine has my pants growing uncomfortably tight in the crotch.

This shit has to stop, I think to myself, standing and stalking into the kitchen. My head chef, Darren, shoots me a wry look when I walk in. "What brings you out of the cave tonight, boss?"

"Got a new recipe I want to sample Friday night. If it does well, I want to add it to the menu."

His expression immediately transforms. Excitement lights his eyes. "No shit?" He turns to his sous. "Javier, cover me?"

"Yes, chef," Javier calls back.

Darren wastes no time huddling up with me where I dive into the nitty-gritty of my new dish. "I want to make Friday night more upscale—a romantic and cozy date-night kind of thing. Not just a meal, but a destination, an experience."

Darren's eyes are filled with intrigue. "But I also want to highlight our local and regional cuisine."

"I'm down with all of that, but get to the good stuff, Boss."

I laugh, appreciating his straightforwardness and passion. "Okay, check it, I want to do a small, intimate tasting Friday night. Fresh fish, blackened shrimp, collard greens cooked with Conecuh sausage, red rice, and a Cajun cream sauce."

"I'm down with all of that. You gonna be able to get the fish in time?"

"Yeah, I talked to the market. I've been toying with this idea for a while."

"What made you pull the trigger?" he asks, but judging from his tone, I'm not sure how much he actually cares.

"I...the new menu has been doing well, and it just felt like the right time." Not to mention, I fucking need a distraction like he wouldn't believe. Then again, maybe he would. I mean, my entire staff knows mine and Nat's dirty laundry. Luckily, Carlos threatened their asses and told them they would continue to act professional or else. Guess their fear of him outweighs the juicy gossip my impromptu office meeting created.

"Yeah, okay, Boss."

"Bring the crew up to speed. I'll prep the front of house." We bump fists and I pivot to head back to my office, only to run smack into Natalie.

And I mean that literally. The momentum of our collision sends her sprawling backward, but thanks to my stellar reflexes, I'm able to catch her with an arm around her waist just in time, leaving us in a tango-esque dip. The only thing missing is a rose clenched between my teeth.

I reach my free hand forward and grab her shoulder, hauling us both upright. We remain locked in our semi-embrace for far longer than necessary. In fact, neither of us moves a muscle—I don't even think we breathe—until

Darren coughs...loudly.

And just like that, the spell is broken. Natalie jumps away from me as if I'm a bonfire and she's a highly combustible solution. *Ha. Highly combustible. If that doesn't describe us, I'm not sure what does.*

"Jesus! Sorry, I wasn't paying attention. Nate texted me."

"It's all good," I say to her. "Plus, I wasn't exactly watching where I was going, either. No worries."

Her cheeks turn the prettiest shade of pink. "Can we talk really fast?" she asks.

"In a bit. Right now, I need you to go ahead and get clocked in." She looks crestfallen, and I feel like an ass, but somehow I know she has the test results with her and me...I just need some time to compose myself.

"Yeah. Sure. Okay." She scurries around me, and as much as I hate to admit it, my eyes stay glued to her ass— her plump, juicy, bitable ass—until she's out of view.

I start again to head for the door when someone else stops me...Darren this time. "Hey Boss!"

"Yeah?"

He snorts out a laugh. "Real smooth."

I shake my head and walk away; I'm not dignifying that with a response. I mean, it's not like I was trying to be smooth. It's not like I even *want* to be smooth around her. Even if she is my greatest temptation—much to my chagrin. She's also my biggest weakness—just look at my inability to stay mad at her. Maybe that's due in part to her being the mother of my child? Fuck if I have a clue. All I know is with every day that passes, my anger decreases.

I've managed to avoid Natalie for most of her shift. Pathetic, I know. But, I swear it's like she's out to make me crazy. From the feel of my hands on her body earlier, as innocent as it was, to the narrow indent of her waist before the sinful flare of her hip...*damn, it's all I can think about.* Which is truly insane, seeing as I should still be upset with her—not lusting after her.

It doesn't help that the first time we crossed paths after her shift started, she was walking in front of me a few paces and dropped her order book. She bent to retrieve it, presenting me with the sweet apple of her ass, and, *oh my God,* I almost came in my pants. Honestly, I think it's the universe punishing me for not manning up and talking to her when she asked.

After that incident, I confined myself to my office, only leaving if absolutely necessary. The fact that I'm hiding out in here pisses me off. This isn't the kind of owner I want to be. My style is hands-on and elbows deep, yet here I am cowering in my office because I'm too chicken shit to face the truth.

Sitting at my desk, I stew. It feels like we're engaged in some form of silent warfare. Logically, I know the notion is insane and completely a figment of my over-agitated and under-sexed imagination. But my heart's not listening to my brain. The muscle in my chest refuses to take this war sitting down and wants retribution. My heart, the foolish bastard, screams *what right does she have to dump the shit she did on you and then prance around looking like every wet dream you've ever had?*

Finally, I decide I'm being ridiculous. In an effort to prove to myself just how crazy I'm being, I head out to the floor. Only, right as I step out of my office, Natalie walks past me toward the kitchen, her hips swaying like a pendulum.

Covertly, I watch as she enters the kitchen, all the while trying to convince myself not to follow her, but I'm helpless to resist her pull. When I enter the kitchen, my little lying temptress is leaning forward with her elbows propped on the counter and her ample cleavage shining like a beacon to every red-blooded male in the kitchen.

The thought of my kitchen crew checking her out has me seeing red. "The hell are y'all sitting around for? I'm not paying y'all to gossip."

Natalie straightens, but it's Darren that speaks. "Nat was just paying compliments to the kitchen from one of her tables."

"Great and now you know. So." I wave my hands, shooing them. "Get back to work. And Natalie, why don't you button your shirt up a little more."

She sputters, shocked by my words, before turning and stomping out of the kitchen.

I pinch my eyes shut in frustration, fully aware I'm acting like a psychotic jackass. When I blink them open, my entire kitchen crew is staring at me—probably wondering if I'm on the verge of a mental breakdown...*well boys, the jury's still out.*

chapter twenty-eight

Natalie

HAND ON A BIBLE, I'M about two seconds away from tearing Alden a new one. I came in tonight feeling the kind of hope I haven't felt in a long time. The still-sealed test results are burning a hole in my pocket.

I thought he would be as anxious as me to open them—but he's running so hot and cold that I'm not sure if I'm going to need sunglasses or a fucking parka when we finally sit down to talk. One second, he's cordial, the next he's shooting me these lingering looks, and all in the same breath he's basically calling me a whore.

What right does he have to tell me to button my shirt up? Not to mention, only the top two are undone. You know, the same way *everyone* wears a button-down shirt.

Thankfully, Alden's pissy, mercurial ass stayed out of sight after that, and I pasted on a fake smile and got through my tables.

It's fifteen minutes to closing time, and I have one table left—a cutesy couple on a date. Their meals are long since finished, yet they're still here, seated at their small table staring at one another all moony-eyed. Normally, this wouldn't bother me. But the longer they stay, the longer I have to wait to storm Alden's office and demand he talk to me

"Maybe they need a little push," I mutter to myself, heading back to my lone table. I'm so incredibly ready for us to open this envelope—I'm ready for him to know I'm not lying, even if he doesn't remember that night at all.

Quietly, I slide their check onto the table. "No rush, y'all. Just wanted to leave this here for whenever you're ready."

Their conversation halts, and they blink at each other and then at me. The girl looks at her phone. "Oh, Andre! Did you see the time?"

Her date checks his phone and immediately pulls out his wallet. He peels off three crisp twenties and lays them on top of his bill.

"Thank y'all so much for dining with us. I hope everything was wonderful."

They both smile and thank me and then they're on their way. I immediately dash to the closet and grab the cleaning caddy and set to work on my station. Memories of last Wednesday filter in, very much uninvited. Things like the way his scruff felt against my face and the way he wrapped my hair around his fist. I shut those thoughts down—the last thing I need to be when we talk is turned on.

I fly through my cleaning and rush to put away my supplies. I'm not giving him another chance to blow me off or avoid me.

Carlos intercepts me as I approach the office. "You ready to cash out?"

"Yup. Ready to go." I edge a little closer to the door

he's blocking. "Just gotta speak to Alden first."

"Nah, let's take care of this first. You're the only person I'm waiting on."

Resigned, I agree. "Fine."

I follow behind Carlos, hoping he's not in the mood for small talk tonight. I'm a woman on a mission, and nothing's going to stop me.

Luck seems to be on my side and my book is settled quickly. I slip my tips in pocket, my fingertips brushing against the envelope as I beeline back to Alden's office. Usually I knock, but tonight I don't. I bust in, full of fire. "I swear to God, if you keep avoiding me, I'm going to lose my ever-loving mind!"

I'm slightly embarrassed by my outburst, but there's no way I'm backing down. We have things to discuss, and he's being a wimp. I prepared for him to try and put me off again, but nope. Instead he chuckles. He. Fucking. Chuckles—that bastard. I pin him with a frigid glare, letting him know that I'm in no way amused.

"Actually, I wanted to apologize. I've been an ass tonight. And yeah, I've totally been avoiding you."

"Is that all you wanted to apologize for?"

He sighs, but it's through a smile. "Also, sorry about the shirt comment. It was uncalled for. Safe to say I'm a bit on edge."

"Why?" I ask, wondering if it's over what I think it is.

He drums his fingers over his desktop. "Are the results in?"

Bingo. "Yeah, I brought them with me. That's why I wanted to talk earlier."

"What do they say?"

"I don't know. Well, I mean, *I know*, but I wanted us to open it together."

He looks mildly surprised by my words. "Oh. Okay."

"Are you ready?"

He pinches his eyes shut and shakes his head back and forth a few times. "As ready as I'll ever be."

I move to his side of the desk and pull the envelope from my pocket. The paper is creased from being folded in half for so long. He stares at it, unblinking and unmoving.

"Well, what are you waiting for?" I ask, nudging him.

He pushes his index finger under the flap, running it along the seam until it's fully opened. I watch with bated breath as he slides the papers out and unfolds them. Together we scan over the page, and there in black and white in the bottom right corner it reads: *Probability of Paternity: 99.9998%.*

"Holy shit." The papers fall from his hands, scattering on the desk and floor. "Holy shit! She really is mine!"

"I told you," I say weakly, knowing this has to be a lot for him to process.

"I...I...wow." Alden shocks me when he grabs my cheeks in his hands and presses his lips to mine. It's not really a romantic kiss, but it lights me up like a Christmas tree all the same.

I smile and twirl my thumbs together, not quite sure how to proceed. "Tatum's really excited about us going to the park."

At the mention of Tatum, his eyes light and then immediately dim. "You think maybe afterward, I could take her to lunch...just the two of us?"

I swallow and look away from him. It's not that I don't trust him—I do, with all my heart. I know he's not only a good father but a good man. And I know Tatum loves him, even without knowing who he is. This hang-up I have is all mine, and I need to get over it. "Yeah, sure." I whisper the words so quietly, yet they fill the room like a shout.

He jerks his head back. "Really?"

I don't ponder it another second. "Yeah, Alden. Really."

The rest of the week drags by, but now, it's finally Sunday. From the moment I told Tatum that we were going to the park today with Alden, it's been all she's talked about. Lucky me, I had the foresight not to tell her too soon, but even still I've been hearing about it since yesterday morning.

We're nearing twenty-four hours of Alden-induced mania.

"Mama! It's time to go now?" Tatum bounces and wiggles at the foot of my bed before climbing up onto it and snuggling up to me.

For the past half hour, I've had my nose shoved into my Kindle, reading while she watched Netflix. But it seems the charm of whatever show she was watching—probably *Trolls*—has worn off.

"Fifteen more minutes, Tater Tot."

"How long is dat?"

I point to the alarm clock on my nightstand. "When

that last number is a five, it will be time to go."

She nods, positioning herself so that she can stare at the clock until it's time to leave. I shake my head at her determination and fall back into my book. I'm at a good part in my book—you know, a *goooood* part—when Tatum gleefully announces, "Time to go! It's time to go! Hurry, Mama!"

"Oh, I don't know. Maybe we should wait a little longer," I say, teasingly.

"No! No Mama! We have to go now! What if him thinks we're not coming and he weaves?"

Her desire to see him simultaneously breaks and heals my heart. I know for certain that when we tell her who Alden really is, she's going to be the happiest girl on the planet. "I'm only joking. Let's go!"

Tatum yelps with joy and throws her arms around my neck before jumping off of the bed and hauling *you know what* for the front door. I, on the other hand, move at a normal speed, pausing to slip on my shoes. I detour to Tatum's room to grab her shoes as well, along with a small bag filled with essentials for going out with a toddler.

"Forget something, Tater Tot?" I ask, dangling her shoes from the tips of my fingers.

"Oh! Yeah! Thanks, Mama!"

I squat and help her into her shoes, and then we're out the door and on our way.

chapter twenty-nine

Alden

EVER SINCE LEAVING THEIR HOUSE on Tuesday night, I've been anxious to see my girl again. Especially now that I'm one-hundred-percent certain she's mine—well, 99.9998%.

So anxious, in fact, I arrived to the playground ten minutes early. Do you know the kind of looks you get being a single, childless dude loitering near the swings? Let me tell you...they're not good.

The thought of fleeing to my car is tempting, but I don't. Honestly, some petty part of me is excited to see the looks on these people's face when my daughter shows up. *My daughter. Damn, that feels...good. Strange still, but so good.*

Things with Natalie and I are running smoother every day. And by smoother, I mean I've quit acting like a split-personality asshole. I still have a smidge of resentment I'm harboring, but, it's more like a tiny, dying ember than the raging inferno it was.

So, yeah, progress.

I'm fiddling around on my phone when the sound of familiar, excited laughter floats my way. I look up just in time to see my Tatum barreling toward me. "Alden!" she screams, and I wrap her in a hug, breathing in her sweet, still baby-ish scent.

"Hey, pretty girl. How have you been?"

"I's good." She does a twirl, causing the little cape attached to her shirt to flare out. "I's a super-he-whoa!"

Natalie claims the seat next to me, smiling at Tatum's pure, unfiltered cuteness.

"A superhero, huh? What's your code name?"

She looks at me like I'm crazy.

"You know, Peter Parker called himself Spiderman. Bruce Wayne was Batman. Who's Tatum...Reynolds?" Calling her by that last name burns in my gut. I wonder if Natalie would ever be opening to having it changed to Warner?

"Uh. Hmm. I's Super Pwincess Sparkle!"

Natalie leans into my shoulder, stifling her laugh. The intimacy of our position sends a million little sparks racing through my veins. The urge to casually sling my arm around her is so strong. I combat it by directing all of my attention to my little girl.

"I think that's perfect." Natalie moves back to her side of the bench, and I mourn the loss.

She smiles. "Yay! I gonna go pway? 'Kay, Mama?"

"Sure. Stay in the little kid area." Tatum runs away, cape flapping in the wind, and Natalie turns to me. "Thanks again for meeting us here."

Pulling out my phone, I snap a few pictures of Tatum as she darts off. "You don't have to thank me for that."

I swipe up my text thread with my parents—yes, we have a group text—and attach the pictures of Tatum. They aren't the first ones I've sent, and even though they haven't met her yet, I know Mom and Dad will both gush like the proud grandparents they are. Hell, I wouldn't be surprised if they print them out and hang them on the fridge.

She lets out a sigh far too weary for someone her age. "Yeah, Alden, I really do. You've been so great and far more forgiving than I deserve. So, like I said, thank you for your willingness to compromise."

I offer her a boyish grin. "That's part of co-parenting, right?"

She laughs and we fall into a companionable silence while we watch Tatum flit around the playground.

Tatum plays and plays, like she has all the energy in the world. But, I guess at three, she does. She's a red-cheeked, sweaty mess when she runs back to our bench. "Mama, I wanna do the big swide! I wanna show Alden how brave I am!"

I glance toward Natalie, and she gives me a subtle nod. "The big slide, huh?"

Tatum's head moves up and down so rapidly she resembles a bobblehead.

"How about I help you up the ladder and Alden can catch you at the bottom?"

"Yes!" Tatum cries before running to the slide. I swear, this kid only has one speed—and it's *fast*.

Natalie climbs up the ladder with Tatum and helps her get situated properly before sending her down the chute to me. The sound of my girl squealing in delight and screaming, "Again!" is the best sound I've ever heard.

On her second go, I tell her to wait a minute before sliding and snap a few more pics of her. She looks so carefree and innocent, and I want to remember this moment always.

We're on our fourth slide trip when an elderly woman lays her hand on Natalie's arm. Without meaning to, I overhear her say, "Your family's beautiful, dear. Especially that husband of yours."

Natalie's cheeks go so crimson it's almost comical. I wait for her to rebut the woman, but she merely smiles and thanks her. My initial reaction is to correct her...to tell her we're not married or a family. But my second and far stronger reaction is one that truly throws me for a loop—longing.

What the hell...

About thirty minutes later, the three of us walk to the parking lot. Tatum whines in her mom's arms. "I not wanna go home!"

"Then I've got good news," Natalie soothes, ruffling her hair. "Alden is gonna take you to lunch."

"For reals? Just da two of us?"

"Yes, ma'am. Doesn't that sound fun?"

"Yes! Dis is da best day ever!"

Tatum's excitement over spending time with me warms my heart. Natalie passes Tatum to me. "Let me grab Tatum's car seat and we—"

"I bought one!" I interrupt her, sheepishly nodding toward my car. "You can check it out first if you want. I, uh, researched the best ones and took it down to the fire department to have them check the install."

Natalie's eyes go glassy, and I worry I've done something to upset her. But then she wraps her arms around my middle, hugging me to her. "You are such a good father. Tatum's a lucky girl." Her words are a whisper meant only for me, but they resonate like a cymbal clanging in my ear.

We walk the few steps to my car and Nat helps show me how to properly secure the five-point harness. "I packed a little bag for y'all."

I take it from her and place it on the floorboard at Tatum's feet. She leans in to kiss her—our—daughter and like the pervert I am, I use the opportunity to once again check out her fine ass. High, firm, and juicy...a work of art. I'm so lost in imagining all the things I could do to that ass that I fail to realize that she's speaking to me, not to mention she's no longer bent over.

"Alden...hello! Earth to Alden!"

I snap my eyes up to hers, willing myself to look innocent. After all, there's no need to complicate things between us further.

"Yeah?"

"I was saying she's not allergic to anything, but can sometimes be picky. Well, not normal kid picky. Maybe... *persnickety* is a better word. Oh, and she'll try and weasel you into dessert no matter where you eat."

A strand of hair blows across her face, and I fight the urge to brush it back. "Sounds great. We won't be late."

Nat smiles and lays her hand on my shoulder. "You're fine. I trust you."

For some reason, her words warm me down to my very

soul.

In the car, I ask Tatum what she wants to eat, and she immediately exclaims, "Burgers and fwys and ketchup and milkshakes!"

"I think I can handle that, pretty girl."

I drive to my favorite burger joint, Homegrown. It's a longstanding local joint, owned by the Bell family, that's been around since my parents were kids. Though their menu has evolved with time, and I'm more than ready for one of their gourmet burgers. They're a farming family and pride themselves on using local ingredients and meat from animals that were both humanely raised and slaughtered. Basically, they're my kind of people.

As we pull into their small lot, I ask Tatum if she's ever been here before. She shakes her head. "Well then, you're in for a treat."

Getting her unbuckled takes me a hot minute—you have to really *squeeze* to get that buckle apart. I try not to let my frustration show, but Tatum catches it...and finds it hilarious. "Ta'mon, Alden! Use your mustles!"

I grin at my girl, my annoyance vanishing. "I am using my muscles!" I get the chest clip opened and go to unhook the buckles, which is just as hard. Finally, I am victorious, and we walk into Homegrown hand in hand.

The interior captivates Tatum. I get it though. The red brick floors have a yellow path painted on them leading back to the kitchen—Homegrown's very own yellow brick road. The walls are a mixture of aged wood and corrugated tin, and the tables and chairs don't match. "Dis place is cwazy!"

"Crazy good," I assure her, leading her back to an open table. I help her up into her seat and then claim the one across from her. "Your mama's never brought you here?"

She shrugs. "Nope."

I snag a menu from the little holder on the table and begin perusing it. Tatum sees me reading it, and grabs one for herself, pretending to read along.

"Whatcha gonna get?" she asks.

"I am gonna get a Rob's classic—a grass-fed patty, local cheese, bacon, sautéed mushrooms, and garlic aioli on a French roll."

She tilts her head and looks at me a little funny. "I only know what some of dose things are. But I can tries it?"

I beam at her adventurous spirit. "Yeah, pretty girl, you can try it. What do you want on your burger?"

"I likes the cheese with the holes in it and crunchy bacon and ketchup and a egg."

"That sounds really good."

"It is. I thought it looked yuck but Mama made me tries it, and it wasn't yuck! It was yum! I love it. With tots."

"Tater tot likes tots, huh?" She giggles, and I wish like hell I could bottle the sound and carry it with me.

Our server approaches us wearing an apologetic smile. "I'm so sorry to have kept y'all waiting. We're short today."

I wave a hand in the air. "Not an issue."

"Thank you. What can I get y'all today?"

I place our order, along with two waters, and our server heads off to put them in. She returns almost immediately with our drinks. After spending most of the morning outside, the cool beverage is more refreshing than usual.

That is, until Tatum busts out with, "Are you Mama's boyfriend?" Except she draws out the word *boy*.

I suck my sip down the wrong pipe, choking. I pound my chest a few times, trying to regain my composure. "Do you even know what that word means?"

She looks at me like I'm an idiot. "Duh. I have two hubbands, remember?"

More coughing. "Ah. Yes. How could I forget?"

She shrugs her shoulders. "Well?"

"I...uh. I'm...we're not. No." A toddler has me utterly tongue-tied. "Your mom and I are just friends."

She pouts. "Oh. Why? You not like her?"

Jesus. This kid. "I like your mama just fine, pretty girl. Where's all of this coming from?"

She sucks in a shuddering breath. "I see udder kids with mamas *and* daddies. And I want a daddy, and if you—"

Our server chooses that exact moment to bring our food—thank fuck—because I was two seconds away from breaking down and telling her the truth. This sweet girl sure knows how to bring me to my knees.

The food is enough of a distraction that she lets our earlier conversation drop. And while it may be out of mind for her, it's all I can think about. One thing's for sure, Natalie and I need to have a long talk.

"You still wanna try mine?" I ask, grabbing a napkin and wiping the ketchup from her face. "I saved you a bite."

"Mmm. Okay, I try."

I fork up the bite and extend it toward her. She gives it a little sniff before touching the tip of her tongue to it. After a few more licks, she finally snags it off of the fork. She spits the mushroom into her palm and happily swallows the rest—not bad for a three-year-old.

Our server returns and clears our plates, and I order us a chocolate shake split into two glasses. "Alden, why you call my mama Small Fwy?"

"Well, when I met your mama she was tiny little thing. Shorter than all the other girls her age. It just slipped out one day, and it stuck. Why does she call you Tater Tot?"

"Her says it's a special name from my daddy." I swallow roughly. Because, *Jesus...I may not have given her the nickname, but I may as well have. It's a play on what I call her mother and couldn't be more perfect.*

When I speak again, my voice comes out scratchy. "Speaking of special..." I reach into my pocket and retrieve another small, organza bag. My girl already knows what it is and wiggles around in her seat making grabby hands.

I pass her the bag and she uses her little fingers to pry it open, spilling the charm onto the table. This time it's a whisk, with little stones embedded in the handle of the whisk. "Oooh. I love it! Thank you so much!" She thrusts her arm my way, presenting me with the bracelet. "Hooked it?"

I oblige and we both admire how pretty it looks next to her crown. After we finish our shake, I pay the bill and we head back to my car. I buckle her in, all the while wondering how Natalie makes it look so effortless.

"You ready to go home?"

"I guess."

"You guess? Don't you miss your mama?"

"I do. But when you go, I'll miss you." And with those

seven words, my heart cracks wide open.

"I'm not going anywhere, Tatum."

"Pwomise?" she asks, her voice small.

"Promise."

I take the long way, driving the backroads, simply to prolong our time together. Still, all too soon, I'm pulling into Natalie's apartment complex.

I put my car in park and kill the engine. I exit and come around to get Tatum, only to find her snoozing far too peacefully for me to wake her up. With great care, I unbuckle her, finding it a little easier this time around. I grab her bag and pick her up, cradling her to my chest. Walking far slower than what's probably necessary, I head for their unit.

I lift my fist to knock, but Nat opens the door before I get the chance. She reaches for her, and I transfer our sleeping beauty from my arms to hers. "Let's talk," I mouth the words, and she nods, leaving the door open for me.

She returns from laying Tatum down and drops down onto the far end of the couch. I follow suit, claiming the opposite end.

"What's up? Did y'all have fun?"

"Yeah, Nat. We really did. She's such an amazing kid."

"She is, huh? Every day she does something that blows my mind. She's so smart, Alden."

"She's the best of both of us," I say to her, meaning it.

Natalie smiles so brightly, which makes the next words a little harder to say. "She asked me if I was your boyfriend today. Wanna know why?"

Natalie's smile wilts away. "Wh-why?"

"Said she wanted me to be your boyfriend because she sees other kids with dads. That shit's not cool. We need to tell her."

"We do. You're right. And we will. I swear it."

I try to be cool, but my impatience rings through. "When, Natalie? When?"

chapter thirty

Natalie

ALDEN'S QUESTION PLAYS ON A loop in my mind. I know he's right and that she needs to know. I also know the longer I put it off, the more his resentment will grow. So, guess it's time to buck up.

"We can tell her next time we're all together. Does that sound good?"

His jaw drops, and he blinks as if stunned by my response. "R-really?"

"Yeah, Alden. Really. You're her father—and a damn good one. She deserves to know."

For the first time since all of this started—well, other than our brief kiss in his office when he read the paternity test results—Alden initiates physical contact between us, scooting down to my end of the couch and bear-hugging me. "Thank you so much." His breath is hot on my neck, and chill bumps cover my body.

I start to squirm out of his hold, but I'm rendered motionless at the feel of his stubble against my skin. His lips quickly follow as he softly kisses my neck. His touch is almost worshipful, so soft but strong, all at once.

I'm almost too scared to move as he drags his lips

higher, nipping at the sensitive skin beneath my ear. I can't help but groan at the heady mix of pleasure with a touch of pain. Alden growls at the sound, and before I know it, he has me laid back on the couch and he's nestled between my legs, his lips sliding against mine as his tongue begs for entry.

My body decides before my brain to simply roll with it, and I open to him as I run my fingers through his hair, tugging on the ends as he sucks on my lower lip. We kiss and carry on like two horny teenagers until my hips shift restlessly against his. It's been so long since anyone's touched me this way...I honestly think I could come just from this.

Which explains my pathetic, kicked-puppy-sounding whimper when he pulls away. "Jesus, Nat."

I stare at him dazedly, my brain far too foggy to come up with a reply.

Naturally, he finds this to be hilarious. "Cat got your tongue?"

I can feel the blush staining my cheeks. "Something like that."

Teasing me, he rolls his hips, and I let out the most embarrassing sound. I want to smack the smirk off of his face as he moves completely off of me and to a sitting position.

An awkward silence falls over the room. Suddenly, I'm unsure of how to act, much less what to say. I settle with an eloquent, "So..."

Which Alden echoes back. "So..."

"Jesus, this is awkward." I mutter the words to myself,

but of course he hears me.

"It doesn't have to be, Small Fry."

"But...it is. You k-kissed me."

Alden nods. "I did. And I liked it. It felt...natural. Right."

I look down at my lap, feeling all kinds of different ways. When I don't reply, he reaches over and takes my hand in his. "Hey, I'm sorry if that made you uncomfortable."

"No, it's not that. It's just—" I break off, trying to find the right words. "Complicated. It's complicated." Really, that's the best word, because how else do I explain that my feelings for him never faded, and that he's always been my gold standard, and that no other guy has ever measured up? Not to mention, I don't want things between us to get messy and have it affect Tatum. *So, yeah, complicated.*

"Right." He swallows roughly before changing the subject. "Maybe y'all can come to my place for dinner one night?"

"That...that sounds good."

Alden beams his pearly whites at me, and once again my heart pangs, knowing all I have deprived him— and Tatum—of. He rises from the couch, and I do too. Together we walk to the door, where things once again turn awkward. After practically dry humping on the couch, do we hug? Shake hands? Nothing at all? I'm too busy overthinking it when he makes the decision for the both of us, hugging me close and placing a feather-soft kiss to my forehead.

He's out the door before I can even process everything that just happened. And my God, it's a lot to process. *Wine!*

I think. *Wine will help.*

I return to the couch, drink in hand, just in time to hear my phone ding. It's a text. From him.

Alden: For real, Nat. Thank you.

I gulp down half of my glass and reply.

Natalie: Don't thank me for doing what I should have done from the start. It's the right thing to do. For you and for her.

He doesn't reply after that, and that's okay; we've said all we need to—for now.

Thirty minutes later, Tatum is still napping. Normally, I wouldn't let her sleep so long, but she's had a big day, and honestly, I need some time to myself.

Sinking back into the couch, I relish in the peace and quiet—until the sound of my phone ringing cuts through the air. A quick glance at the screen shows my mom's name. We've chatted a few times here and there since all of this happened, but my dad and I have yet to talk, which freaking kills me.

Not in the mood to deal with her, I send the call to voicemail. But she's persistent and calls right back. I swipe my thumb across the screen. "Hey Mom."

"Natalie." My name comes out as more of a sigh than a greeting.

"What's up?" I ask, already feeling exasperated. I get that I let everyone down, but at this point, I feel like my parents need to accept what happened and move on. Every time my mom and I talk, it feels like we're both walking on eggshells.

"Oh, your dad and I just wanted to check in."

"Don't."

"Don't what?"

"Don't speak for Dad when we both know he hasn't made an effort to speak to me since everything went down at Bayside."

"Your father loves you, Nat. He's just struggling."

"He's struggling? Really?" I count down from ten in an effort to not flip my shit. "I get that me being a teen mom was hard for y'all. I get me refusing to name the father was hard for y'all. But guess what? It. Was. Hard. For. Me. Too!

"I freaking lived it. *Every day*, I lived it. And I know I made mistakes and messed up, but I'm doing my best to right my wrongs in a way that's best for Tatum. Because here's the thing: she comes first. Now and always. Dad can either decide to forgive me and accept things for what they are or not—I'm not going to beg. But, Mom, I will not let this drama affect my daughter—*your granddaughter*—and y'all shouldn't, either."

Mom's quiet for a long time, and patiently, I wait her out. Finally, she says, "Okay Natalie. Okay," and ends the call. I'm not sure which part of my tirade she's *okay*ing, but whatever. I'll take it. Okay is better than nothing, I guess.

As the week progresses, work, home, and school all run smoothly—even things with Alden seem to be looking sunny. You know, aside from lingering glances and a crackling sexual tension that we're both determined to ignore. Which is why my defenses are up—I've learned by now that anytime life looks this bright, I should expect a black cloud to dump rain on me, pronto.

Or maybe it's just nerves over our dinner at Alden's tonight. Nerves over telling Tatum who he is. Yeah, that's probably it. "C'mon Tater Tot! It's time to go," I say, poking my head into her room.

Only she's not there.

Panic rushes through me, and I holler her name, sprinting from her room.

Relief fills my lungs just as quickly when I find her sitting on the floor at the front door. "I's been ready," she states in that no-nonsense way of hers. "I's been waiting on you!"

"You scared me, Tater Tot. Why didn't you answer me when I called for you?"

"You said we not yell through the house. I sorry."

I crouch down and kiss her pudgy cheek, unable to argue with her logic. "It's okay, baby. Let's go. I bet your— Alden made us something tasty."

The drive from our apartment to his house is quick— he lives much closer than I realized—walking distance, in good weather. His house is a split-level white brick ranch with a yard so picture-perfect the Cleavers would be jealous.

Tatum and I walk up the little stepping stone path that leads from the driveway to the front porch. Well, I walk; Tatum runs. Her little fist is pounding on the beautiful blue door before I even make it halfway. Needless to say, the kid is excited.

The door swings open, and a very nervous-looking

Alden appears. I've never in my life seen the man look more frazzled. Tatum flings herself into his arms, and right before my very eyes, his stress melts away. It's beautiful and completely reaffirms it's time to tell her. So, those rainy clouds I was worrying about can take a hike because tonight is going to be nothing but rainbows and happy tears.

Reminiscent of his first time at our house, I have to ask if he's going to invite us in. Which he promptly does, a slight blush coloring his cheeks, making him look younger than he is.

"What you cooks us?" Tatum asks, smelling the air like a dog sniffing out its dinner. "It smells like pizza."

Alden reaches a hand over his left shoulder, rubbing at the space between his shoulder blades. "Ah, about that. It *is* pizza. I planned on grilling steaks, but they...didn't turn out."

Oh, my. I might just die from the cuteness. "Alden Warner, did you get nervous and burn our dinner?"

He studies his feet like they're the most fascinating thing he's ever seen. "Maybe."

"Ha!" My laugh bubbles up and out before I can stop it. He glares at me for about two seconds before he starts laughing, too.

Meanwhile, Tatum's looking at the two of like we're insane. "Peoples! Pizza is no laughing matter. My tummy wants it! Now!"

"Yeah, true that," Alden agrees, hoisting her up and flying her, airplane-style, all the way to the kitchen.

We waste no time digging into the gloriously cheesy pie. We're all on our second slice when I decide it's time.

"Tater Tot, there's something we want to tell you."

"Der is? What?" She takes another bite, cheese stringing from her lip down to the slice on her plate.

Alden reaches over and severs it, leaving Tatum to happily slurp it up into her mouth. "What, Mama? What!"

"We wanted to say...to tell you that...um." Alden trips over his words in the most endearing way.

Tatum though, she's fed up with waiting. "You Mama's boyfriend now?"

"No!" Alden rushes out, his eagerness to correct her is a small arrow to my heart. "No, pretty girl. That's not it." *Guess I'm good enough to kiss but not to date.* The thought invades my mind uninvited, but I send it packing. Tonight is not about me.

Tatum pouts and her shoulders slump forward. "Why does that make you so sad, Tater Tot?" I ask.

"A'cause if Alden was you boyfriend, he could be my daddy."

We both inhale sharply. All this time, I thought Tatum was content—happy with it being just the two of us. The knowledge of all that I've truly deprived her of is another arrow to my heart, only this one splinters and embeds itself into the very core of the muscle.

"I am." Alden chokes out the words. "I am your daddy."

Tatum swivels to face him so fast her movement is a blur. With her eyes wide and her heart on her sleeve, she asks, "You are? For reals?"

"Yeah, pretty girl, for really reals."

She shoves her chair back from the table so hard it topples over, but that doesn't stop her. She's on a mission—and that mission is to hug her dad. She flings herself onto his lap and wraps her arms and legs around him in a monkey hold.

He hugs her close and presses his lips to the top of her head. I feel like I'm intruding on a magical but private moment, so quietly, I excuse myself and retreat to the kitchen. But as I go, I hear my girl whisper through her happy tears, "I lub you, Daddy Alden. A lot."

Tears wet my cheeks as I cry silently. I'm not sad. I'm happy—so incredibly happy. And remorseful. And full of regret. It's funny how back then, I was so convinced I was doing the right thing...how I planned this all out to make sense in my mind. But, we know what they say about the best-laid plans.

The sound of their muffled talking floats into the kitchen. I'm tempted to listen in, but I know that this is their time. Still, the temptation is strong. In an effort to fight it, I let myself out onto the back porch.

But the nighttime silence is too much. I need a distraction. Fumbling, I slide my phone from my back pocket and dial my brother. No answer—duh, he was switched to night shifts last week. Unsure of who else to call, I find myself scrolling to Jenny's contact info. I hit the green button, and she answers on the first ring.

"Nat! Hey girl!"

"H-hey." My voice breaks.

"Are you okay? What's wrong?"

"Nothing." I sniffle. "Everything."

"Nat, you're kind of freaking me out."

"S-sorry. It's just..." More sniffles. "It's just too much,

you know?"

"No babe. I don't know, because I have no clue as to what you're talking about." We're both quiet for a moment. "But...something tells me this is about Alden."

At the sound of his name, a small sob breaks free, and I slide down the side of the house until my ass hits the wood of the porch. "We told Tatum tonight." Since the entire café knows our drama, that's all I have to say. Jenny remains quiet as if she knows I have more to get off of my chest. "He's such a g-good man, Jenny. He's stepped into his role as Tatum's d-dad like a duck to water. He's so kind and compassionate and just...good. Even with my bullshit and lies, he's k-kind to me. He sh-should hate me for keeping his daughter from him."

I'm mortified by the words falling from my lips, but I can't seem to stop. "I thought I was d-doing the right thing. I thought I was protecting him. But I was selfish and stupid. I took so much from them." My words dry up as my tears fall harder.

"Babe, I'm gonna stop you right there. From what I've gathered here, you were still a kid. We all do stupid shit that seems smart when we're young—learning from our mistakes is how we gain wisdom. And sure, he missed out the first couple of years, but they have their entire lives together ahead of them. You're a good woman, and a good mother, and Alden forgives you because he can sense that. Just breathe, sweetie."

Her words are just the balm I needed. They wrap around me and soothe my hurt. "I...thank you, Jenny. Sorry to dump on you like that."

"No problem, babe. But know this—my ass just got promoted from your work wife to your real-life bestie. Deal with it."

Her sassiness turns my cries into laughter. She's the exact medicine I needed. "I can handle that."

"Wasn't asking. Talk later. Oh, and Nat...you've got this." She ends the call, and I lean my head back against the side of the house, staring up at the twinkling stars in the night sky. Is Jenny right? Do I *got* this? I sure hope so.

chapter thirty-one

Alden

SWEAR ON EVERYTHING I'VE EVER cared about, my daughter hugging my neck and telling me she loves me is the most amazing feeling on this earth. It's everything I never knew I wanted, yet everything I ever needed, all at once.

The feeling punching around in my chest is like nothing I have ever felt before—it's sadness, joy, hope, elation, and reverence, all rolled into one. That this kid could truly accept and love me is the greatest gift I've ever been given.

When Tatum finally draws back from our embrace, she touches the tip of her little button nose to mine and places her palms flat on my cheeks. "You really my daddy?"

I nod, my throat too clogged with emotion to attempt to speak.

"And you wub me? Forever?" More nodding. "Den where you been all my life?"

Her questions cause an ache all the way down to my soul—*dammit, Natalie.* "I..." my voice is gravelly. "I was away...studying and working...on becoming the best man I could be so that I'd be worthy of being your daddy."

She studies me for a minute, and I swear she's, at all of three years old, about to call me on my shit. But instead, she snuggles in close to my chest again, nestling her head beneath mine. "Okay...Daddy."

We stay just as we are for a few more quiet minutes before she pulls away again. "I's still hungry. You got ice cream?"

I shake my head and smile. Damn, toddlers are resilient. "You know what, I think I do. Wait here, and I'll go find your mama, and we'll scoop up some ice cream."

My girl nods and moves back to her chair, helping herself to another slice of pizza. For such a small thing, the kid really can put away some food.

I walk into the kitchen, fully expecting to see Natalie. What I'm met with though, is completely different. The door leading to the porch is ajar, and drifting in on the breeze is the sound of Nat breaking down. Her tears and sobs and sorrow are so visceral, it's almost as if I'm the one experiencing them. I can *feel* just how much she regrets the decisions that led us here. I once accused her of being selfish, but the reality is, she is anything but. She was a scared kid who didn't fully comprehend the ramifications of the decision she made.

I shouldn't stand here and listen to her pour her heart out like this, but I'm a shit, because I do. I listen to every word until I hear her end the call. I let a few seconds pass, and then I step outside and join her.

"You okay, Nat?"

The smile she aims my way is watery. "Yeah. Totally fine."

I don't bother calling her on it. Instead, I extend a hand down and haul her to standing. "Our princess is requesting ice cream."

"Oh, well, we better—"

Natalie doesn't have the chance to finish her sentence because a very impatient Tatum bursts through the doorway, joining us.

"I want ice cre—you have a pool!"

We both snicker at her abrupt subject change. "Yes, I do."

"I lub swimming!"

"Tater Tot, you don't know how to swim."

Totally undeterred, she stops her little foot. "So! I still lub it! It's like a really super big bathtub, and baths are da best!"

I wink at Natalie. "Girl's got a point. Y'all will have to come over and swim soon before the temperature drops."

"Yes! Please, Mama! Please, can we?"

"Of course, baby. Alden—your dad and I will figure out a date, okay?"

"Okay! Now we can has ice cream?"

"No," I gently correct her, "we can *have* ice cream. Not has."

Tatum gives her mama an eye roll worthy of a teenager. "Fine. Can we have ice cream? I fink I might die without it!"

I snort at her antics. If she's this dramatic now, I can only imagine her at thirteen. "Yeah, kiddo, let's head inside. I have chocolate, vanilla, and chocolate chip cookie dough."

"Dat one! I want dat one!"

chapter thirty-two

Natalie

THE PAST TWO WEEKS HAVE been nothing short of pure bliss. Thanks to Alden hanging out with Tatum on the days I do my classes, my grades are top notch. They've also had several solo outings. I'm so totally impressed with the way Alden makes Tatum his number one priority, even over the café.

One day last week, she was sick, and the preschool called me to come get her. My section was crazy busy. Even though things with my parents are still rocky, I tried calling them, but they didn't pick up. Alden, though—he rearranged a whole day of vendor meetings and picked her up. He stopped by my place and grabbed her blankie and her Poppy Troll and set her up with his tablet on the couch in his office.

Hell, he even had Darren whip up some chicken noodle soup for her and sat on the edge of the couch where he fed it to her—when I walked in and saw that, swear to God, my ovaries exploded. *Ka-boom.*

As promised, Alden has kept me off the schedule on the third Saturday of every month. And on this particular Saturday, we're headed to his house to swim. To say that

Tatum is over the moon would be an understatement.

Me, on the other hand? I'm a too-deep-in-my-own-thoughts mess. After the handful of heated kisses we've shared, the silly teen inside of me wants to look good for him...she wants him to notice me as more than the mother of his child.

Pathetic, right?

Even knowing what a sap I'm being, here I am, standing at the foot of my bed looking at every swimsuit I own. Do I play it safe and go with my black one-piece that screams *I am mom, hear me roar!*, or do I walk on the wild side and don my sexy, rust-red bikini with cheeky bottoms? Maybe I should just split the difference and go with my high-waisted bottoms that hide—as Tatum calls them— my tiger stripes?

I blanch at the thought of Alden seeing my stretch marks. High-waisted it is. The bottoms are a gray-ish blue, and even though they don't match, I pair them with my rust-red top. It pushes my boobs together, and Lord knows, after nursing, they need all the help they can get. I toss on a simple black cover-up and grab some towels, Tatum's floaties, sunblock, and some after-sun lotion and toss it all into a bag along with a change of clothes for each of us.

Just like every time we go to Alden's, Tatum is ready and waiting at the door. "Are you fine-ah-wee ready?"

This girl...she loves her daddy. "Yes, Tater Tot. I'm *finally* ready. Let's go!"

The entire drive is spent with Tatum chattering excitedly to her Poppy Troll and me worrying about how I look in my swimsuit—especially after eating a heavy lunch. Oh, God, I should have gone with my mom-suit.

My worry stays with me right up the walkway and to the front door...where Alden is waiting, clad in only his swim trunks. Oh, Jesus. This man is the perfect male specimen. With his smooth, tanned skin stretched taut over his lean muscles, he looks more like a sculpture you'd find in a fine art museum than standing here in nowhere Alabama.

Behind the safety of my sunglasses, I stare at him without any shame. At least, until he says, "You're drooling a little, Nat."

Mortified, I rush past him and into his house, straight through to the backyard. *Strike me down now, God!*

His throaty chuckle follows behind me, taunting.

"We swim now?" Tatum bursts through the back door, struggling to remove her cover-up.

I start to go to help her, but Alden beats me to it. "Sunblock first."

I retrieve the bottle from my bag and pass it to him. He sprays her down and then uses it on himself. I watch, tantalized by the way his abs flex and bunch as he does so.

"Hey! Earth to Nat!"

I snap out of my Alden-induced lust-fog. "Huh? Yeah?"

He laughs again. "You want some?"

So, maybe I'm still in said lust-fog because it takes me a minute to realize he's referring to the sunblock and not... well, you know. "Sure," I croak out.

Except he makes no move to hand over the bottle. I gesture for it, but he smirks. "Can't put on your SPF if you're still clothed."

"Y'all go ahead," I tell him, desperate for his attention to be off of me.

"Nah, we'll wait."

Hello, rock and hard place. Nervously, I peel my cover up over my head, depositing it onto the porch near my feet.

Alden

I know the game I'm playing is dangerous, but for some reason, I can't stop pushing her buttons.

But when that piece of fabric hits the deck, I damn near swallow my tongue. Natalie has grown up right. "Damn, girl," I mutter under my breath as I step a little closer.

She's looking anywhere but at me, and yet I can't look away. She's all lush curves, and the way her tits look in her swimsuit top is almost pornographic. They're full and bouncy and jiggly and...*fuck.*

I have to get my shit together, for several reasons. One, because our daughter is *right fucking here* watching our every move. Two, Natalie and I aren't like that. I mean, the last time we kissed, she practically begged me not to do it again. Which, not going to lie, sucks. And three, I'm about two seconds from pitching a tent in my shorts, and that's the last thing any of us need.

Quickly, I toss her the sunblock and move to grab Tatum, hoisting her up onto my shoulders. She squeals as

I walk us into the pool, the cool water instantly cooling my raging, underused libido.

I lower Tatum, moving her to balance her on my hip. She splashes happily as we wait on Natalie to join us. And join us she does, gliding down the damn pool steps like a runway model, with Tatum's floaties clasped in her hands. She walks to us, the water moving around her, splashing up onto the exposed hint of her midsection. Her two-piece is classy and shows just enough to make me want to peel it away.

Fuck. What am I thinking?

I school my features as best I can, trying to keep her from seeing the X-rated thoughts dancing in my mind. When she reaches us, she dips one floatie in the water and then slides it up Tatum's arm, repeating the action with the second.

With me at her shoulders and Natalie at her feet, together we help Tatum float on her back. When she gets tired of that, I teach her to hold her breath via the classic puffed cheeks and nose-pinch method, and I softly dunk her a few times.

Every time she resurfaces, she cackles like it's the best thing she's ever experienced. Turns out my girl's a water baby. Once she's fairly comfortable with that, I let her jump from the edge and catch her.

We play and splash and splash and play until Tatum's tummy rumbles, and she demands a snack. The three of us climb out of the pool, and Nat dries Tatum off while I run inside to grab her something to eat.

Armed with the perfect late afternoon snack—

lemonade and fresh-cut fruit—I head back to my girls. *Oh, shit. Did I just say* my girls? *Yes. Yes, I did, and I'm not sure how I feel about it.*

I find them laid out on side-by-side loungers. Tatum is wrapped in her towel, while Natalie lies on top of hers, soaking in the sun, looking every bit like a goddess. *There I go again. Jesus. It must be all the skin she's showing that's got me so keyed up.*

"Who's hungry?" I ask, setting the platter down. I pass each of them a small plate and glass—well, a sippy cup for Tatum.

While Tatum is happily munching away, I ask Nat, "Do you mind if we Skype my parents? They've been dying to meet her."

"No, not at all." She downs the last of her lemonade. "I'll give y'all some privacy."

"Oh, you don't have—"

She holds up a hand, stopping me. "I want to." She leans over and presses her lips to Tatum's temple before leaving us for the refreshing water of the pool.

"Hey, pretty girl. How do you feel about video calling your grandparents with me?"

She scrunches up her nose in the most adorable way. "Nana and Popsie? Dey already know me."

Damn, this kid is cute. "No, I mean my parents."

Tatum's eyes widen. "You mean I have two?"

"That's right."

"Dey get me Christmas presents too?" I bite back a smile at her innocent question. God bless the kid that her biggest worry is getting extra presents under the tree.

"I bet they will. They're so excited to meet you."

She eyes me expectantly, and I stand and move to the end of Tatum's lounger, grabbing my phone off the table and dialing them. I had sense enough to warn my parents that this call was a possibility, so when they answer, it is with bright smiles.

"Oh, my goodness!" My mom's voice croons through the speaker. "She is absolutely precious!"

"Pretty girl, this is Phyllis and Bob, your grandparents." Tatum smiles at them, and they smile right back. "Mom, Dad—this is Tatum."

"Well aren't you the prettiest little girl ever?" Dad asks, sounding sappier than I've ever heard.

Tatum nods seriously, causing them to smile. "My daddy says I'm a pwincess!"

I swear, my dad wipes away a tear. "Then it must be true." His voice is scratchy. It does something to me to see my dad, who is usually so stoic, this choked up.

They chat back and forth for a while, with me adding input when needed. More than once, my gaze flits to Natalie and her lithe body cutting through the water. *Good God, I think I'd give my left nut to get her under me.*

After about fifteen minutes, Tatum yawns and her eyes droop shut, so I end the call with a promise to do it again soon. After setting my phone back onto the table, I turn to ask Tatum what she thinks of my parents, but she's out like a light, curled up on a lounger in the shade. I sit with her for a few more minutes, stealing surreptitious glances at Nat as she swims laps from one end of the pool to the other.

Eventually, the heat wins out, and I head for the pool. I make sure to stay in the shallow end in case Tatum wakes up and needs either of us. Though, judging from the logs that kid is sawing, she's *out*.

I strategically position myself to the right side of the steps, propping up against the wall. Not-so-coincidentally, this also happens to be the side where Natalie's been swimming her laps. I watch her sinful body slice through the water like a hot knife through butter. Her movements are fluid, effortless.

As she nears me, I realize my error. But it's too late for me to move. I only wanted the best view of her, not what I know is about to happen. Though, let's be real, I'm not gonna complain, either.

Natalie surfaces, taking a breath before heading back under. She reaches out for the wall, but her hand connects with the hard planes of my abs instead. Her head pops out of the water and she rears back, struggling to find her footing. I reach for her, wrapping an arm around her waist and pulling tight to me.

"I've got you, Small Fry."

Breathlessly, she blinks up at me, water clinging to her lashes. "That's the first time you've called me that since— well, you know."

"Is it now?" I try and think back, but it's an impossible task with her skin touching mine.

She nods, the up and down movement causing her breasts to shake and like the dog I am, I watch. I'm so totally transfixed by the sight of her, pressed against me beneath the surface of the water, that I'm not even sure

I'm aware of my actions as I trace the contour of her body with my fingertips.

"Alden," she whispers my name like a prayer. "Wh-what's happening?"

Starting at the edge of her swim top, I gently work my way down, skimming my fingers over her skin, loving the way she rocks the curves that motherhood gave her. My fingers roam over her hip and around to the swell of her ass, not stopping until they meet the seam of her bikini bottoms.

Her breath shutters.

"Fuck, Nat, I don't know. But I'm tired of fighting this." With that, I pull her even closer and seal my mouth to hers, flicking my tongue against her bottom lip until she grants me entry. Our kiss is every bit as heated as the air outside, and when I feel her nipples pebble through the triangle of her bikini top, I damn near lose it.

I slide my hand beneath her bottoms, palming the flesh of her ass, pulling her against my hardness. With only the thin nylon of our bathing suits separating us, I can feel her heat, her outline. I nestle my erection against her and use the hand on her ass to guide her as she eagerly rolls her hips. We meet thrust for thrust, grinding on each other like our lives depend on the orgasms we're both chasing.

Ready for more, I withdraw my hand from the backside of her swimsuit and she whines in displeasure. That is until I slip it down the front side instead. I trace her seam with my index finger, teasing and rubbing until she's a panting mess, and I'm about to blow my load in my swim trunks just from the sounds she's making.

"Fuck, Nat, you feel so good."

She moans her agreement, the sound a direct line to my pleasure, frantically tugging at the waistband of my trunks. She frees me, and tingles start at the base of my spine. I move to shift her bottoms to the side, ready to slide home when a wail sounds from the porch.

Tatum.

Natalie flies away from me, hurriedly righting her bikini before rushing to our daughter. I linger, waiting on my erection to fully die down. Thankfully, toddler tears are a total boner killer.

By the time I make it over to them, she has Tatum soothed and napping again. I'm tempted to see if she wants to pick back up where we left off, but the moment is gone.

I take in the sight before me, Natalie with her cheeks all flushed, gently rubbing Tatum's back. Swear to God, she's never looked more beautiful than she does now.

"Stay for dinner?" I ask, my tone just shy of begging.

"Yeah, okay," Natalie whispers. "What about Tatum?"

As softly as I can, I lift my sleeping girl up into my arms and head for the house. Natalie picks up the platter and our towels, following behind me. She looks at me quizzically as I begin to climb the stairs.

I gesture for her to open the first door on the right and when she gets a glimpse inside, she audibly gasps. I try and take in the view from her perspective, from the pale aqua walls to the twin bed outfitted with a white quilt with rows and rows of neon-colored pompom balls. I even remembered to get a rail for her bed.

"You...you did all of this?"

I stride across the room to the bed. Natalie rushes over and pulls down the quilt, allowing me to tuck my daughter in bed in my own house for the first time ever. I draw the covers up to her chin, brush her chlorine-scented hair off of her face, and drop a soft kiss to her forehead. "Love you, pretty girl."

Out in the hall, Natalie repeats her earlier question, sounding on the verge of tears.

"Yeah, I—uh...I wanted to be prepared in case she ever spent the night. I wanted her to feel at home here, too."

Natalie shocks the shit out me when she presses a hard but chaste kiss to my lips, retreating before I can even react. "You're a good man, Alden Warner."

chapter thirty-three

Natalie

WE'RE DOWNSTAIRS, WITH ME SEATED on a bar stool and Alden pulling out ingredients. We've probably been down here for at least ten minutes, but *gah*, my lips are still tingling from our brief kiss outside of Tatum's room.

Then again, the rest of me is still tingling from our bump-n-grind session in the pool. And the fact that we're both still wearing only our swimsuits isn't helping.

And my heart...my heart is fluttering over how entirely Alden has accepted Tatum into his life. I mean, that bedroom was fit for a princess. I even noticed a few *Trolls* toys in the corner, along with a box marked *Dress Up*. Seriously, could this man be any more perfect?

"Whatcha making?" I ask, drumming my nails on the hard surface of his granite countertops.

"*We* are making brown butter scallops with parmesan risotto."

"Ooh, fancy," I tease.

He gives me a lopsided grin and walks back over to the fridge, where he grabs a bag of marinating chicken. "And grilled chicken for Tatum."

"Good call. She's adventurous, but maybe not that

much."

"You gonna come help me?"

"Yes, chef." I give him a salute and come around to the other side of the island. I try not to get distracted by all of the smooth skin he has on display, especially since he seems so in the zone.

Alden has me start the risotto while he heats grapeseed oil in a non-stick pan and pats the scallops dry. I'm in the process of adding the arborio rice to my shallots and garlic, and the smell alone is drool-worthy.

I let out a little moan at the scents filling the kitchen, and no lie, Alden growls. Goodbye, metaphorical panties, it was nice knowing ya!

After adding my white wine, I slowly add in broth. Simmer, stir, pour, over and over, until my rice is soft and creamy. "Small Fry, think you can start the spinach?"

"Yeah, I can do that!" I grab a pan from the ceiling-mounted rack that hangs over the island. I ignite the burner and oil the pan, letting it heat before adding some garlic. I alternate between the risotto and the spinach while Alden works on the scallops, brown butter, and Tatum's chicken. We move around each other in the kitchen like it's a dance we've been doing together our entire lives.

Our timing is so in sync, we reach simultaneously to shut off our burners, our hands brushing in the process. Little jolts of electricity race from where we touched, heading straight to my heart—and other places.

"Why don't you go wake up sleeping beauty, and I'll plate everything."

I nibble my lower lip—God, he is so sexy. "Sounds

good." I turn and head for the stairs before I can do anything dumb. Like throw myself at him, and beg for him to finish what we started earlier.

In her room—*gah, that sounds weird still*—Tatum is still fast asleep. "Tater Tot, it's time to get up." I kiss her temple. When she doesn't stir, I tickle her ribs and shake her lightly. "C'mon sleepyhead, your daddy made a yummy dinner!"

At the mention of food, her eyes pop open.

"Let's get you out this swimsuit first, though. Be right back." I run down the stairs, grab our bag, and dash back up. Once we're both dressed, we head down, ready for dinner.

"Plates are on the table," Alden says. Apparently, he found time to change too, as he's now dressed in a pair of navy sweats—still no shirt, much to my delight.

They way Alden has plated our dinner is worthy of a Michelin-star restaurant. The seared, perfectly golden-brown scallops rest atop the risotto along with the spinach. It truly is picture perfect.

And holy shit, it tastes even better. Even Tatum agrees, happily devouring her risotto and chicken. "Dis good, Daddy."

Every time I hear her call him that, my belly swoops low and my heart does a little dance in my chest. If it makes me that giddy, I can only imagine how he feels. Probably like the king of the world, if I had to guess.

After dinner, I clear our plates, rinsing and placing them in the dishwasher. I already know it's going to be a struggle getting Tatum loaded up to head home. She loves spending time with her daddy and is not going to go quietly.

Stalling, I also scrub the pots and pans, as well as wipe down the counters. I guess I stalled too long though, because when I reenter the dining room, they aren't there.

I follow the sounds of my girl's high-pitched laughter, finding them in the family room. Alden is queuing up a movie—*Boss Baby* from the looks of it.

"We's gonna watch a moobie!" Tatum informs me, patting the spot to the left of her on the oversized couch.

"Is that all right?" Alden asks, sounding unsure.

"Sure. But only if we have popcorn."

"That I can handle. Have a seat."

I drop down next to my girl, and she immediately leans into me while Alden goes to make us some popcorn.

He quickly returns, claiming the spot on the other side of Tatum. Like the little diva she is, she snags the popcorn bowl from him and kicks her feet up into his lap. And like the sucker he is, he sets to work massaging her little toes.

She sighs dramatically and tosses a few pieces of popcorn into her mouth before focusing her attention on the screen.

As much as I hate to admit it, the movie is cute—even if it is my one-millionth time seeing it. It would seem that Alden agrees, because Tatum has long since fallen asleep—again—yet here we are, still watching. And we keep watching all the way until the end credits.

"I guess we better get going," I say, trying to maneuver out from under my snoring toddler.

"Or, y'all could stay." Alden's eyes widen at his suggestion. "I mean, Tatum's already out cold, and she has her room here, and I have a guest bedroom set up too. You don't have to though. It's just an idea."

His nervous rambling is endearing. "No. That's fine, we'll stay."

"Really?"

"Yeah, really."

"Let's tuck her in, and I'll show you to the guest room."

I smile and nod as he scoops her up into his strong arms. We once again head up the stairs and together we tuck her in, taking turns kissing her forehead. Poor thing must be exhausted; I hope she's not getting sick.

"C'mon," Alden whispers, grabbing my hand. "Guest room is right down here. You have your own private bath. My room's at the end of the hall if you need anything."

He turns the knob and opens the door, and I'm thoroughly impressed by how inviting this room is. The floor is covered in a plush, sheepskin rug, the bed is decked out with a fluffy, inviting down comforter, and the walls are the most relaxing shade of gray—so pale it's almost white.

"Bathroom's through there." He nods to the door on the far side of the room. "Towels are stocked. Probably some soap too. You want a shirt or something to sleep in?"

I glance down at my ensemble of linen shorts and a tank top. "Nah, I'm good. Thank you, Alden."

He looks me up and down, smiling. "Yeah, you are. G'night. I'm the next room over if you need me."

"Okay. Thank you." Things are feeling awkward now. Without Tatum as a buffer, it's safe to say both of our minds are venturing back to earlier today.

Alden turns to go, giving the door frame two taps as he passes it. "Sleep tight," he murmurs and then he's gone.

chapter thirty-four

Alden

THE THOUGHT OF NATALIE SLEEPING under the same roof as me—especially after us damn near fucking in the pool—has me way too keyed up to sleep.

I'm hard enough to pound nails—though I'd rather pound Natalie—and hornier than a fourteen-year-old boy with his first nudie magazine. Basically, shit is dire over here, and I have no choice but to relieve some of this tension flowing through me.

I shuck off my sweats and lie back onto my bed, propped up against my headboard. I let my eyes drift shut as my right hand trails down my abdomen, lower and lower, calling my go-to Natalie fantasy to mind.

We're finally alone together after exchanging looks all night long; you know, the kind that says let's get naked. *I sit on the edge of the bed and pull her between my legs. I pop the button to her skin-tight jeans, loving the way she blushes as I pull them down, revealing her pale pink lace thong to me—*Goddamn. *I waste no time removing her shirt and matching bra. Girl's a goddess.*

She nibbles her lower lip and asks, "What about you?"

"What about me, Small Fry?" I run my hands over the firm swell of her ass, up her sides and palm her tits. They're barely a

handful, but that's okay—just means they'll be a perfect mouthful.

"Are you gonna take your clothes off too?"

I lean forward and suck her left nipple into my mouth, nibbling and kissing it before showing her right side the same attention. "Do you want me to?"

"Y-yes," she moans, her head thrown back.

Once I'm naked, I slide her thong down and press a soft kiss to her right hip, trailing my tongue across and dipping low before kissing the left hip as well.

I pull her into me and roll us so that she's on her back and I'm hovering over her. We're both a little tipsy, but damn, I think it's making us both feel more. "You sure, Small Fry?"

"More than ever." She sounds like she means it and I press forward, meeting resistance. "Keep going," she gasps out, sounding almost in pain.

"Oh, holy shit!" My erection dies a painful death. I feel fucking sick. I race from my bed to my en-suite bathroom, where I promptly lose the delicious dinner and popcorn from earlier tonight.

All this time, that's been my go-to spank bank material—a fucking fantasy. Except, I'm pretty sure it's not make-believe. I'm pretty sure that's a memory of the night Tatum was created.

A few dry heaves later, I'm in the shower, trying my best to chill the fuck out. That couldn't have been a memory, right? Nah. Unless...

Fuck.

I shut off the water and throw my sweats back on, not bothering to dry off. I need to talk to Nat. *I have to talk to Nat.*

Singularly focused on getting to the bottom of this... *epiphany*, I tear out of my room and rush into the guest bedroom, not even bothering to knock.

The sight of her lying in bed, with the covers pushed down around her hips, wearing only her tank and panties while reading on her phone, just about does me in.

"We gotta talk."

She tosses her phone down onto the bed and pulls the blanket up to cover her. *Pity.* "About what? Is everything okay?"

I sit on the edge of the bed. "Fuck, Nat. I don't know. I...I think I remembered."

She looks at me like I'm spouting off complex math equations in Mandarin. "Remembered what?"

"That night. Us. Together."

"I'm sorry. But, what?" She shakes her head. "Alden, I'm not following."

Oh, Jesus. I'm going to really have to spell this out for her. "I...ahem. I was taking care of business, and there's always been this one fantasy I would play in my head." *Kill me now, I just admitted to jerking off to her for* years. "But tonight...tonight was different. Tonight, I realized it was a memory."

Realization dawns. "Are...are you sure?" she whispers, her voice hoarse.

"About ninety percent. I was hoping you could clear it up for me."

She nods, unshed tears glistening in her eyes.

I go through my fantasy with her, as painful as it is, and by the time I'm finished, she's all-out sobbing. "Nat, are you okay?"

She flings off the blanket and crawls to me, wrapping herself around me. Her tears are cool on my overheated skin. "You re-remember." The words are soft and broken sounding. Right here, in this moment, the weight of her relief is palpable.

"I do," I murmur, kissing away her tears.

We sit just like that, with her quietly weeping while I rock her and whisper sweet nothings into her ear. Finally, she calms and pulls back, and I wipe the moisture from beneath my own eyes...*what the hell? When did I start crying?*

I'm scared she's going to vacate my lap, but she snuggles into me deeper and asks, "What now?"

We both do our best to ignore the way my untimely erection is pressing into her, begging for the release he's twice been denied today. "This might sound crazy, but I want to give us a chance. I don't care how it complicates things. I want you, and I think you want me too."

"Wh-what?"

"Me. You. Together."

It's kind of cute the way her brain isn't processing what I'm saying. "Like together? For real?"

"Yeah, Small Fry, for real. I think we'd be doing us—and Tatum—a disservice not to see where things go. I've always been attracted to you, long before it was socially or morally acceptable. I want to try and see if things will be as good between us in real life as they are in my head."

"I...Yes," she breathes out the word on a shaky exhale. I lean in for a kiss, but she pulls away. "But, we need to tread carefully. Because as amazing as this *could* be, there's also the potential for it to end horribly—and we'll still have to co-parent, even if things go south. We don't need to get Tatum's hopes up until we know for sure."

Here she is, once again, showing me what an amazing mother she is to our girl. Even now—especially now—she's putting her first. "Agreed. We play it casual when Tatum's around. But, Nat, I'm not holding back."

"Okay." Her voice is soft and breathless—a direct line to below my belt.

"We're gonna do this right. I know we're all kinds of out of order, but I want to date you. To woo you."

"Th-that sounds good." She sounds overwhelmed, in the best possible way and I love it.

"But, there's something I gotta do first."

"Wha—" I swallow her words with a kiss, molding my lips to hers, my tongue demanding entry, which she immediately allows. I taste and savor her, drinking down the soft noises she makes like a sweet nectar. Her hips begin to shift restlessly, signaling to me that it's time for me to pull away.

Which I do, much to her and my dick's dismay. The little wanton moan she gives as she chases my lips makes me feel like I'm on top of the fucking world. "Dream of me, Small Fry," I say, brushing my mouth against hers once more before retreating back to my bedroom.

chapter thirty-five

Natalie

YOU KNOW WHEN SOMETHING SEEMS too good to be true, and you have to pinch yourself to make sure you're not dreaming? This is totally one of those moments. Using the nails of my thumb and index finger, I squeeze at the skin of my thigh. "Ouch!" Definitely not dreaming then, and yet all of my dreams are coming true.

I quickly set an alarm on my phone to make sure I'm up before Tatum. The last thing I want is for her to wake up scared. I grab my spare charger from my bag and plug my phone in.

I toss and turn for a few minutes, unable to find sleep. Restless and overly excited, I slide out of my bed and creep down the hall to check on my sweet girl. I'm relieved to find her curled up in a ball and snoring like an old man.

Back in the guest room, I crawl under the covers and will my mind to shut down. Finally, after what feels like forever, sleep takes me.

I wake feeling more relaxed and rested than I've felt in a long time. A quick glance at my phone tells me why. It's nine-thirty—well past the time I set my alarm for.

As fast as I can, I step into my shorts and dash toward

Tatum's room. But she's not there. I fly down the stairs, only to come up short at the sight of Tatum and her daddy in the kitchen cooking up a feast.

I stay put in the shadows, observing them together, my heart swelling with emotion. Their relationship is so effortless. I can only hope mine and Alden's will be the same.

At the sound of their combined laughter, I step into the room. "I see y'all got the party started without me."

"We's not at a party. We's making breakfast. Pamcakes!"

"Ooh, I love pancakes. What kind?"

"All da kinds!" Tatum gleefully yells.

"And by that, she means, banana walnut, chocolate chip, and old-fashioned buttermilk." He waves his arms Vanna-White-style toward the island. "In the way of toppings, we have sliced bananas, freshly made whipped cream, and strawberries."

"Y'all went all out, huh?"

"Yes! Daddy said we was gonna make it for you and surprise you in bed. But, you waked up."

"Breakfast in bed, really?"

"Thought you might enjoy being taken care of for once." Swear to God, I'm a puddle of swoon at this man's feet. "I heard your alarm going off, and I might have turned it off and woke Tatum up. Hope I didn't overstep."

"Well, you aren't gonna hear me complain. Thank you. It's been a long time since I've slept in."

"You deserve it, Nat. Now, let's eat!"

We dig in, each of us choosing a different flavor. I go for the banana walnut, Tatum obviously devours the chocolate chip topped with whipped cream, and Alden opts for the buttermilk doused in syrup and covered with strawberries. All in all, it's been the perfect morning, and if I play my cards right, there will be a lot more of them.

The rest of the day is spent poolside, breaking only for lunch—grilled cheese and tomato soup. We swim and soak up the sun until it starts to dip below the horizon.

Alden makes good on his promise of wooing me. So much so that here we are, two weeks out from what I like to call *Remembrance Day*, and he's just now taking me out on our first real, official date.

Now, that's not to say that just because we haven't had our date yet that he hasn't been wooing me. Because, sweet baby Jesus, he has. From fresh coffee waiting for me on my opening shifts, to shoulder rubs, and even a spa day, that man has been wooing my socks off.

Our dateless status is not from lack of trying, either. He's been slammed at work, trying his hardest to revive our sweet little café, and my class load has been kicking my ass—who knew accounting was so damn hard? The only highlight in all of this is even though we're moving at a snail's pace, he's still a regular fixture in my and Tatum's lives.

Any time I need a little extra help—and even when I don't—he's there. We eat dinner together most nights—sometimes at my place and sometimes a quick bite at the café. Lord knows Tatum thinks going to Mama and

Daddy's work is the best thing ever.

But back to the date thing. I've cycled through every outfit in my closet. Usually I would break out my trusty wrap dress, but maybe on this first date, I *do* want to put out. I'm in a downward spiral of fashion despair when my doorbell rings.

"Come in," I holler, knowing good and well it's Jenny. Since I'm still not on the best of terms with my parents, and Nate's still working nights, she agreed to keep Tatum for us tonight.

Jenny's cheery voice fills my apartment as she greets Tatum. "Hey Lil Mama!"

"I's not a mama!" Tatum informs her, mild toddler outrage coloring her tone.

"My bad. Are you excited for us to hang out tonight?"

I can't see my daughter, but I can vividly picture her reaction. Most likely she's tapping her pointer finger against the sweet, little dimple in her chin pondering the question.

"That a'pends. Will you paint my fingernails? Can we have dessert first? And can we watch *Trolls*?"

"I will even paint your little piggies. No ma'am, dinner first. And you betcha."

It's quiet for a minute and then Tatum says, "Two outta free, not bad. Oh. You go helps Mama?"

"Help your mama with what?"

"Her says she has nothing to wear, but Miss Jenny, her has lots of clothes. Not as much as me, but lots!"

Jenny laughs. "I'll get her sorted. Maybe you can think about whatcha want to eat?"

"You can cook?"

"Lord no, but I can order takeout like a boss."

"Uh. Okay."

Jenny laughs again as she makes her way down the hall to my room. At the sight of damn near every stitch of clothing I own strewn across the room, she doesn't even blink. Nope. She just sets to work organizing it and creating outfit choices out of items I would have never ever thought of pairing together.

I watch in awed silence as she works until she has three outfits laid out on the bed for me. The first one being a flouncy, burgundy-colored chiffon skirt with a black button-down blouse. The second is a little slip dress I forgot I even owned. It's a silky emerald green and shorter than sin. The third is by far the most out of my comfort zone, which is saying a lot seeing as number two looks like sexy pajamas. Somehow Jenny managed to find an old crop top of mine that I only wear when I'm cleaning and has paired it with a pair of pale pink, high-waisted linen shorts.

"The first is really cute," I murmur, my eyes straying back to option number three.

"It is," she agrees. "But let's start with this little number." She grabs the shorts and crop top and shoves them into my arms and then me into the bathroom. "Get changed, babe. Now."

I do as she says because, at this point, someone else calling the shots is a weight off my chest. I'm already clad in sexy undies—not that he'll be seeing them, but a girl can hope. I slide my legs into the shorts and pull them up, instantly appreciating how the rise accentuates my waistline.

It's the crop top that has me out of sorts. It's almost cut like an elongated sports bra, stopping at the bottom of my rib cage. Due to the cut, an actual bra is out of the question. *Hope he doesn't take me anywhere chilly.*

All in all, the outfit is good. It doesn't show nearly as much skin as I was imagining—just a sliver of my abdomen. Feeling inspired, I quickly turn on my curling iron, tease my crown, toss my hair into a low pony and curl the ends. After that, I dust on some bronzer, apply a hint of eyeliner, coat my lashes in mascara and gloss my lips. *Hell yeah. I'd do me.*

I step out, and Jenny appraises me like I'm a piece of art and she's a critic. I'm worried she hates it but said worry dissolves when a brilliant grin splits her cheeks. "Yesss! Bow to your queen!"

I give her a little bow and we both giggle.

"Now you need to accessorize." A statement necklace and a few bangles later, I'm just about ready. I cross the room to my closet in search of the perfect shoes, settling on a pair of nude-colored wedges.

"Are you meeting him or is he picking you up?" Jenny asks, as Tatum barrels into the room.

"Mama! You look so pretty. But why your tummy showing?"

Her question catches me totally off guard. Luckily, Jenny answers for me. "Because she's a grownup and wants it to."

"Can I show off my tummy when I grow'd up?"

"As long as you're over eighteen, go for it, kid."

"Yay!" Just as quickly as she entered, Tatum exits the

room in a tornado of excitement.

We both laugh and then I say, "And to answer your question, he wanted to pick me up, but I figured it would be confusing for Tatum if I went somewhere with her daddy and left her behind..."

"Ah. Smart, Mama." She ushers me toward the door. "Have fun. We'll call if we need you."

On the way out the door, I stop and pepper my girl with kisses, hugging her tight. "I love you, Tater Tot. Be good for Miss Jenny?"

"I always good Mama."

I smile and give her one last kiss. "Love you."

"Love you too."

And with that, I'm out the door and on my way to my first real date with the father of my child.

chapter thirty-six

Alden

IT'S FUNNY HOW THE HUMAN mind works. I've known Natalie most of my life. I've shared countless meals with her. I've seen her bare-ass naked. Hell, I've been inside her...created life with her. Yet here I am, nervous as fuck over this date.

I made it to Cobalt about fifteen minutes before our reservation time. Talk about being eager. But, better early than late, I guess. Especially when I'm trying to make an impression. Which honestly seems a bit strange—because once again, I've known the girl since she was knee-high to a grasshopper, whatever the fuck that means. My grandpa used to say it, and it seems right.

As I wait in my car, my mind drifts. Unwelcome thoughts of Mia invade my brain and I shudder. *Nope. No way. Not letting that bitch ruin my night.* I bolt out of my vehicle and head for the entrance. Maybe they'll have our table ready. Because if I let my thoughts stay on the path they were on, tonight's going to be a total shitshow. Nothing— and I mean nothing—brings out the worst in me quite like my ex.

I manage to regain my composure on the walk over, but seeing Natalie standing near the entrance dressed to kill—yeah, I promptly lose what little chill I had.

My feet carry me directly to her, and I don't stop until were toe-to-toe. She looks absolutely radiant, and I can't help but to lean down and kiss her. When our lips meet, it's deep and slow and delicious. She tastes like melon-flavored lip gloss and something inherently Natalie.

I groan and pull away. "C'mon, beautiful, we don't want them to give our table away."

Seated, with menus in hand, we peruse them together, commenting on the various dishes. It's so refreshing to be able to talk about food with someone who's just as passionate about it as I am. Unlike Mia. She rolled her eyes and checked out every time I mentioned a new technique or flavor profile. *No. Bad, Alden. Cut that shit out. You know good and well Natalie is nothing like Mia.*

But it seems I don't cut it out quite fast enough, because Natalie picks up on my change in demeanor. "You okay?" she asks, placing her hand on top of mine.

The gesture brings me completely back to the here and now. "Totally fine. What sounds good to you?" I ask, changing the subject.

"I think I'm gonna go with—" Our server comes by, cutting her off. We place our drink orders, along with an order of their black-eyed pea dip. The server jots it all down with a smile and heads off to ring it in.

"As I was saying, I'm gonna go with the chargrilled beef medallions. Something about those loaded mashed potato cakes and fried oysters has my mouth watering. Gonna skip the Tabasco hollandaise though—that stuff is gross."

"Not a Tabasco fan, Small Fry?"

"Hell no. Cholula or bust."

"Girl after my own heart," I murmur, and she blushes the prettiest shade of pink.

"What about you?"

"Def going with the shrimp pasta. There's no way to go wrong with fresh shrimp paired with roasted mushrooms, chargrilled lemon, greens, and spicy marinara. A match made in culinary heaven."

"Ooh. That does sound good."

"Play your cards right, and I'll share."

Her returning smile is so beatific, it almost hurts to look at it dead on.

Our server returns, drinks and app balanced on her tray. The grilled French bread accompanying our dip looks divine. After we place our order, I spoon some onto a slice and lift it to Nat's lips.

She parts them in acceptance of my offering, moaning as the flavors burst across her tongue. The sound is so sensual my pants start to feel a few sizes too small.

Throughout the rest of our dinner, we cover all of the usual first date topics—from our favorite foods to our favorite colors and everything in between. It's actually refreshing, getting to know more about the woman Natalie is now, learning about her little quirks and what makes her tick.

Our server returns with the dessert menu, but we both pass, too full from our dinners. I pay the tab and together we exit the building. I guide her with my hand pressed to the small of her back. My pinky finger brushing over the exposed skin is almost like an adrenaline rush.

Outside, we linger, neither of us wanting our night to end. I check my watch, noting that it's already after eight. "What time did you tell Jenny you'd be home?"

Natalie shrugs. "I told her I wouldn't be too late, but we didn't really settle on an exact time."

I grin. "Wanna go for a drive?"

She smiles up at me, looking ten kinds of mischievous. "Sure."

Quickly, I guide her to my car, opening her door and helping her in. "Such a gentleman," she murmurs, her voice low and suggestive. Jesus, this woman oozes sex appeal, and I'm not even sure she knows it.

I crank the engine and reverse out of my spot. At the stop sign for the main road, I ask her, "Have you ever play Left-Right?"

"Uh, no. What's that?"

"So, every time we come to a turn, you tell me if I should go left or right and we'll see where we end up."

"Ooh! Okay. Go left."

I flip on my blinker and pull into traffic. At the next light, she directs me to go right. We continue on like this, weaving a maze until we find ourselves on an unpaved backroad. It leads to a small parking lot at the water's edge. It's dark, secluded, and...perfect.

"What is this place?" I ask, scanning our surroundings.

"It's a boat launch."

"You been here before?" I ask, petty, school-yard jealousy prickling my tone. After all, this place practically screams *make-out spot*.

"No."

"Then how do you know where we are?"

She giggles. "The sign, you doofus."

"What sign?" I look around again, and sure enough right outside her window is a freaking sign telling us exactly where we are. *Oops*. "Ah. That sign."

She laughs again, the sound light and infectious. I reach out and brush my fingers over her cheekbone. "You're really beautiful when you're happy." That didn't come out right. "I mean, you're always beautiful, but when you smile, it just radiates."

Thanks to the moonlight spilling in, I can see her blush. I know from our time in the pool just how far that blush reaches, and damn if I don't want to see it again. Feeling bold, I palm the back of her neck and draw her nearer to me.

Our lips meet in a kiss so soft and sweet it puts every fairy tale to shame. But it's not enough. I want more. And judging from the little noises Nat's making, she agrees. I reach over and click the button on her seatbelt, releasing it. "Backseat?" I ask, like an over-eager teenaged boy.

She doesn't answer with words. She simply climbs over the console and into the back. I follow suit. Thanks to the car seat I have for Tatum, it requires a bit of tricky maneuvering, but finally, I get her straddling me.

Our lips come together again in a clash of teeth and tongue. This kiss isn't sweet. It's fierce and full of want. I bite down on her bottom lip before sucking it into my mouth to soothe the sting away. She grinds into me, and I grip her ass—a cheek in each hand—like a lifeline.

The feeling of her moving over me and her hands in my hair has me so wound up, and even though I promised her we would take things slow, the head on my shoulders is at war with one below my belt. All I can think about is how fucking good it would feel to slide into her, to feel her squeezing me as I push us both toward release.

"Touch me, Alden, please."

Keeping one hand on her ass, I bring the other to her breast, tweaking her nipple through her sexy-as-hell top. Her eyes all but roll back in her head—so fucking responsive.

"More," she moans, and before I can do a thing, she removes her shirt, bearing her beautiful, full breasts to me. I waste no time giving my girl what she wants, kissing and sucking and nipping at her tits until she's trembling in my lap.

"More," she demands again, guiding my hand to the edge of her shorts. I pull back and look her in the eye, making sure she means this. She nods, and I pop the button and work my hand beneath her panties.

I find her wet and ready. Gently, I stroke two fingers over her seam, parting her. She rolls her hips and rides my hand like a fucking rodeo pro. Before I know it, she's coming apart, calling my name, and I'm about ready to blow my load in my pants. *What is it about this girl that gets me so hot?*

Once she comes back down, she slumps down onto me, her cheek landing on my shoulder. I withdraw my fingers, and the sensation causes her to rock against me. "What about you?" she asks, sleepily.

"Don't worry about me, Small Fry."

She lifts her head and looks at me with a wicked gleam in her eye. "That doesn't seem fair."

I watch in fascination as she scoots back on my lap as far as the seat in front her allows and undoes my pants. I hiss as she frees me and fists me, running her hand from root to tip. What really gets me, though, is when she releases me, licks her palm and gets back to work, jacking me like she knows exactly what I like—like she was made for me and me alone.

"Fuck, Nat...feels so good."

She moans as if pleasuring me pleasures her. "I still want more, Alden."

I'm so close to release I can hardly think. "We...we said sl-slow."

"I've been waiting for you for what feels like forever. Fuck slow. I want you."

I haul her up to me, pushing her shorts down as I go. She's poised above me, and as she sinks down, encasing me with her heat, I swear I've died and gone to heaven.

She swivels her hips, and a tremor works its way up from the base of my spine. "Nat. Wait. Protection."

"I have an IUD."

And with that, I thrust up from beneath her, setting our pace. She rides me without any abandon, seeking her pleasure and taking it until she's a writhing mess, calling my name as she comes. An embarrassingly short amount of time later, I find my own release, loving the way it feels to finish inside of her.

"Jesus, Small Fry," I groan out the words, and she looks

so proud that I don't even care that I just got off in my backseat like a sixteen-year-old. All I care about is keeping that smile on her face forever.

Holy shit, did I just think *forever?*

Natalie fumbles around until she finds her top, pulling it on. I'm expecting her to climb into the front seat—and excited for the view it will give me—but instead, she carefully exits the car and rushes to open the passenger door. Standing between the two open doors gives her a bit of privacy as she roots around in her purse until she finds baby wipes. She flips the pack open and grabs a few and uses them to clean me off of her thighs. *Huh. Who knew those things were so useful?*

I scoot over and climb out as well, and she passes me a wipe. I take care of business before tucking myself back into my pants and buttoning up. With us both redressed, I cage her against the car and kiss her deeply. "Tonight was more than I could've ever imagined."

She smiles up at me and then ducks into the car, where she promptly buckles up. "Tonight was perfect. Absolutely perfect."

"Damn straight it was." My chest puffs up like a proud peacock. "Now, let's get you back to your car so you can get home to our daughter."

chapter thirty-seven

Natalie

I'M SO HIGH ON ALDEN, the entire drive home feels like a blur. I can still feel the way he moved inside me, and while tonight was amazing, my body already craves more. More of him, more of his touch, more of the pleasure only he can give me.

In my parking lot, I sit in the car for a few moments, pulling down the visor and flipping open the mirror to make sure I'm presentable. Other than some seriously messy sex hair, I'm good to go. I finger comb it back into place the best I can and exit my vehicle.

Inside, the house is quiet and dark. Jenny is on the couch watching television, the volume barely audible, and Tatum fast asleep in her lap.

"Hey," I whisper, bending to scoop up my girl.

"She fell asleep on our second round of *Trolls*. I was too scared to move her."

My shoulders shake with silent laughter. "How long?" I ask, walking back to Tatum's room.

"Long. At least three hours. I can't feel my left arm or my ass."

Jenny waits in the hall as I tuck Tatum in. I pull her

door to behind me, leaving it partially open. "Three hours? You poor thing! Good thing about Tatum is, once she's out, she's out."

"Now you tell me!" Jenny rolls her eyes.

I roll mine right back, adding a valley-girl-worthy scoff.

"Speaking of telling, why don't you tell me about tonight, Miss Sex Hair?"

Gah! I guess I did a lousy job of smoothing it down. "It was amazing." I delve into our date, sparing her the dirty details—they're only for Alden and me—much to Jenny's disappointment.

"Well, I'm glad y'all are figuring this out. You two deserve it."

As the weeks pass, and fall rolls in, Alden and I seem to find our dating stride while he and Tatum continue to grow their bond. I don't think I'll ever tire of seeing the two of them together. Their connection is magical—the kind of relationship every girl wants with her daddy. The kind I had up until I became a teen mom.

To say I miss my parents would be an understatement. And more importantly, Tatum misses them. I get that I let them down and that this is hard for them, but my God, if Alden can forgive me, so can they.

But, they're both as stubborn as the day is long. So, it's going to be up to me to extend an olive branch.

I'm in the middle of a shift when the idea strikes. I quickly check on my tables before dashing off in search of Alden. I find him in the kitchen chatting with Darren about some menu changes.

Like he can sense me, he turns and looks at me. His stare is heated as it drags over my body, lingering in all the right places. We've gotten down and dirty a few times since our second first time, but I still want him. Bad. I'm talking *if that man doesn't sex me up soon, I might die* bad.

When his eyes finally meet mine, I mouth, "Need to talk to you." He holds up his index finger and nods.

I know he'll find me when he finishes up in here, so I head back out to tend to my tables. One table is ready to order, one table is fine and dandy, and two are ready for their bill.

Cashing out is a breeze since Alden upgraded us to an all-electronic system. Gone are the days of handwritten tickets and adding totals on a calculator. Hallelujah, because unless I'm halving a recipe, math is not my thing. Like, at all. So much so that I foresee Alden being the one to help Tatum with her homework when the time comes.

Butterflies erupt in my belly at the thought of Alden being in our lives that far down the road, but I know he will be, and if I'm a really lucky lady, he and I will still be together—maybe even married. *Jesus, girl. Slow your jets,* my logical brain shouts at my overactive imagination. *A few weeks of dating and a whole lot of sex does not a marriage make,* or something like that.

As I walk the dining room again, I see that all of my tables are content and not in need of me. Which is a good thing, because two strong hands are gripping my elbows and pulling me back into the office. The door shuts behind us, and I turn, melting into Alden.

He slides his lips against mine in a kiss so sensual my knees feel weak. I'm slightly dazed when he pulls away—so much so that it takes me a minute to realize he's speaking to me.

Naturally, Alden finds this to be hilarious. "You with me, Small Fry?"

"Ha ha, funny. I can't help it if your touch makes my brain all fuzzy."

"Does it now?" He tilts his head to the side, a look of faux seriousness painted across his face. "Tell me more."

His antics make me laugh—I love this playful side of him.

"Seriously though, you said you wanted to talk to me. I'm all ears."

I nibble my lower lip, nerves zinging through me. "I...I was thinking—no, hoping—we could do a cookout this weekend. And invite my parents."

He groans and kisses me again, nibbling softly on my lower lip before pulling back just enough to speak. "If that's what you want, you know I'll support it. And I think it's the right thing to do for Tatum."

"Really? You're cool with it?"

"Of course I am. They're your family. They're Tatum's family."

"You're so good to me. I don't...I don't deserve you."

"If you're gonna say shit like that, then I'm gonna put your lips to better use."

He kisses me again, licking, sucking, and biting until I'm a writhing mess. It kills me to do it, but I pull away. "I need to check on my tables," I pant, far too turned on to be at work.

Alden presses his hardness into me, and I moan. "Yeah, you better. But, damn, I wish you didn't have to."

I smile at him and step back. "But, I do."

He gestures for me to go ahead without him, which is probably for the best since he's sporting some major wood.

chapter thirty-eight

Alden

NATALIE HAS BEEN A KNOT of tension and stress since telling me she wanted to have her parents over. I know they have a lot of shit to sort through and a lot that was left unresolved. So, I'm hoping this will be good for them and help get their relationship back on the right track.

In an effort to defuse a little tension, I told her to invite Jenny and Nate. She lit up at the suggestion, which made me feel all proud and caveman-y.

Currently, she's in the kitchen obsessing over the sides she is making to go with my grilled chicken and sausage. She actually started prepping everything the night before at her place, and I swear, my eyes about my bugged out of my skull when she and Tatum got here this morning and she sent me to her car to help bring things in.

There is an apple crumb pie in the oven, along with scalloped potatoes. On the stove, she has homemade baked beans simmering and a pot of water boiling for her macaroni—she made the cheese sauce last night.

"Gonna go check the grill," I call over my shoulder, Tatum following along behind me like a pint-sized shadow. But I don't mind—I love that she wants to be around me, and I especially enjoy her enthusiasm for cooking. It's almost crazy how much alike we are, even without her knowing me for most of her life.

"How you knows when it's ready?" Tatum asks, standing on her tippy-toes in an effort to see.

"Careful, pretty girl. It's hot."

She watches with wide eyes as I hover my hand, palm side down, over the grate of the grill. "You be careful too, Daddy."

I grin at her. "Will you help me count?"

Together we begin counting, only making it to five before I have to pull my hand away. "Why we did dat?"

"How long I can keep my hand there tells me how hot the grill is. It still needs a bit more heat to get a good sear on the chicken."

"Whoa!" My girl sounds thoroughly impressed. "I try it?"

"Maybe when you're a little bit older."

She sticks her lower lip out in the cutest pout known to mankind. "Fine. I go help Mommy." She pivots and runs toward the house, leaving me to chuckle in her wake.

Back inside, Natalie is chopping away at a head of lettuce, presumably for a salad. "Where's Tatum?" I ask, coming up behind her and dropping a kiss to her neck after checking the coast was clear.

"She didn't like that I didn't have a job for her, so she is up in her room playing."

"It's sweet how much she likes to help."

Natalie nods her agreement, too focused on making uniform cuts on her tomatoes to reply verbally.

I'm about to ask her how she's feeling when the sound of my doorbell rings through the house. Tatum comes flying down the stairs. "Nana! Popsie! Der here!"

I catch her at the landing and swoop her up and around my shoulders like a toddler scarf. Her giggles are contagious, and by the time we make it to the door, we're both laughing.

I swing it open, only to be met with a triple whammy— all of our guests have arrived together, and poor Tatum doesn't know who to greet first. She wiggles and I set her down on the floor. "Nana! Popsie! Uncle Nate! Miss Jenny! Dis is the best day ever!"

We all stand there awkwardly, until Luke—Mr. Reynolds—drops to his knees and engulfs his granddaughter in a bear hug. Melanie is quick to follow suit, peppering Tatum's face with kisses, murmuring in between then how much she has missed her.

After their reunion, Tatum wraps herself around Jenny's leg, tugging on the hem of her top, begging her to hold her. "Miss Jenny! You're here! You watch *Trolls* with me?"

Before Jenny can reply, Nate slaps a hand over his chest. "Hello? What am I? Chopped liver?"

Tatum cracks up. "Ew. No. Liber is yuck."

"Then get over here and hug me, Tater Tot!" Jenny passes Tatum to Nate, and I notice her giving him a slow perusal—*how interesting*. Nat will have a field day with that.

"Uncle Nate, you wants to see my room?" Tatum asks, batting her lashes up at my best friend.

"You know I do."

She squeals in his arms. "You too, Miss Jenny! You'll love it!"

Together, the three of them set off up the stairs, while I shut the front door and head back toward the kitchen. The tension is so thick you could cut it with a knife.

Natalie and her mother are making small talk, while her dad silently bores a hole into her head with his laser focus.

"We're glad y'all could make it," I say, and Natalie smiles gratefully.

"Thanks for inviting us," Melanie says, but her tone lacks the warmness it used to hold when she spoke to me. As much as I love Tatum, and as much as I would never trade her or give her up for anything, I can't say it doesn't hurt to get the cold shoulder from Melanie and Luke. They truly were like second parents to me growing up.

"Can I get y'all something to drink?" I walk over to the fridge, swinging the double doors open wide. "I've got beer, wine, lemonade with fresh mint, tea, water."

"You drink in front of Tatum?" Mr. Reynolds barks out, and my hackles rise.

"Do we have *a* drink with a meal in front of Tatum? You betcha. Do we get *drunk?* Absolutely not." I'm not sure what he's getting at, especially seeing as a drink or two—especially during football season—was a common occurrence in the Reynolds household growing up.

He steps a little closer to his wife as if looking for back up. "You think that sets a good example?"

I take a deep breath, trying to stay calm. Natalie, on the other hand, looks ready to spit fire. Gently, I place my hand over hers—something both of her parents catch—letting her know that I've got this. She pauses and looks down at the now mangled carrot she was chopping and rolls her eyes.

"You know," I say, trying to keep my tone level. "I certainly don't think it's a bad example. We never over-imbibe. We never have more than a drink with dinner. Nothing wrong with that."

Natalie's dad huffs like a bull about to charge a red flag. "And you know what's best for her after being a father for all of ten minutes?"

Melanie looks torn between being horrified by her husband's behavior and wanting to support him out of obligation.

"Why can't you just get over this?" Natalie screams. "Even excusing that I'm your only daughter, are you so prideful and stubborn you'd risk your relationship with Tatum over something that really has nothing to do with you?"

"Natalie! Luke! Enough!" Melanie yells forcefully. "I've allowed this to drag on far too long. Your daughter is right."

At the sound of our raised voices, Tatum flies into the room, with Nate and Jenny hot on her heels. She flings herself into her mother's arms before reaching out and grabbing my sleeve to pull me closer. "Why's eb-ry one being so loud? I don't like it." Her eyes are brimming with tears, and suddenly, I feel like a rotten jackass. What the hell are we thinking hashing this out where she can hear?

I place my hand on her cheek and guide her eyes to mine. "Sometimes grownups disagree and argue. We're sorry we upset you, pretty girl."

She sniffles and clings tighter to Natalie. "Why you mad? Did Popsie break your toy?"

Nat buries her face in Tatum's hair. "No, Tater Tot, Popsie didn't break one of my toys. We're just...having a disagreement. Kind of like when I ask you to pick up your room, and you don't want to. Everything's okay."

I'm hoping like hell Tatum's presence will be what it takes to break this ice and to get us on the path to a resolution, but a glance over to Luke tells me that's not going to be the case—he looks utterly repulsed.

"How sweet," he sneers. "Playing house doesn't make up for all of the—"

I have no desire to hear whatever this man has to say. In the brief amount of time he's been under my roof, he's made both Natalie and Tatum cry, and that shit's not going to fly with me.

"That's enough." I keep my tone low, as not to scare my daughter, but it's also deadly, showing just how serious I am. "With all due respect, sir, your daughter was faced with a situation far beyond her years, and while she definitely made mistakes, she handled it in the way she thought was best at the time. There's no way in hell I'm going to let you sit here and make the woman I love feel even worse than she already does. We're both moving forward, and you can either move with us or get left behind."

All of the women in the room are misty-eyed, and when Nat palms my cheek and turns my face toward hers, the full impact of what I just said hits me like a freight train.

"You love...me?" Her voice is so small and unsure.

As I look at her, cradling our daughter close to her chest, I swear to God I see our past and our future flash before my eyes. "I do. I really do love you, Nat."

A small sob squeaks past her lips. "I-I love you too." She looks down at her feet and then back at me. "I always have."

"Does dis mean your mama's boyfriend now?" Tatum asks, reaching for me.

I take her into my arms and touch my nose to hers. "Yeah, pretty girl, I guess it does."

"You need to talk to them," Melanie hisses at her husband under her breath, but all I can focus on is what Jenny murmurs from behind them.

"Lord Jesus, remind me to never settle for anyone who doesn't look at me the way you look at Natalie."

Natalie's brows pinch together. "H-how does he look at me?"

"With fire and forever dancing his eyes, babe. He looks at you like you're his lifeline."

Melanie places her hand lightly on her husband's arm. "I mean it, Luke. I've been patient, but this has to stop." He gives her a terse nod. "Jenny, sweetheart, could you take Tatum out in the backyard to play?"

"Of...of course. Come on, girlfriend, let's go." She makes her way over to where we're standing and takes Tatum from my arms.

"I go play, but no more yelling, okay?" Tatum demands, crossing her arms over her chest.

Natalie boops her nose. "Deal."

chapter thirty-nine

Natalie

A HEAVY SILENCE SETTLES OVER the room after Jenny and Tatum leave. Nate tries to follow, but Mom stops him. "You should stay too."

Looking resigned, my brother nods.

I'm a yo-yo of emotions right now: Elated to learn that Alden returns my feelings; he wouldn't love me if he hadn't let go of my transgressions, right? Sad and confused over the way my dad is behaving. And nervous for whatever bomb he's about to drop.

Alden places his hand on the small of my back, rubbing his thumb in soft, soothing circles. "Let me turn off the grill and then we can head into the living room to talk."

"I've got it, man. You stay with her," Nate says, clapping Alden on the back as he walks past us.

The four of us go ahead and get settled in the living room. I'm so thankful to have Alden at my side. I know with him I can face whatever is about to come our way.

My parents snag the club chairs and when Nate joins us, he lowers himself down to the floor and leans back against the far side of the couch.

When neither of my parents make a move to talk, I

lose the little bit of patience I have left. "Are we just going to sit around and stare at each other? If so, I'm gonna pass."

"Just give your dad a second, this is hard for him," Mom says, her voice as calm and even as ever.

I stifle the urge to roll my eyes, but just barely.

"Your aunt Linda," Dad starts and I can't help but wonder my deceased aunt whom I've never even met could possibly have to do with anything.

He seems to get choked up over the mere mention of her name, and Mom reaches over and clasps his hand in a show of support. He clears his throat and continues. "Your aunt Linda and I were really close growing up, kind of the way you and Nate are. She always wanted to tag along with me and my friends."

Nate and I exchange baffled glances but keep quiet.

"When she was a senior in high school, I brought her with me to a college party and—" His words break off again, and I swear he has tears gathering. "I didn't want her to hover like a shadow all night, so I grabbed her a beer and sent her on her way...a few of her friends were there."

When his tears actually fall, I know this story doesn't have a happy ending. Dad drops his head to his hands and sobs openly while my mother soothingly rubs his back, murmuring words of comfort.

"Sh-she was a-a-assaulted. Raped. By the man I called my closest friend." He pauses again, and my heart aches for him. Alden reaches an arm around me and pulls me into him, silently giving me the comfort I desperately need.

"She didn't tell anyone what happened that night. Not

until about eight weeks later, when she found out she was pregnant. She ended up losing the baby, and she blamed herself. She never was right after that. And Natalie, oh my sweet Nat Bug...everything with you was so reminiscent of her. Then we find out Alden is the *responsible* party, and all of the sudden it's like history's repeating itself right before my very eyes."

"But Dad, Alden didn't—"

He waves me off. "I know. *I know.* But I couldn't help but draw parallels. Every parent wants the best for their child, and I couldn't help but feel I had somehow failed you the same way I failed her. You got pregnant. As a minor. Under my roof. How can I not hold myself responsible?"

I rush off the couch and throw myself into my dad's arms. "Oh, Dad. No. You've always been such a good father. You've always been there for me. And Nate. And even Alden. We're all so lucky to have you." His large frame shakes as he continues to cry.

I ramble on, trying my best to give him peace. "Alden would never hurt me, Dad. He's a good man, and what happened between us was consensual, even if we were under the influence. I knew what I was doing, and as much as you don't want to hear this, I initiated it. I had this...this plan. Over the years, my feelings morphed from a childhood crush to more. So much more. I knew even then that I loved him, Dad. And I thought that if we...you know...that he would see we were meant to be together. Obviously, things backfired a little. But, I got my sweet Tatum and now...now things with Alden are falling into place. I'm so sorry this brought back all of those memories, but I promise you, it was *not* the same thing."

Nate stands and joins us, wrapping the both of us in a hug. "What happened with Aunt Linda wasn't your fault, Dad."

"No," Dad argues. "If I hadn't—"

Alden speaks up, cutting him off. "Luke, you've always been like a second father to me. Thanks to your influence in my life, I know I'll be the best dad to Tatum possible. Throughout my childhood, you taught us through your actions that fatherhood is a privilege and not a right. You're a good man who has suffered through unspeakable loss, and I hate that. But, sir, I can guarantee you, I love your daughter, and I would *never, ever* hurt her in any way or take advantage of her in any way. She's precious to me." Alden's feelings for me, and our daughter, are clearly on display for the entire room to see—and when his eyes also cloud over with emotion, I know bone deep he means every word.

By this point, there's not a dry eye in the room. "I know, son. I know."

Nate gives us one last squeeze before returning to his spot on the floor, but I stay with my dad, hugging him tight for a few more minutes. "I'm so sorry, Nat Bug," he whispers gruffly into my hair.

"It's okay—"

"No, it's not. I...I think maybe I need to talk to someone about this. Your mom has been begging me to for years. I think now it's time."

I pull back from our embrace and look him in the eye. "I think that's a really good idea, Dad. And I...I'm proud of you." I kiss his forehead and move back to Alden's side.

For a few minutes, we all sit in silence, absorbing the reality of all of the truths that just came to light. That is, until we hear the sound of little feet running across the hardwood accompanied by Tatum yelling, "I know, Miss Jenny. But I gots to potty now!"

We all laugh and take that as our cue to disband.

"Y'all still hungry?" Alden asks.

My dad pats his belly. "I could eat. If you still want us to join you."

"Wouldn't be the same without you, Luke." Internally I beam at Alden's words, loving that he loves my family the same way they love him.

"I'm gonna go check on Tatum," I say, excusing myself. I head to the half bath, knowing that's where my girl will be.

I find Jenny in the hall outside of the half bath. "Sorry," she cringes. "I tried telling her to wait."

"You're all good. It was actually perfect timing."

Jenny's tight facial features visibly relax. Poor girl—we haven't really made the best first impression as a family unit, have we?

We both grin when from behind the bathroom door Tatum hollers, "Miss Jenny! I all done. I did a poop!"

"I've got this," I tell my best friend, and Lord knows, she doesn't need to be told twice. She makes a hasty retreat, bumping into my brother on the way. I watch, fascinated, as she tries to stop in time, but trips and faceplants into his chest.

He catches her and steadies her on her feet. "Whoa, girl. Slow down."

She smiles up at him dazedly before moving around him and scurrying away. He turns my way, smirking. "Your friend's an odd one."

"She is not!" I start to argue, but Tatum interrupts.

"Hello! I did a poop! Helps!"

Nate laughs, backing away. "That's all you."

I open the bathroom and immediately bust out laughing. Tatum has practically the entire thing of toilet paper unrolled and is in the process of bunching it. "Tater Tot, what on earth are you doing?"

"No one came to help me, so I do it. I'm big!"

"Oh my, you *are* big. But, sweetheart, that much toilet paper will clog the toilet."

I show her the proper amount to use, but she pushes it back my way. "No, you here now. You do it." *Good Lord, this kid.* I help her take care of business, and we both wash our hands, humming the *Happy Birthday* song as we go, before heading out to join everyone else.

Back in the kitchen, the atmosphere is notably lighter, and my heart soars. This is how it should be when family gets together—easy and fun, not rife with tension and aggression.

Tatum notices it too. "Oh! Eb-ry one is happy now!" She claps her hands and twirls. "Dis is much gooder!" She walks over to where my parents are seated at the bar. "Nana. Popsie. I show y'all my room?"

"We would love that very much," my mom tells her, and the three of them set off up the stairs.

Alden and Nate are chatting about God knows what by the back door, while Jenny is—wait a minute. "Alden, where's Jenny?"

"She stepped outside to make a phone call." He walks over to me and pulls me into him, nestling my head in the crook of his chin. "You okay?"

I sigh. "Yeah. I am." His earlier declaration whispers to me. "You really meant it when you said you loved me?"

"With every fiber of my being."

I pull back and look up at him. "You're not worried about...complications?"

"Natalie, I. Love. You. I love our daughter. I want us to be so tangled up together that I don't know where you end and I begin. I want all of the complications. I want you. I want this. For now, and forever."

I push up on to my tip-toes and kiss him, not caring one bit that my brother is still in the room. Or at least I don't care until he groans and mutters, "I'm glad y'all are happy, but I don't need to see this shit."

I pull away and smirk at him before leaning in and kissing Alden one last time. "I guess I'm going to get all of the side dishes reheated."

"Sounds good. I'll get the grill going again."

Alden heads out back and Nate follows—*men and their grilling.*

chapter forty

Alden

WE'VE JUST FINISHED OUR LATE lunch turned early dinner when Tatum wiggles down from her chair and crawls up in Melanie's lap. "Nana," Tatum whines. "I come sleep at your house? I miss you. And Popsie too."

"Oh, sweet girl, I would love that. But, it's ultimately up to your mama...and Daddy." My heart clenches in the best way when he tacks me onto the end of her sentence.

Tatum swivels her head around to face Natalie and me. "Pweeeeaaaasssse?" she begs, poking her lower lip out like a sad little puppy. "I'll be extra good!"

Natalie and I exchange a look. "Sure, Tater Tot. I think that would be great."

In my head, I'm thinking *Yes! Maybe I'll get a sleepover too?*

Tatum bounces around, shimmying her shoulders in her version of a happy dance.

"Oh, but wait!" Melanie exclaims, halting my girl's dance. "I promised to set up the church breakfast tomorrow."

Thankfully, Nate's got my back. "Don't worry, Mom. I'll swing by and grab her in the morning, and we'll go to breakfast."

"And da park?" Tatum asks, turning her pleading eyes

on her uncle.

His shoulders shake with silent laughter. "Yeah, kid. And the park."

"Yes!" Then she decides to push her luck—either that or she's playing toddler Cupid. "Can Miss Jenny come too?"

Jenny's gaze shoots up to Tatum and then to Nate before she blushes and looks back down. "No can do, little one. I already have plans tomorrow."

Tatum pouts, but Nate quickly cheers her up. "Don't be sad. We'll get hot dogs too, okay?"

"I guess," Tatum grumbles, not completely satisfied. "Maybe cupkates too?" The kid drives a hard bargain.

"Sure, cupcakes too." Nate catches my eye and winks. Thank God for the funcle!

Natalie speaks up. "I have a change of clothes in her bag, I'll send it with you."

Everyone takes that as a hint to leave, and no lie, I'm totally okay with that. I'm more than ready to spend a little one-on-one time with Nat—preferably naked.

After everyone leaves, and the kitchen is clean, Natalie and I collapse onto the couch together in heap of tangled limbs. "Are we gonna talk about...everything?" she asks, rubbing her nose against mine.

"We can talk about anything you want to, Small Fry."

"Today was just...a lot. I'm glad Dad clued us in. It makes understanding his actions so much easier."

I drop a kiss to her temple. "I can't even imagine."

Changing gears, Natalie pushes on my shoulder until I'm flat on my back and she's straddling me. "I know I keep asking, but...you really love me?"

I grin at her reluctance to believe me. I guess I can see where she's coming from though. "Yeah, I really love you. Wanna know what else I love?"

"What?" she whispers.

"Waking up next to you."

She draws her head back and sits up so that she's looking down at me. "But...what? We've never—"

I tunnel my fingers into her long locks and draw her face to mine, where I speak my next words against her lush lips. "Then let's change that. Stay?"

"Yes." She nods, and I roll my hips, showing her just how much her answer pleases me. The motion also turns her *yes* into a long, low, "God, yes." I fucking love how responsive she is, but I can't help but wonder if she's always this way or if it's just with me.

I try my best to banish the unwelcome thought and to simply be in the moment with her, but like a weed—it has taken root and I have to know.

"Hey, Nat, I have a question. You may not like it."

She moves back to sitting and looking down at me. "What's up?"

"I, uh. I guess what I wanted to ask is, uh. How—how many other guys—"

Her hysterical laughter cuts me off. "Alden Warner, are you trying to ask me my *number*?"

I turn my gaze away from her, embarrassed. "Yes," I

grumble.

She's not having any of that though, and palms my cheek, turning it back. "Oh, Alden. It's always been you. Sure, I've dated around, and I even tried to have a one-night stand once, but I chickened out. None of those men were you."

My heart swells with pride as the caveman inside of me stakes his claim—my dick swells, too, at the thought of being the only man to ever have been inside of her.

"Wh-what about you?" She nibbles on her lip, and I reach up and free it.

Damn. Should have seen that coming. "Since Mia, just you." We both cringe at the mention of the she-witch, but then the entirety of my confession hits, and she beams the most magnificent smile I've ever seen.

Natalie lunges at me, attacking me with her lips. I eagerly reciprocate, palming the round, firm globes of her ass, squeezing and guiding her movements as she rocks against my hard length.

"Fuck, Nat, you're so hot. I need you."

"Have me," she pants out.

"In my bed. I want you in my bed."

Wordlessly, she moves off of me and stands. Her eyes never leave mine as she strips off her shirt, followed quickly by her bra. She pivots and heads for the stairs, shedding the rest of her clothes along the way.

I jump up and follow behind her. Her head start leads me to find her naked at the foot of my bed, looking like a fucking goddess meant only for me.

I rake my gaze over, visually devouring her. She looks

good enough to eat. I'm about to tell her just that when her sudden boldness vanished, self-doubt and insecurity taking its place.

She averts her gaze and wraps her arms around her middle. I step closer and slide my hand down her jaw before tilting her head back so that our eyes are locked. "What's wrong? Don't hide from me."

"It's...I just. All of our other times together have been in the dark, and my body..." She trails off, and I think I get where she's going with this.

I pull her hands away and drop to my knees. Feather soft, I trail my fingertips over the fine white lines that mar her belly. "Are these what you're worried about?"

She nods as a small sniffle escapes her.

I press my lips to her stomach, kissing a path from hip to hip. "You're so beautiful, Natalie. And your stretch marks in no way detract from that. If anything, they add to it. They're visible proof that together, we created life, and there's nothing sexier than that to me."

She smirks down at me, her confidence returning. She gestures for me to stand, and I do.

"Thank you, Alden. So much," she murmurs, trailing the tip of index finger across her right clavicle and then down the valley between her breasts.

I just about swallow my tongue. "Just speaking the truth."

She presses her lips to my neck and speaks against my skin. "You have on too many clothes." She steps impossibly closer to me and slides her hands beneath the material of my shirt, sliding it up. I help and pull it over my head. We toss it to the floor together.

"Better?"

She shakes her head. "No. Still too many." Her hand drops to my pants, reaching down to palm my erection before unbuttoning them and dragging them down. She repeats the motion with my boxers, leaving us both gloriously naked. She appraises me like a tiger does its prey right before the kill

But I'm ready, and when she pounces, I catch her, and she wraps her legs around me. I can feel how hot and ready she is for me, but still, I want to make her feel good.

I secure her to me with an arm around her waist as I lower us both to the bed. I position us so that I'm on my back, and she's straddling me. "Come up here," I direct her, tugging on her hips.

She quirks a brow. "Up where?"

"Up here," I say, lifting and pulling her to my face. The movement causes her to pitch forward, which works out just fine for me. With her on her knees and her hands braced on the headboard, I set to work making her feel good, using my tongue and fingers to draw every ounce of pleasure I can from her. All too soon, she's a trembling mess, rocking against my chin and chanting my name.

Right as she's about to explode, I reposition us so that she's on her back, and in one swift movement, I enter her right as her climax finds her. She clenches around my dick, and—no lie—I see stars. As her orgasm ebbs, I set our pace, loving her in long, slow strokes until she's on the brink again.

Only this time, when she crashes over, I'm right there

with her.

After we get cleaned up, I leave Natalie in bed and head downstairs to whip us up a little snack to restore the energy we burned. I return with a platter of meats and cheeses and fresh fruit along with two bottles of water.

All too soon, eating turns to playing, and we're both ready for round two. This time, it's slow and sensual—we don't fuck, we make love—murmuring sweet nothings until we're both sated and spent.

We continue in this holding pattern of rest and sex and touching until we're both far too exhausted to continue. Tonight has been so damn perfect that I'm not sure which will be better, falling asleep with Natalie draped over my chest, or waking up with her—only morning will tell.

I wake with the sun, basking in the delicious weight of Natalie's body wrapped around mine. I'm still not sure which is better—falling asleep with her or waking up. If pressed, I'd say it's a tie and that both are an honor.

Slivers of light filter in through the blinds and the way they hit her skin creates an almost angelic glow. I could lay here and stare at her forever, but the desire to make her breakfast outweighs my need to catalog her every feature.

As quietly as possible, I disentangle our limbs and slip out of the bed. I slip on a pair of gray sweats and give her one last glance before trotting down the stairs. Hopefully this time she sleeps long enough for me to actually serve her in bed.

I start a pot of coffee and quickly get to work whipping up some from-scratch cinnamon rolls from a chunk of dough I prepared earlier in the week. She loved them something fierce growing up—I hope that hasn't changed.

While they bake, I start the icing. When my timer sounds, I pull the fluffy rolls from the oven and ice them instantly. I know some people like to let them cool, but I live for the way the heat sort melts the icing, making it into more of a glaze. I lick a little off of my thumb, and instantly I'm imagining licking it from Natalie's body—preferably her tits...or her thighs.

With deliciously dirty thoughts swimming around in my mind, I quickly plate us up two each and pour two mugs of coffee before heading back up the stairs with a tent in my shorts and a spring in my step.

In my room, I place the tray at the foot of the bed and walk over to her side of the bed—*her side, damn, I like the sound of that*—where I kneel and simply admire her for a minute. The covers are pushed down around her waist, revealing her breast and stomach to me. I study the stretch marks she was so worried about, and before I know it, I'm imagining how she'd look with her belly rounded out again. The thought is shockingly sexy, which totally catches me off guard.

I trail the pads of my fingers over the dip in her waist—up and down, up and down—until her eyes flutter open. "Alden," she murmurs, her voice husky with sleep.

She stretches and sits up, propping herself against the headboard. "Something smells good."

I don't even try and fight my grin. "I made us breakfast."

I move and retrieve the tray. "Cinnamon rolls and coffee."

Her eyes light up. "One of my favs!"

"I know." I pass her a plate and the mug with her coffee in it before rejoining her in the bed.

I watch eagerly as she takes her first bite. The moan she lets out is enough to get me hard as concrete. "Oh my God. This is divine. Why is this so good?"

"Homemade," I offer simply.

She nods and moans again with her next bite. "I could get used to this."

My stomach clenches. "I'd gladly do it daily if it kept that blissed-out look on your face."

She sucks the icing from her middle finger. "There's a lot of ways you can achieve that look, Alden Warner."

The way she says my name—so teasingly—has me tossing my half-full plate down onto my nightstand. Like a mind reader, she does the same and simultaneously we lunge for one another.

Our kiss is heated and sweet tasting, which begs to my earlier thought of how the icing would taste directly from her skin. Too curious to not find out, I reach over and swipe two fingers through a pool of it on her plate.

She watches, wide-eyed, as I smear it all over her left breast. Her breath hitches when my mouth follows.

"Oh," she hisses as I bite down. She squirms beneath me as I soothe the sting. "Feels so good." Her words are staccato with desire. I'm positioning myself between her legs when the sound of my phone ringing somewhere in the house stops me. "Ignore it," she pleads, lifting her hips, begging me with her body to fill her.

Then her phone rings.

"Dammit, that's Nate's ringtone."

Resigned, I move off of her, and she flies out of the bed in search of her phone. She returns a few minutes later, with it pressed to her ear. "No, it's okay. I get it." A pause. "I promise, it's fine. I'll meet you at the apartment."

She ends the call and turns to me. "Nate got called into work."

"Call him back and tell him to come here."

"I would, but I have an online study group. We were supposed to meet on Thursday, but a few couldn't log in then, so we pushed it."

"Well, why don't I take Tatum today, and you can focus totally on that."

She ponders the offer for all of two seconds. "That would be amazing. Thank you, Alden." She walks over to my side of the bed and crawls onto my lap, still magnificently naked. She kisses me long and hard but pulls away before we can get too heated.

I groan at the loss of her heat, but she just smirks. "C'mon. We gotta get showered. And I need to let Nate know the change of plans."

We share a shower, and much to my disappointment, no shenanigans take place. Then again, Tatum comes first, so really, it's okay.

Once we're both dry, I give Nat a pair of my sweats and a shirt to wear home. It's a bit chillier than normal for this time of year, so I throw on a pair of jeans with long-sleeved T-shirt.

We walk down the stairs together and kiss goodbye at

the door. All in all, it's incredibly domestic—and I really, really like it.

chapter forty-one

Alden

I MEET NATE AT THE diner a few blocks down from the park. He and Tatum are already inside, seated at the bar. I plop down onto the stool to the right of my girl. Her eyes widen at the sight of me. "Daddy! You comed for breakfast!"

"I sure did, pretty girl. Uncle Nate has to go to work, but I wanted to make sure you still had your big day."

She pitches herself my way and hugs me tight. "You're the best daddy ever."

My heart pinches. This kid. She is everything.

Nate stands and hugs his niece before clapping me on the shoulder. With eyes locked on mine, he says, "I'm glad it was you."

His approval hits me all the way down to my marrow. My eyes glisten with emotion, and he doesn't miss it. He chuckles and mouths the word *pussy* before heading out the door.

"Whatcha gonna get?" I ask my daughter.

"I want a big bowl of cheese grips!"

"Cheese grits, huh? I think I want the same thing." I place our order, and within minutes, two large bowls of steaming, cheesy goodness are placed before us. I doctor them both up with butter, salt, and pepper, and we happily devour them.

I pay the tab and help Tatum down from her stool. "Let's see. You wanted to go to the park today too, right?"

She jumps up and down—which I understand is the universal toddler sign for *yes!* and occasionally for *I have to potty!*

"Wanna walk there?"

She nods rapidly, and hand in hand, we set off for the playground, which is luckily less than a block away. This isn't the same one we went to last time, but Tatum looks excited all the same. At first, I keep right on her, moving from one piece of equipment to the other. Eventually, she tires of my stalking. "Daddy. I'm big. I'm"—she holds up four fingers—"three! I can pway alone."

"Are you sure? I'm having fun playing with you!"

She looks over toward a group of similarly aged kids all playing together. "I'm sure."

I hesitate, but ultimately give in. After all, Natalie and I hung out on a bench the last time we came to the park. "All right, pretty girl. But stay where I can see you, okay?"

"I will, Daddy!" She kisses my cheek and darts off toward the group of kids playing.

I keep my eyes laser-focused on Tatum as she plays. She and two of the other kids are playing on a little jungle gym. It's decked out with two slides, a mini suspension bridge, and a pint-sized plastic rock wall. The sound of her laughter floats my way on the breeze. She looks so happy and carefree that I can't help but want to capture the moment forever.

I shift slightly and grab my phone. When I unlock the screen, a text from Natalie pops up. It's nothing more than a blowing kisses emoji. I smile and toggle over to my camera.

Except before I even have a chance to snap a pic, a scream rings out, coming from Tatum. I shove my phone back into my pocket and haul ass to my girl. A few other parents rush over as well. When I reach her, she's on the ground, wailing and clutching her arm to her chest.

I drop down to my knees. "Tatum! Tatum, baby, are you okay?"

She's crying too hard to reply, and the sound of her sobs is soul shattering. I only looked away for one minute. Oh, Jesus. This is all my fault. Natalie is going to murder me—and rightfully so.

Tatum tries to reach for me, but the motion sends her into another fit. She's crying so hard she can hardly breathe. As carefully as possible, I gather her into my arms. She clutches my shirt with her uninjured hand, her tears wetting clear through my shirt. "Daddy, it h-h-hurts!"

Guilt churns in my stomach like the sea during a raging storm. "I know, pretty girl. I'm so sorry. Daddy's gonna make it all better."

The mom of one of the kids she was playing with stops me. "She was about to slide and tripped. Fell from the top." I thank her for the info—info I should have known without being told, because I should have been watching.

My heart sinks. How could I have let this happen? All of this because I wanted to take her picture. *How stupid could I possibly be?* And then I remember we walked here.

"It's okay pretty girl, Daddy has you."

With painstakingly careful steps, as not to jostle her, I set off for the car. What was a quick, two-minute walk here feels like an unending journey back—like in a horror movie when the hallway keeps getting longer, extending on endlessly.

When we finally reach my car, I'm faced with an entirely new debacle. Her car seat. As softly as possible, I place her in the seat. She doesn't want to let go, though. "I have to put you down, pretty girl. We need to go to the doctor, and you need to be safe." I keep my tone soft, whispering the words into her ear.

She releases her hold on my shirt and allows me to set her down. I slide her good arm through the harness, opting to leave her rapidly swelling arm that is very obviously broken out. I secure her buckle as best I can and fly around to the driver's seat.

"I want Mama!" Tatum wails, and my heart splits clear in two. Of course, she wants her mom—and truthfully, I do too. Natalie would probably be cool as a cucumber, whereas I'm on the verge of Hulking out or breaking down. Hell, I doubt this would have even happened on her watch. Which reinforces the fact that she's so going to kill me.

I turn on my flashers and pull out into traffic—luckily, it's Sunday and still church hours, so there's next to no traffic. As soon as my phone connects to my car's Bluetooth, I dial Natalie.

She doesn't answer.

I call again.

No answer.

Fuck. Nat, answer!

Tatum's cries have turned to heaving sobs.

I try Natalie one last time, and when she doesn't pick up, I have no option but to leave a message and to try her parents. "Nat, you need to call me. I'm on the way to the emergency room with Tatum. I'm pretty sure she broke her arm. Please call me. Better yet, meet me there."

Here's to hoping she gets that.

Immediately, I dial Luke, remembering that Melanie was helping at church.

He answers on the second ring. "Yeah?"

"Luke, Tatum is hurt. We're on our way to the E.R. I can't get ahold of Natalie."

"I'm on my way," he says, ending the call. *Thank God!*

All of this is strangely reminiscent of when Natalie broke her arm—mainly because that, too, happened on my watch.

I make it to the hospital in what has to be record time, and I manage to score a parking spot near the entrance. I use the same great care to unbuckle and lift her into my arms.

She turns her face into my chest. She's still crying and begging for her mama, and I'm still an emotional disaster of epic proportions. "Just hang tight, Tatum. We're almost there. The doctors here will be able to help you. And Popsie is on his way."

"B-but I want Mama!" She conveniently screams the words at the top of her little lungs just as we pass through the automatic doors. Several heads swivel our way—some with concerned looks, some offering empathy, and others looking perturbed by the noise. Let me just say, that last group can fuck right off.

I march directly to the sign in desk, clutching my crying girl to my chest. "She needs a doctor. My daughter needs a doctor!"

The nurse looks up. "Sign in."

"My hands are a little full," I grit out. I mean, Jesus, would it kill her to help?

She huffs and spins the clipboard to face her. "Patient's name? Date of birth? Reason for visit? Your name?"

I rattle off her info, and the nurse tells us to have a seat in the waiting area. My blood boils. Doesn't she see my girl is hurt? "We need a doctor!" I implore, but it falls on deaf ears.

"Yeah, and so does everyone else here."

My shoulders sag in defeat, and I walk over to a small cluster of chairs. In between trying to calm my still sobbing daughter, I'm shooting death stares to nurse and checking the clock on the wall, wondering when Luke is going to get here and when Natalie is going to call. Basically, I'm damn near crawling out of my skin.

After what feels like two lifetimes, the nurse calls my name, her voice monotone. I'm hopeful she's calling us back, but my hope deflates like a sad balloon when she passes me a clipboard and a pen. "If you could fill this out."

I'm sure this lady has seen it all and then some, and that this job is trying on the best day. But right now, I don't have it in me to care. I clench my jaw to keep from telling her exactly where she can shove her paperwork and softly shift Tatum so I can take it from her.

The movement causes Tatum to let out a high-pitched, ear-piercing squeal, once again earning us a mixed bag of looks. "Shh, it's okay, pretty girl. Daddy just had to get this paperwork that is apparently more important than actually helping you." My attempt at comfort ends in a feral growl.

Back in our seats, I try my best to fill out the forms, which is no easy feat with a whimpering toddler in your lap.

The forms themselves present an entirely new problem. *Insurance...no clue. Social security number...nope, don't know that either. Family medical history...well, I know the paternal side. Allergies to any medications...that's going to be another nope, with a capital 'N.'*

My panic spirals as I realize how little I know about my own child. My head swims, and my vision blurs. I think I'm shaking, but it could be Tatum, too. It's probably both of us. Why didn't I ever think to ask Natalie any of this? A good dad would know these things. Hell, a good dad would have never let this happen. Will Natalie ever trust me with her again? Should she?

I'm about twenty seconds away from passing out when the *swoosh* of the doors followed by Luke's bellowing voice. "Alden!"

I lift my hand, alerting him to where we are, and he rushes over to us, swooping in and saving the day—or at least a piece of my fragile sanity. "What happened?" he asks, gruff and all business.

"She fell at the park."

"Popsie," Tatum cries and I pass her to him.

"I swear, I was watching her. I didn't mean—"

"Son. Take a breath. It could have happened to anyone."

"No, this is my fault. If I—"

"Alden. Listen to me. You're a good man—a good dad. You didn't hurt Tatum. It was an accident and could have happened to anyone."

My shoulders slump. "But it didn't. It happened to me."

"Did Natalie ever tell you about the time Tatum fell in the bathtub?"

I shake my head, wondering where he's going with this.

"Tatum wanted out, and apparently Natalie wasn't moving fast enough, so she tried climbing out on her own. Nat only turned around to grab the towel from the sink, but in that blink of an eye, Tatum slipped, fell, hit her head on the faucet and went completely under the water. Natalie called us, crying her eyes out, saying she was an unfit mother, which we both know is untrue. My point is, accidents happen. It sucks, but that's life. At the end of the day, Tatum's okay. She's happy, healthy, and loved. Cut yourself some slack, son."

His words make me feel marginally better. "That may be true. But that doesn't change the fact that I can't even fully fill out these forms—there's still so much I don't know."

Luke chuckles. "Son, I'm gonna let you in on a little secret. I couldn't fill them out either—to this day, Melanie even fills out mine. Quit worrying."

Easier said than done.

"Did you get ahold of Natalie?"

"She didn't pick up for me. Mel didn't answer either,

but I called the church and got ahold of her that way. She's on her way to Natalie's place. They'll be here soon, I reckon."

We slip into a comfortable silence. It's strange how just his mere presence is comforting to me. After what feels like another eternity, Tatum's name is called. Luke and I both stand and walk to the desk. The nurse motions for us to step behind it into this little triage area.

"All right, we're gonna get a few vitals really quick."

"And then we'll see the doctor?" I ask.

"And then you'll head back to the waiting room."

I inhale deeply, trying to remain calm—mostly because I don't want to scare Tatum. The nurse verifies our identities and slaps matching bracelets onto Tatum and me before checking her temperature. She attempts to clip some little device to the index finger of Tatum's uninjured hand, but my girl's not having it. She thrashes and screams so hard it takes both Luke and me to calm her down.

The nurse moves to try again, but I'm pretty sure my snarl stops her in her tracks. "Let's...let's try her big toe."

I remove one of Tatum's shoes, and the nurse is able to successfully get the readings she needs.

Once she logs all of Tatum's stats, she turns to us and asks what happened.

"We were at the park, and she was going to slide but tripped and fell from the top."

The nurse looks from me to Tatum and then asks her, "Is that what happened?" I'm sure it's something she has to ask, but it pisses me right off—as if she doesn't believe me.

Tatum sniffles and mumbles, "Yes."

The nurse hesitates briefly and then enters the information into her computer. "Okay. Y'all can go have a seat."

I want to rant and rave and riot and demand for someone to see her immediately, but I know it won't help. In truth, the only thing it will accomplish is the nurse calling hospital security on me—and then Nat would *really* kill me. As is, regardless of Luke's reassurances, I'm fairly certain she's going to have my balls.

chapter forty-two

Natalie

I HAVE MY HEADPHONES IN, and I'm deep into our study session when I hear a loud banging on my front door. I slide my headphones off just in time to hear the lock turning and the door opening. "What the..." I push back from my desk and slowly venture out into the hallway.

"Natalie!" Mom yells. "Natalie!"

I meet her at the end of the hall. "Jesus, what?"

"Why haven't you been answering your phone?"

The fine hairs on the back of my neck stand on end. "It's on silent. Why?"

"Tatum fell. Alden took her to the E.R. No one has been able to get ahold of you!"

My heart races and stops all at once. I race back to my room and throw on a hoodie and my slip-on Keds, not caring one bit that I'm still dressed in Alden's clothes.

Mom and I break every traffic law driving to the hospital. I'm a nervous wreck when we enter the emergency room, but my fears calm when I see my dad holding Tatum and Alden at the nurse's station, demanding to know why they haven't been seen yet.

"We've been here for damn near an hour. My daughter

is in agony. How much longer is it going to take for her to be seen?" He's a mixture of distraught and rabid—a true papa bear if I've ever seen one. I know it's far from the right moment, but seeing him so worked up over our daughter kind of gets me hot.

I step closer to him and place my hand on the middle of his back. "I'm here."

He spins to face me, the nurse long forgotten. As if driven by pure instinct, he draws me into his arms and holds me close. "Oh, thank God. Where were you?"

His tone isn't accusing in the least—if anything he sounds concerned—but I still feel like crap for missing all of his many calls.

"I was doing that study session, and my phone was on silent."

He nods, and I step up to the desk to let them know who I am. The nurse takes my information and clacks away on her keyboard. Moments later, the printer spits out an I.D. bracelet for me. She fastens it around my wrist and then Alden takes my hand, guiding me to where Dad and Tatum are. My dad glances up upon our arrival. "She's pretty much cried herself to sleep."

I look down at my beautiful girl, sleeping fitfully on his lap. Her left arm is swollen to twice its size at the wrist, and her skin is a mix of angry purples and blues. Tears cloud my vision. "Oh, Tater Tot." I lower down into the seat next to my dad, and he passes her to me. She stirs and whimpers, but doesn't wake.

Mom grabs the chair on the other side of Dad while Alden paces back and forth in front of us, yanking on the ends of his hair. "He's taking this pretty hard," Dad whispers to me.

My nose scrunches. "It was an accident."

"He's blaming himself. Also, he needs a little help on the intake form."

My heart sinks. Accidents can happen to anyone, and I know Alden would never let anything happen to our daughter intentionally. I call his name and pat the chair next to me. He shakes his head and keeps pacing. I try again, only to get the same results.

My shoulders slump. If I'd have had my ringer on, I would have answered his first call and been able to reassure him—not to mention, I could have been here from the get-go.

Dad passes Mom the clipboard. She knows most of the info and even has a copy of Tatum's insurance in her wallet—thank God for nurse mamas.

She glances over at Tatum a few times while jotting down answers on the form. "It's definitely broken. Don't need no X-ray to see that."

He paces a few more times before finally slumping down into the seat next to me. I place my hand over his on the shared armrest, hoping the motion will give him comfort. Right as I'm about to let him know I'm not upset, Tatum's name gets called.

Alden and I both stand and head back with the nurse. She leads us down a series of hallways before bringing us to your typical E.R. room—small and cold, with a bed, a single chair, a sink, and ceiling-mounted television that gets fuzzy reception.

Alden helps me onto the bed, where I lie with Tatum curled up beside me. He claims the chair in the corner. The nurse asks all of the standard questions and lets us know that radiology will be by soon.

The three of us wait in the cold room for about fifteen minutes before there's a knock at the door. "Come in," Alden calls.

Two women and a man wheel in a large, portable X-ray machine. I slide out of the bed and don one of the lead aprons. They get to work positioning the machine and then they ask Alden to step out.

I seriously think he's going to combust, but he eventually relents, looking none too pleased.

Tatum wakes up with a scream that quickly turns to heaving sobs when they begin positioning her to get the best image. I comfort her as best I can, but I kind of feel like breaking down and sobbing with her.

I glance out into the hallway, where an incredibly angry Alden is standing with his hands fisted at his sides and his eyes brimming with tears. This man looks ready to go to war for his daughter, and it makes my heart flutter in my chest.

Finally, they tell us they've gotten what they need and that the doctor will be in soon. *Thank God.* I haven't been here nearly as long as Alden, and it's already been too long.

Alden reenters the room and rushes to us, helping me and Tatum back into a comfortable position, murmuring words of love and comfort all the while.

Twenty minutes later, there's another knock at the door. This time, it's the doctor and a nurse. He introduces himself as Dr. Murphy. "The good news is it's a clean break. The bad news is we're going to need to cast her."

"How long will she need to wear it?" Alden asks, not missing a beat.

"Six weeks to start, and then we'll have her follow up with an ortho for another set of X-rays. They'll determine then if she'll need to wear it longer."

The nurse speaks up. "What color would she like?"

Once again Alden beats me to the punch. "Pink."

The nurse smiles and heads off to retrieve her supplies. She returns and asks me to sit Tatum up in my lap. She positions Tatum's arm into a sideways 'L' with her inner wrist facing her stomach. Tatum is *not* a fan of this and loudly lets everyone know.

"Stop!" she screams, tears trailing her cheeks. "It hurts!"

Alden jumps out of his chair and moves to stand behind us. He leans over and kisses her cheek. "It's okay, pretty girl. Remember when we talked about being superheroes? This is just going to help you get even stronger. I know it hurts now, but it's going to get better."

"P-promise?" she asks, sounding so small.

"I absolutely promise. But you have to sit very still and be a very brave girl. Can you do that for Daddy?"

She sniffles and nods.

The nurse begins wrapping the liner. She then wets the outer cast material and wraps it over the first layer. "It's hot," Tatum cries.

"I know, sweetie," the nurse coos. "That's the fiberglass getting hard. It'll cool in about fifteen minutes."

Tatum sniffles again.

The doctor goes over aftercare instructions and reminds me to make a follow-up appointment in six weeks. Alden and I both thank him and stand to leave. Tatum is still teary, but she's no longer bawling.

The nurse leads us to a set of double doors that exit back into the lobby. "Be sure and stop by the desk to pay your co-pay. Have a nice night."

Alden gives her a tight smile, grumbling under his breath all the while. Out in the lobby, we do as she says, and Alden whips out his wallet and pays before I can even argue.

We say goodbye to my parents and head back to my apartment.

chapter forty-three

Alden

NATALIE SAYS SHE'S NOT MAD, but the entire drive back to her place, I worry she's going to change her mind. I mean, why wouldn't she be at least a little upset? Tatum got hurt on *my* watch.

After I park, I help Natalie get Tatum inside. I trail behind, expecting Natalie to go to Tatum's room, but she continues on to hers. "She likes being in my bed when she doesn't feel good," she explains.

Once she's tucked into her bed, I kiss her forehead and turn to leave. "I'll see you later, yeah?"

Nat rushes after me. "Wait! Where are you going?"

I look down at my feet. "I figured you'd want me to head out."

She steps closer to me and pressed her index finger under my chin, tipping my head up to face her. "Why would you think that? Because she broke her arm?"

"Yeah, I guess."

"Come sit with me." She takes my hand and tugs, guiding me to the couch. "You're her father. You're the man I love. There's no other place we'd want you to be right now. When she wakes up, she's going to want both of us here."

She brings her hands up to my chest and pushes me back onto the couch, where she promptly straddles my lap. "I always want you here, Alden." She seals her mouth to mine, her tongue flicking against my lips. I open, and she deepens our kiss. He fingers tangle in my hair, and she rocks against me. "Seeing you so protective and worried about her really turned me on."

Holy. Shit. She's really not mad!

I dive back into our kiss, licking and sucking and nipping until we're both wound tight with desire.

"I need you to make me feel good," she purrs. Unable to deny her, I make quick work of stripping her and laying her down on her back. I kiss my way down her body, paying special attention to her breasts, before reaching my final destination, where I don't just make her feel good—I make her feel divine.

Over the next week, Tatum returned to her normal sunshine-and-rainbows self. There were definitely some rough patches—a lot of meltdowns—from it hurting, not having the use of both arms, not being able to wear certain outfits thanks to her cast.

But then she learned she could ask people to sign her cast. Talk about a happy kid. Everyone at the café and all of the staff at her daycare has signed it. And, anytime anyone asks her what happened, she tells them she was trying to fly but forgot her cape. Swear to God, she's the cutest, most imaginative kid in the world.

Since her big tumble, Tatum hasn't wanted either of us out of her sight—which has been both a blessing and a curse. At first, we alternated whose place we stayed at every other night, with me always sneaking out to the couch before Tatum woke up. Then, one day, Tatum surprised us all by asking why Natalie and I didn't share a bed like Nana and Popsie did.

Talk about awkward.

I played the novice dad card and let Natalie handle that one. She sat Tatum down and explained to her that we didn't share a bed because we didn't live together and because we weren't married.

To which Tatum replied, "Why not?" I'm unsure whether she was asking why Natalie and I wasn't married or why we didn't all live together—either way, it got my wheels turning.

Why don't we live together? I mean, we are a family.

After swapping houses for the fourth time in as many days, I convinced Natalie that the two of them should just stay with me—she seemed on the fence at the first, but Tatum's enthusiasm sold her.

That was step one in my Convince Natalie to Move in with Me Grand Plan. As of right now, we're still pretending to sleep in separate beds, but baby steps and all that.

Now, here we are on day seven. Tatum's still sleeping. Natalie's whipping us up some breakfast, and I'm folding our laundry at the dining room table—literally never something I thought I'd say, and yet, I wouldn't change it for the world. After Mia, I planned on being a lifelong bachelor, but now I can't see myself being anything other than a family man.

Which is all the more reason to take a step to make our little family more concrete. I plan to pop the question. Well, not *that* question, but an important one nonetheless. I want my girls to move in with me, and I'm hoping like hell Natalie says yes.

I'm halfway through the second load of the day—early bird gets the worm and all that—when the scent of bacon lures me to the kitchen. I come up behind Natalie, admiring the way she looks in her flannel pajama pants and tank top. Then again, she could make a sack sexy.

I drag my lips across her neck, speaking against her skin. "Mmm. Smells good."

She wiggles her ass against me. "Gonna taste good too. Bacon, soft boiled eggs, and toast."

I grip her hips and place another lingering kiss to her nape. "I'll go wake Tatum up."

"Sounds like a plan."

I make a pit stop at the table and transfer my piles into their coordinating baskets before setting off up the stairs with a hamper in each hand. I go to drop our basket off in *my* room when noise from behind the closed guest room door snags my attention. I shoulder the door open and immediate lose my hold on both baskets, spilling my freshly folded clothes all over...*oh, holy shit.*

Tatum is sitting in the middle of the floor, looking proud as punch.

"Wha-what is that?" I ask, gesturing to the wine-colored goop covering her from head to toe.

"Lipsticks," she answers bluntly.

"Lipstick, huh?"

She smiles a wide, beauty queen smile at me. "Yup. Don't I look hootiful?"

I shake my head back and forth, laughing under my breath. *This kid.* "You look...why don't we go show Mama?"

"Yes!" Moving from sitting to standing takes her an extra second or two thanks to her cast, but before I know it, she's racing down the stairs.

"Oh, good Lord! Not again!" I hear Natalie holler, and I grin. Apparently, this is not a first-time offense.

I step into the room and see Tatum trying to twirl like a ballerina. "Don't I look hootiful?"

"Tatum. We talked about this," Natalie says, using her mom voice.

My girl's eyes fill with tears, and it takes everything in me not to play good cop and come to her defense. But then I'd be the one in the doghouse—no thanks.

When her lower lip wobbles, my knees do too.

"I just wanted to look pretty, Mama."

Natalie lets out an exasperated sigh. "You always look pretty, Tater Tot. You know better than to play with my makeup."

"I know. I sorry. I just wanted to be pretty like you!"

That's when I step in; I can't stay silent a second longer.

I squat down so that Tatum and I are eye level. "What do I call you?"

She tilts her head and blinks before smiling. "Pretty girl."

"That's right. You're my pretty girl. I know Mama's

lipstick seems shiny and fun, but it's for grownups. Not little girls. Okay?"

She pouts a little but agrees. "Okay. I sorry."

Nat grins at me; I hope that means I nailed this. I'm thinking we work great as a team.

Natalie takes Tatum upstairs to the bathroom, leaving me to plate up our breakfast. Really, this couldn't have worked out better had I planned it.

I bring our food out, along with the silverware and drinks. Only, I leave something extra special on Nat's napkin.

They join me at the table, both digging into their food right away. It's agony waiting for her to notice the little box. I was really counting on her putting that napkin in her lap.

Finally, she makes a grab for it. "What's this?" she asks, looking at it quizzically.

"Open it."

She looks nervous, and I kind of love it.

She cracks open the box, revealing a key on a silver keychain. She lifts it from the box and reads the engraving— *You already live in my heart. Share my home too.*

Her eyes fill with tears, and I worry I've messed this all up.

Natalie quickly dispels that worry when she nods and rushed over to hug me. Not one to be left out, Tatum wriggles down and joins our embrace. "Mama, why you crying?"

"Happy tears, Tater Tot. Happy tears."

Tatum pulls back and scrunches her nose. "Why?"

"How...how would you feel about us living here with

Daddy?"

"Like a family? Like Nana and Popsie?"

"Yes, pretty girl," I answer her, "just like that."

"Yes! Please! Yes!" She launches herself back at me, burying her face in my chest. This is hands-down the best day of my life.

It's been a month since I asked my girls to move in with me. As much as I'd love to say life has been perfect, I'd be lying. We bicker from time to time like an old married couple, and sometimes Tatum misses her old apartment. All in all, though, the transition has gone well, and really, when toddlers are involved, a few hiccups along the way are par for the course. And honestly, I wouldn't change a thing; it's our own kind of perfect.

I was truly more apprehensive over telling our families than about us actually moving in together, but they took it shockingly well.

Nate simply shrugged and said, "Treat her right, brother."

Her parents were excited. Melanie wrapped me in a hug and rocked us side to side. I'll never forget my shock when Luke wrapped an arm around me and said, "Now you better make an honest woman out of my baby girl soon."

Hell, I'd do it today—right this very second, in fact—and Natalie would probably be down with it too. But she deserves the fairytale every little girl dreams of, and I'm damn sure going to give it to her. Not to mention, Lord help us all if we deny Tatum the change to dress fancy and be the center of attention—she would never forgive us.

My parents were over the moon—so much so that they're flying in today and are staying through the first of November. I'm actually on my way to the airport now to pick them up, making this day one of five that they'll be occupying my guest room—which equates to five days of Natalie being weird about sex. But, such is life.

Natalie and I tried getting them to hold off until Thanksgiving or Christmas, but they weren't having it—they're way too excited to meet Tatum face-to-face. According to them, they've waited long enough. Three years too long, to be exact. I know it wasn't a dig toward Natalie, but I could tell it hurt her feelings. After that, I had a private talk with my mom and dad and asked them if they could refrain from making comments like that. Mom felt awful when she realized it had upset Natalie. She was insistent on apologizing, but I convinced her to let go and to just move forward.

Hopefully she doesn't try and spring an ambush apology on her in person—with my mom, you never know.

I pull my car into the pick-up area, and sure enough, Mom and Dad are waiting, eagerly scanning every vehicle, like they don't know what I drive—even though Dad consulted with me on which make and model to buy.

Gotta love parents.

I idle the car and pop the trunk before hopping out to help them. Dad waves me off, insisting on stowing his own luggage, and Mom wraps me in a bone-crushing hug. "Oh, my baby! It's been so long!" She kisses both of my cheeks and then peers around me into the backseat. "Where's Tatum?"

"She's at the house with Natalie."

Mom pouts, looking much like Tatum does when she doesn't get her way. "C'mon, you'll see her soon enough."

Dad shuts the trunk and comes around to hug me. It's not one of those back-slap-man-hugs—no, it's every bit as bone-crushing as Mom's. "Son. You're looking good. But take me to my grandbaby."

I snort out a laugh. He's every bit as bad as his wife—the two really are a match made in heaven.

The drive home is full-on nonstop chatter. We catch up on everything that's happened since we spoke last, which isn't much, seeing as we talk at least every two days.

They're both anxious to meet Tatum; their excitement practically rolls off of them in waves. I have clearly been demoted in the hierarchy of importance.

I pull into the driveway, parking behind Natalie's vehicle. My mom has her door open before I even shift the car into park.

She all but sprints toward the house, my dad not far behind her. The front door flies open and Tatum darts out, throwing herself in my mom's waiting arms.

"Grammy! Grammy! Yous here!" Guess it's safe to say they're equally excited.

Mom squeezes her tight before placing her hands on her shoulders and holding her an arm's length away. "I sure am. Now, let me look at you." She scans Tatum from toe to top, her eyes wet with tears. "Oh, you are just beautiful."

Dad crouches down next to them, and Tatum happily flits over to him, hugging his neck. "Paw Paw!" He smiles and kisses her cheek. She cackles and pushes his face away. "You ticklers tickle."

Dad twitches his nose. "You mean my mustache?"

Tatum shrugs. "I guess. I think dey look like whiskers. Like a puppy!"

Dad's expression grows dead serious, and then he lets out a bark, much to Tatum's delight. God, who knew my parents would be such good grandparents?

I look up from my parents and Tatum to see Natalie on the porch watching their interactions. She looks a steady mix of nerves and joy. I wave her over and hesitantly, she comes.

Mom notices her first. She stands and wastes no time embracing her. "Natalie Reynolds. Look at you, all grown up."

"Hey Mrs. Warner—"

"None of that. Call me Phyllis."

Nat scrunches her nose and ducks her head. "Sorry. Hey Phyllis. We're glad y'all are here. Was your flight okay?"

Dad stands and hugs Natalie too. "Aside from them serving pretzels and not peanuts, it was fine."

Mom smacks his chest. "Fine? There was enough turbulence to bring the thing down!"

My dad chuckles. "There was one bump, dear. One."

"Hush. Let's not argue in front of the kids."

"Let's head inside," I say. "Natalie made dinner."

Dad pats his stomach. "Good. Those damn pretzels didn't fill me up."

I know what's about to happen before it does. "Paw Paw! That is a no-no word! We do *not* talk like dat in dis house!"

My dad's eyes widen, and he apologizes to his granddaughter as we all head inside to enjoy good food and even better company.

Natalie

Halloween is officially upon us. From the minute her little eyes popped open, Tatum's been asking if it's time for *twick or treat* yet. Needless to say, she's excited.

It's been all we could do to keep her entertained throughout the day. Having Phyllis and Bob here definitely helped. This morning, they made caramel popcorn, and after lunch, they had a spooky—but child appropriate—movie marathon. Tatum's favorite was Halloween Town; she's truly a kid after my own heart.

Now, it's time to start getting ready, and she's practically bouncing with excitement. She and Alden came up with her costume, and they've kept totally quiet on what she's going to be.

I'm currently camped out in the hallway, along with Alden's parents, while he helps her get ready. The three of us have been tossing out our best guesses, but so far, no dice.

"A princess?" Phyllis tries.

Tatum scoffs. "I already a pwincess. Daddy says so."

Bob takes the next guess. "A ballerina?"

"Nope," comes her reply.

"A witch like Marnie!"

Tatum giggles. "No, Mama."

The three of us continue tossing out suggestions until finally her bedroom door opens and they emerge.

I let out a little gasp when I see my girl and Alden dressed in matching chef whites. "I wanted to be like Daddy!" she exclaims, and I swear to God, Alden looks so proud.

My voice is heavy with emotion. "I think that's perfect, Tater Tot. Absolutely perfect."

"Tell her what else, pretty girl," Alden urges.

Tatum's eyes go round, and she dashes back into her room. When she returns, it is with an apron clutched in her grasp. She thrusts it toward me. I take it and shake it out, my eyes honing in on where the words *Sous Chef* are embroidered.

"Oh, I love it! It's—" My words die in my throat when I glance up from the apron. Alden is down on one knee. Oh, my God. Is he...

"Nat, I've known you my entire life, and I've loved you just as long in one way or another. Every day my love for you grows and we've had enough missteps and missed time. Be my sous chef for life...my love, my partner at home and in business."

I try to contain my sobs, but it's a fruitless effort. Tears stream down my cheeks and my knees buckle, bringing down next to Alden.

He drops down and pulls me into him. "Make me the luckiest man on this planet and say 'yes.'"

Tatum crawls onto my lap and hugs us both. "Yeah, Mama. Say 'yes.'"

I nod. "Yes! Oh, God, yes!" The three of us stay on the hall floor wrapped in an embrace until the sound of Alden's parents' muffled tears remind me that we're not alone.

I'm the first to pull back, pressing a chaste kiss to Alden's lips, followed by one to Tatum's cheek before standing. After a round of hugs and a few more tears, I stand and loop the apron around my neck and tie it at my back.

"Oh, one more thing!" Alden exclaims, sliding his hand into his pocket, retrieving a small velvet box. "The ring!" He flips open the lid, revealing the most beautiful emerald cut cushioned yellow sapphire on a platinum band encrusted with tiny little diamonds. It's truly breathtaking.

Alden takes my left hand and slides the ring onto my finger. A whole new bout of tears starts—this is every childhood dream I ever had, coming full circle. "I love you with every ounce of my being, Alden Warner."

He grins and takes my hand in his. "I love you too, soon to be Mrs. Warner." He reaches down and ruffles Tatum's hair. "Now, let's go score some candy."

epilogue

Alden

Two Years Later

"I LOOK LIKE A WHALE!" Natalie laments from behind the closed bathroom door.

I smirk, knowing damn well she *does not* look like a whale. Her belly is barely rounded with our second child—a boy. She looks sumptuous and glowing and so damn sexy I can hardly stand it.

"Open the door and let me see."

I hear her huff. "No. You'll just tell me I'm beautiful."

"That's because you *are* beautiful."

"Ugh! Alden!"

She sounds so frustrated, and like the ass I am, I smile. Thank God she can't see me. "Small Fry. You're the love of my life, and, to me, you'll always be beautiful. Even when you're wrinkly with gray hair and tits that sag to your belly button."

She laughs, and my chest swells with pride. The only sound on earth that comes close to comparing is Tatum's giggle. "Okay, fine. I'm coming out."

She steps out. As predicted, I'm right. She looks like

a goddess. Her hair is styled in those waves that all guys love because they look like sex hair. Her makeup is muted, except her lips, which are a bold red. The flowy, champagne-colored dress she's wearing hugs her chest, pushing up her breasts, and glides over her belly. It's long enough that the hemline touches the floor, but knowing her, she's going to rock some ungodly heels that I'll undoubtedly imagine digging into my back all night long.

"Well?" she asks, nibbling on her candy-apple bottom lip.

I fist my hands at my side to stop myself from touching her. I know if I don't keep my hands to myself, I'll destroy her carefully crafted look, and since Tatum's with a sitter, it's an all too real possibility.

"You...you look—" My words fail me.

"Oh, God. You're right. I can't show up to Nate's engagement party looking like this!"

She turns to lock herself back in the bathroom, but I stop her. "You look so far beyond amazing. There's literally not a word to describe it."

She pivots back to face me. "Really?"

"Really, really. Hell, you look so radiant we may have to worry about you upstaging the bride to be."

Her stress visibly melts away, and she steps closer to me, bringing her left hand up to my cheek. The sparkling rock on her ring finger catches the light just right, and my mind races back to the day we said 'I do.' It's mind-blowing to think our one-year anniversary is just around the corner.

But that's kind of how life works, isn't it? It's crazy and messy and chaotic and nothing like I thought it would be. The universe took my best-laid plans and turned them upside down and now...now life's better than I ever thought it could be.

The End.

acknowledgements

To my nutsicles...you two are my people. Y'all get me a freaking spiritual level. I'm not going to get mushy here, because *gross*. But just know, I love y'all so damn much. #Tripod4Life

Joy, I lurve you. That is all.

Jodie, I love our talks. Especially the ones that involve your kids saying, "You're talking to Kate? Again?"

Dani, I love you big. You're one the kindest ladies I know and I'm so blessed to call you a friend. WE WILL MEET SOON!

Jennifer Van Wyk, NEVER LEAVE ME! BE MY FRIEND FOREVER! Just saying.

Kiezha, you're too good to me. You take all of my crazy and make me feel sane. Thank you for putting up with me.

Ellie McLove, just like I'm not allowed to quit you, you can't quit me.

Jules, you're like this amazing mind reading genius. You always take my vague requests and turn them into something incredible.

Harloe, you're the sweetest ever. Thank you for your friendship.

Danielle R, thank you for letting be needy AF and for letting me blow up your inbox at all hours.

Kathy, I love you and all your Aussie slang. <3 Your

notes always makes me teary.

Allyson, I'm so glad you found me!

To all my DND babes, <3 <3

And most of all, to the bloggers and readers who pick up my books...THANK YOU! SERIOUSLY, THANK YOU! Your support is everything to me.

about the author

LK Farlow (A.K.A Kate) is a small town girl with a love for words. She's been writing stories and poems for as long she can remember. A Southern girl through and through, Kate resides in beautiful, sunny LA—that's Lower Alabama, y'all—with her amazing husband and three wonderful children. When she's not writing, you can find her snuggled up on the couch watching nature documentaries while she crochets or with her nose in a book. All Kate really wants in this life is her family happy, strong coffee, a good book and more Happily Ever After's

www.authorlkfarlow.com